THE DIAMOND

COBRA

Yvonne Whittal

MILLS & BOON LIMITED
ETON HOUSE   18-24 PARADISE ROAD
RICHMOND   SURREY   TW9 1SR

First published in Great Britain 1990
by Mills & Boon Limited

© Yvonne Purves 1990

Australian copyright 1990
Philippine copyright 1990
This edition 1990

ISBN 0 263 76805 8

Set in Times Roman 10 on 12 pt.
04-9005-71977 C

Made and printed in Great Britain

CHAPTER ONE

'BLESS me, Father, for I have sinned.' Leonora whispered the words automatically, her burgundy dress rustling as she knelt on the velvet pad inside the confessional.

'Yes, my child?' The familiar, gentle voice came from the Portuguese Jesuit hidden behind the partition.

Leonora shifted uneasily on the kneeler, settling the lace mantilla more firmly on her black hair, piled high on the crown of her head, and clasping her white hands tightly. 'It is I, Leonora Maclean, Father Dominic. I fear I haven't come here for Confession.'

'Ah, Leonora. If that is so, then why did you not arrange to see me at the rectory? It is there that I discuss non-religious problems.'

At the rectory Father Dominic employed an Indian Christian servant, Daniel, who had the reputation of being a gossip, according to Leonora's ayah, and she did not care to take the risk of him overhearing. 'It's more private here.'

'But *menina*, you will have to wait till I've heard the last penitent,' the priest said on a weary release of breath. 'It is late.'

'I'm the last one. I know you're tired, and I'll try to be as quick as I can.'

'Is your mother waiting for you?'

Leonora swallowed to ease the dry guilt locked in her throat. 'No. I—I came alone.'

'But you cannot roam Calcutta without a chaperon, *menina*.' He sounded horrified. 'Respectable European ladies do not go about unaccompanied. No matter, I'll see you home when you've had your say.'

'No, Father, thank you, please don't trouble yourself. I'll be all right. There is a trustworthy servant waiting at the carriage to drive me back.'

'So you have come here without your people's knowledge? You had better explain, Leonora,' he said, his tone faintly disapproving.

Her face grew hot with shame. 'They think I'm in my room. I often read there before dinner. I locked the door from the inside and climbed out of the window. Earlier, I had bribed a servant to get me a hired *ghari*. As I had ordered, the coach was waiting behind the peepul tree near the gate of the bungalow. I don't think anyone saw me leave.'

Leonora sensed the priest's censure and wished she had not come, but his next words gave her consolation.

Father Dominic clicked his tongue in sympathy. 'You must be greatly distressed, *menina*, for this behaviour is not typical of you. What is the trouble?'

Leonora took a deep breath. 'I've run away.'

Shocked silence followed.

A few seconds elapsed, then she spoke. 'You must help me, Father Dominic,' she pleaded. 'You see—I want to become a nun.'

He spluttered, coughed and finally recovered his speech. 'Are you aware of what you're saying, Leonora?'

She grew a little impatient. 'I thought you would welcome a nun to help out in your mission, Father. I would be the ideal person—after all, you were responsible for most of my education. Often in your sermons you have asked for helpers.'

'True, true! However, I was appealing for lay persons. You, I surmise, wish to use the Church to escape from your troubles. You must have dedication to become a nun, not exploit it for your convenience. You already help in the school. Why do you wish to run away from the people who love you?'

Leonora inhaled an anxious breath, absently absorbing the faint scent of incense and candle smoke, reminiscent of the church. She hesitated, reluctant to confide further in the priest, since he had turned down her request to become a nun. And that was all she had come to ask him.

'Come, child, tell me what disturbs you. Don't be afraid. I will not betray your secret; it shall be guarded under the Seal of Confession.'

'But this is not a true confession, Father.'

'No matter, I'll treat it as such.'

Leonora felt heartened. She squared her tense shoulders, and began. 'My mother wishes me to marry Senhor Pedro Fernandez.'

'You mean the rich merchant from Macau?'

Her knees began aching and she sank back on her heels. 'Oh, Father Dominic, he's an aged widower with married sons older than I am. I'm aware my mother wants to see me safely wed for my own protection, but I don't love him. How can I? He's *so old*. What does an ancient man like him want with a girl young enough to be his granddaughter?'

She heard the priest move restlessly. 'It is the usual question. He needs a young and beautiful bride to compensate for his age. There are some men who refuse to accept that they are old. Or perhaps he wishes to thwart his greedy sons—oh, yes, he has told me about them. If he should die after he marries you, they will not receive any of his wealth—you will. Have you known Senhor Fernandez long?'

'This month past,' she said, shuddering as she recalled the bent and fawning merchant. 'He accompanied us to the Governor's ball two weeks ago. I was relieved he didn't stay long as he was taken with a fit of coughing and had to leave. Though not before my mother had given him an assurance of the betrothal. Father Dominic!' Leonora implored. 'Please, please save me from marrying him. Help me!'

She heard the Jesuit come round to her side of the confessional. He slid aside the black curtain and motioned her to rise.

Leonora stepped out of the cubicle and, in the light of candles flickering in front of statues, she looked at the only man she had ever trusted and respected since her father had died.

The same height as herself, Father Dominic was a thin figure in his black cassock. With nervous fingers he fiddled with a large rosary of wooden beads dangling and clacking from the rope wound round his middle. She looked at him with sad affection as his dark gaze rested kindly on her and the scoured forehead wrinkled in consternation. 'Come, *senhorinha*, you must leave now. I'll see you out. Promise me you'll return straight home and I give you my pledge that I'll speak to your mother.'

She longed to tell him more: about her stepfather and his lustful gaze following her whenever he was at home—which, thankfully, was not often. But it would smack of disloyalty to her mother. Besides, the priest looked fatigued.

They both crossed themselves and genuflected towards the altar where a small red lamp burned above the tabernacle, then turned and fell into step in the aisle, their footfalls ringing on the flagstones.

'What exactly will you tell her, Father?' Leonora asked, affected by nervous expectancy.

'I'll mention that you wish to teach the new converts at my village mission, and that I have arranged for you to be accommodated by the Sisters of Mercy who are already working there. But you——'

Not waiting for the priest to finish, she darted in front of him, knelt, caught his hand and kissed it. She did not stop but raced on tiptoes out of the door and down the steep church steps into the chill of the winter night and to where the hired coach waited. She heard Father Dominic call out, 'Go straight home, *menina*!' Leonora waved in acknowledgement of what he had said, quickly entered the carriage and gave her servant, swathed in a blanket on the box, the necessary order.

As the squeaking coach moved off, Leonora clutched the wooden handle of the large canvas bag in which she had packed some jewellery and a few belongings in the hopes of leaving home indefinitely. Feeling easier in mind, sure that Father Dominic would keep his word, she decided to climb back through the low window once she reached the bungalow. Her mother and hateful stepfather would be none the wiser. The most trying time would be awaiting the good priest's visit.

Leonora leaned back on the hard seat, deep in prayer. She prayed to be free from her stepfather's lustful touch whenever he found the opportunity to brush her 'by accident', and free of doddering Pedro Fernandez. Leonora also prayed that somehow her unhappy mother would find contentment. Perhaps I can persuade her to come with me, she dreamed. She sighed. Whatever had made Dona Julia marry that scoundrel? In Leonora's eyes no man could equal her handsome father.

She for certain had no intention of marrying, and if Father Dominic could not help her then, with careful planning, she would abscond on her own.

A sudden lurching startled Leonora out of her unpleasant reverie. The vehicle had changed its usual, slow, rumbling gait to that of top speed, as if it was competing in a race or the horse had bolted. She lifted aside the ragged calico curtain to look through the slats in the door, and saw, with a shock, that the route led nowhere near the sector where she lived. Instead, the carriage swayed and sped down a track flanked by trees—deeper and deeper into the jungle. Soon that was lost from view and the blackness of the wilds greeted her alarmed eyes. All she experienced now was the smell of luxuriant vegetation and the sound of twigs snapping beneath the wheels.

Panic assailed her.

She hammered with her fists on the front panel of the carriage. *'Rokho!'* She yelled at the driver, perched on the box, to stop. Surely he could hear. She kept up the hammering and commands till her fists and arms ached and her voice grew hoarse and cracked. With a sob she tried to open the door, but the latch held fast and she flopped back exhausted on her seat.

Her heart pounded in terror when realisation dawned that she could well be a victim of kidnapping—or worse, the captive of a roving gang of *thuggees*, religious fanatics who tortured, robbed and murdered their victims, whom they regarded as sacrifices to their blood-drinking Goddess Kali. It was rumoured that a gang resided in the jungles surrounding Calcutta. A few of the men had no doubt climbed up on the roof of the coach, she envisaged morbidly, and in all probability had already claimed one victim: her driver.

Leonora squeezed her heavily fringed eyelids tight and willed herself to calm down. Then with shaking hands she delved in her canvas bag and sought her purse. Inspecting the contents, she counted out the twenty pieces of jewellery she had hurriedly dropped in and the ten silver rupees. Her first thought had been to hide the valuables somewhere in the carriage. What good would that do, since she would be killed anyway? Leonora licked her slightly full pink lips to alleviate their dryness, and swallowed hard in an attempt to master control over her shattered emotions. The frozen façade she had hitherto presented to the world, and which had protected her, even to some extent from her stepfather's obnoxious advances, would be useless now because she was up against a ruthless cult to whom murder proved a blessing. God forbid that her suppositions were correct.

She drew the black lace mantilla lower to cover her face, and sat stiffly in the corner of the carriage, staring up at the swaying lamp, praying that no harm would befall her.

The *ghari* began slowing down, and so did her heart. Dizziness made her head reel. She tried to ignore it, and gripped the heavy canvas bag ready to hurl it at whoever opened the door and make a dash for freedom. Finally the coach halted, and she braced herself. As her heart

restarted its drumming, the giddiness subsided. Deathly
stillness prevailed.

Leonora sat as petrified as the statues in a graveyard
as she heard the handle click and watched it move slowly.
Then the door opened on a sharp tug. Her indigo eyes
widened, her brain froze, her brave resolution to use the
bag as a weapon was forgotten.

The man whom she stared at was no *thuggee*, but an
elegantly dressed European. He bowed to her and leaned
into the carriage, stretching out his hand courteously to
assist her descent. In the light from the overhead lamp
and a lantern held by a servant standing behind him,
she saw his gleaming flame-gold hair, the deep waves
caught back at his nape with a broad black ribbon.
'Good evening, ma'am,' he said, leaning further into the
vehicle. 'Allow me.'

By now she had salvaged sufficient mobility to press
into her corner and lift her chin, indented with a slight
cleft, in a show of defiance. The action caused the
mantilla to slide back, revealing the widow's peak on
her rounded forehead, a magnolia-pale face and deep
blue eyes grown large and filled with angry fright. Aware
that if she was to survive she must not be too hasty and
make imperious demands, but act with discretion,
Leonora said coolly, 'I think, sir, that you mistake me
for someone else. I fear the driver has brought me to
the wrong place. He was supposed to take me home. So,
if you please, close the door and let us proceed.'

He dropped his hand, lifted a predominantly red-
tartan-trew-clad leg on to the floor of the vehicle and
rested his elbow on his knee.

She observed the sharp angles of his jaw, the sweep
of his high forehead on which a wayward lock fell, and

his faint, mocking smile. If she had not been so alarmed, she would have admitted that he was indeed a handsome man. The sudden shortness of breath she experienced she attributed to fear, and warned herself not to be deceived by his courteous behaviour. Her gaze strayed for a fleeting moment to the dense thickness beyond him. The jungle seemed alive, breathing, waiting... for the unknown.

He offered her his hand again, the fingers long and strong-looking. 'I assure you, ma'am, there has been no mistake. Now please be good enough to descend.'

She ignored his hand, her own trembling so much that it would have betrayed her terror if she had accepted his offer. Gathering up her skirt and bag, she glanced at him coldly. 'I am quite capable of getting down without help, sir.'

He raised a neat eyebrow and moved to let her pass. She did so with aplomb, her manner wholly deceptive; she felt desperately afraid and his courtesy only increased her wariness and apprehension. The amused expression he wore conveyed nothing of his intentions. She stood stiffly on the rough path waiting for his next move, ready to shy away should he attempt to touch her.

To her relief, he pointed to a copse of trees and said calmly, 'This way, ma'am.' He led the way to a small, low building with a flat roof and a sturdy door.

Leonora hung back, her skin prickling. 'Would you be so good as to tell me why you have abducted me, sir? It's apparent that this is what you've planned.'

He pushed open the door and stood with his back against it, waiting for her to precede him into the dwelling. She hesitated, wondering whether it would be worthwhile making a break for freedom. Behind her stood a couple of his men who held lanterns. Every-where else surrounding the lodge lay thick jungle. She decided against any rash action which might result in her degradation by being manhandled by this man and perhaps his servants. And if she did manage to escape their clutches, there remained little chance of her surviving for long in the wild.

'You're right,' he said. 'This has been well planned. Now please hand me your bag and come in.'

She shook her head and held the bag to her. 'No, thank you,' she said, and stepped inside.

He laughed shortly, and the moment she crossed the threshold he shut the door. She looked forlorn, vulnerable and very beautiful, and he disliked the quick-ening of his heartbeat which warned him that he was softening towards her. The young man hardened his jaw—he must not let her cultured behaviour deceive him. She was the means by which he could strike Angus Grant where it would hurt most. He had never harmed a woman, and had to salve his conscience where this one was concerned. She was his enemy's daughter, known as the frozen madonna, who could no doubt be as hard and ruthless as her father. Both would suffer.

Her nerves as taut as stretched cord, Leonora glanced round the room, visible in the feeble naked flame of an earthenware oil-lamp which stood on a rough wooden table. The place looked clean, she was thankful to see, but that in no way compensated for the shock of her unforeseen predicament, intensified by the presence of her captor who towered awesomely nearby.

Laying the bag carefully on the string bed, covered over with a clean cotton quilt, she straightened and faced him squarely. 'Tell me, sir, why have you brought me here, and what have you done with my driver?'

He waved an elegant hand, with lace at the wrist, to a wicker stool. 'Pray be seated, ma'am.'

She wanted to refuse, but her legs trembled so much she thought it prudent to obey, lest she collapse and give him the impression that she was using feminine wiles to entice him, or that she was so weak and lacking in character that he could do what he wished with her. Heaven forbid! To convince him that she was not afraid, she walked unhurriedly to the stool, settled herself on it and smoothed down her voluminous taffeta skirt.

'Your driver received handsome payment for his vehicle and was only too pleased to part with it.'

'It wasn't his to give,' she said, more to herself.

'Your so-called trustworthy servant has been in my pay for the past fortnight. Money, ma'am, is a great incentive for good or evil.'

'And, I am sure, you have not brought me here to confide your philosophies,' she said drily, displaying a calm that was in contrast to her inner turbulence. 'Who are you, sir?'

He shrugged wide shoulders which fitted snugly in the black velvet jacket. 'You won't know me, but my name is Craig Mackintosh.'

She frowned and shook her head. In cold anger she asked, 'And why have you kidnapped me? I don't recall having met or harmed you in any way. Why are you punishing me for no reason?'

He did not answer but slowly, deliberately, let his gaze meander over her. She chose to ignore his frank appraisal and looked through him.

'Yes, it suits you,' he commented blandly.

'I beg your pardon?' She blinked and now stared directly at him.

He folded his arms across his broad chest and leaned negligently against the wall near her. In his golden eyes she saw contempt. 'You're known as the frozen madonna. Frozen for sure. Cruel as your father.'

The caution she had hitherto practised was tossed aside. She could not tolerate anyone speaking ill of the only man she had idolised. Leonora's eyes grew black with amazement and fury. 'If you have abducted me to slander my father and myself, I declare you have made a grave mistake, Mr Mackintosh. I insist that you return me to my home!'

'Insist, did you say?' He laughed softly, derisively. Then he strode forward, placed his palms on the table and leaned towards her, his expression grave. 'Lady, you are going nowhere. You will stay with me, day and night, till your papa pays me a five-figure ransom!'

CHAPTER TWO

LEONORA dragged herself upright, her face white as candle wax. Over the years she had taken pride in her ability to conceal her emotions behind an impassive veneer, and believed that she could maintain this attitude in front of others in every traumatic situation. She was mistaken; tonight this man had the power to strip away the covering to her soul and gloat at the havoc he had created.

'I might have known that money was behind your scheming. That is no problem, sir,' she said, her breathing difficult. She lifted up her bag, drew out the purse of jewels, and placed it gently but firmly on the table. 'Those are worth more than a five-figure sum. One of them is priceless.'

To her astonishment he did not snatch up the purse, but pushed it towards her. 'You didn't listen, ma'am. I said your *papa* must pay the ransom—not you.'

A faint, sardonic smile touched her pink lips. 'Then I fear, sir, that you will have to wait till you enter another world, because my father is dead.'

In the ensuing stillness she heard a jackal howl and an owl hoot somewhere in the depths of the Indian jungle.

She saw the stunned look on her abductor's face and experienced a faint glow of satisfaction. But she soon knew chagrin when his expression changed to one of mock understanding. The magnificent amber eyes gazed

17

at her with a hint of pity. 'You're trying to save him, ma'am,' he said almost kindly. 'I know for a fact that he's very much alive. I saw him myself at Lord Clive's farewell ball.'

Her indigo eyes, slightly tilted at the outer corners, returned his gaze triumphantly. 'I regret you have been misinformed. The man you saw isn't my father, Mr Mackintosh.'

'Who was your father, ma'am?'

'My father was Andrew Maclean. My name is Leonora Maclean.'

'Maclean? That's Scottish.'

'Yes, sir, he was a Scot,' she said with a wry twist of her mouth. 'A Jacobite, exiled from Scotland for his radical beliefs. He went to Portugal trying to drum up support for the Stuart cause—that is, for Prince Charles——'

'Aye, I know; pray continue, ma'am.'

'He married my mother, Dona Julia Aviz, a noble-man's daughter, and I was born a year later. But when the rebellion broke out he was determined to return to his country.' She remembered with a spasm of pain in her heart how, as an eight-year-old child, she had begged him to remain. He had cried, promised that when the trouble was over he would return to them, despite the fact that her grandfather had disapproved of Dona Julia's marrying an impoverished exile. She could feel the tears pricking behind her lowered lids and, remembering where she was, forced them back. 'My father, sir, died fighting at Drummossie Moor, Culloden. We received the message from a fellow Highlander who had fought alongside him but managed to flee to Portugal, where he still resides.'

She closed her eyes and once more lived the traumatic scene. On hearing of her husband's death, Dona Julia had screamed and fallen into a deep faint and, when she had eventually been brought round by grandfather Dom Aviz, she had sobbed, stormed and raved, blaming the old man for being against the marriage, which she had believed was responsible for her husband returning to Scotland. And there she had been, a young widow with a daughter to bring up alone. As for Leonora, she had felt as if her heart had been torn out. So stricken had she been that for the first few days after the tragedy she had not been able to speak, eat or sleep. Finally, when the tears had come, they had not stopped. From a happy, laughing child she had turned into a sad, quiet being with an unusual reserve. The death of her beloved grandfather a few months later had deepened her reticence.

She opened her eyes and observed that Craig's well-shaped, thick brows had drawn together. He delved into the inner pocket of his jacket and extracted a folded sheet of paper, which he smoothed out carefully on the table and stared at. In his eyes she saw the glow of deep hatred. Her scrutiny dropped to his beautiful hands—it was then that she spotted the jewel of white fire on his right index-finger. The ring of diamonds shaped like a coiled cobra, its hood outspread resting against his skin, had eyes and forked tongue of blood-red rubies. She shuddered, an instinctive reaction to her fear of snakes, but had no time to contemplate further as he held the paper out for her inspection.

'Then who is this man?'

Leonora started as she stared at the sketch of the man's face. The likeness was so accurate, the black strokes sweeping and deft, that she had difficulty hiding her admiration. Though Craig had not executed the drawing in colour, he had emphasised the outstanding characteristics of the image: the thinning, pale hair, bulbous and scoured forehead, high-bridged, long nose with flaring nostrils, puffy cheeks, heavy jowls, thin lips, thick, lined neck. But the most realistic features of all were the eyes: small, mean, the visible whites mapped with lines denoting over-indulgence in liquor and debauchery. 'Did you draw this?' she asked expressionlessly.

He gave a quick nod of impatience. 'Aye. Now tell me, who is this man?'

'He is Angus Grant, my mother's husband.'

Craig smiled broadly, showing an array of white, strong teeth. 'Ah . . .'

'And my *stepfather*.'

The smile vanished. 'Is that so?'

'Yes. And you are wasting your time, for he will pay no ransom for me, sir. Take me home now and I promise I shall not mention a word about the kidnapping. If it's money you want——'

He brushed the air with an elegant hand. 'You have already offered me your priceless jewels. Nay, it is not wealth I want, lady. I don't need it. I have plenty of my own which I earned legally.'

She lifted her shoulders and spread her hands in a gesture of puzzlement. 'I don't understand. Then why——?'

'Revenge. I mean to see that cur ruined, extract every *pice* from him, and see him die a pauper.' He spoke with bitter hatred through clenched teeth, his eyes staring at the rough whitewashed wall above her head but seeing another view in the distant past.

Leonora's fear returned. This man was using her as an innocent pawn in his obsession for retribution. Yet she felt curious about what had occurred between Angus Grant and Craig Mackintosh. Thoughtfully she sank back on the stool. 'What did my stepfather do to you?'

He laughed with about as much mirth as is manifested at a funeral procession. Folding up the sketch, he placed it in his pocket and began restlessly pacing the room, one hand behind his back, the other displaying the ring, fiddling with the fine lace jabot at his neck. 'Well might you ask, ma'am. He was responsible for my father's death.'

Leonora felt a stab of empathy for him—she had loved her own father dearly. Even so, it did not mean that he could use her to satisfy his own ends. She stifled her compassion and asked quietly, 'What happened?'

Craig stopped at the far side of the room with his back to her and stared out of the iron-barred window. At last he turned and looked across at Leonora. She could see the lines of pain etched on his face.

'I was sixteen when Prince Charles Stuart stepped on to Scottish soil and roused the Highlanders to rebellion against the Elector of Hanover. To us, King George was the usurper and Charles the rightful heir to the English throne.'

She could feel the blood leaving her face and had to clench her hands tightly in her lap to stop them trembling. This Scottish rebellion seemed to have affected both their lives.

'Are you all right?' he asked, and Leonora gave him a withering sidelong glance.

'It's a mite late to enquire about that considering the circumstances, sir. But I find your tale interesting. Do proceed.'

'Let me impress upon you, lady, it is not my habit to relate my life story,' he attempted to assure her with a hint of irony. 'I am doing so now to show you what manner of fiend your stepfather is. Perhaps then you'll agree with my motives.'

She yearned to tell him that kidnapping an innocent woman was no way of going about revenge. Her curiosity to hear his explanation, however, overrode the desire for argument. 'Carry on, sir.'

He began pacing again, a frown wedged between his brows. 'My father disapproved of the rising, stating that no good would come of it. Indeed, Scotland was split: part of it on the side of the Elector and part on the side of Prince Charles. My father and I quarrelled seriously for the first time in our life together.'

'You left home to take up arms with the Prince?'

'Aye. I left my father without even saying goodbye. At that time I wasn't sorry. Patriotism for the Stuart cause became a fixation with me. We, the followers of our Bonnie Prince, swore to lay down our lives for him.' Nostalgia in his voice was as sharp as a sword blade.

Leonora moved restlessly. She felt guilty. Her father had returned to Scotland for the selfsame purpose: to lay down his life for the Prince and the 'King over the water'—the prince's father. She had underestimated the power of patriotism. Till now she had carried in the deep recesses of her heart an ingrained bitterness for the father she had idolised and who had thrown away his life for a lost cause. She could not understand why loyalty to a prince he had never met had superseded his duty and responsibility to his wife and daughter. Listening to Craig, she gleaned the meaning of patriotism.

'But it all ended in a bloodbath on Drummossie Moor on a cold April day—an unequal contest between the hungry Highland clans and the well-fed, well-armed troops of that fat Butcher of Cumberland, the Elector's German brother.' Bitterness had crept into Craig's deep voice, the burr in his accent more pronounced. Lightly he punched his left fist into his right palm. 'The Prince and a few of his lords became fugitives and eventually reached France. We ordinary Highlanders had no choice but to flee the battlefield, the Butcher's dragoons at our heels with the command to give no quarter.'

He paused for so long that Leonora thought he had decided to say no more. 'Where did Angus Grant come into all this?' she prompted.

'He was one of our number on the run.' He sighed and ran a hand through his bright hair, but could not control the rebellious lock that dropped on to his brow again. 'If I had but known,' he muttered. 'I led our small band of fugitives to my father's house in Inverness and begged him to shelter us. He was a prosperous merchant trading with France and owned his own vessel, which was out at the time. He didn't hesitate to hide us in his spacious warehouse near the wharves on the Firth of Moray, and promised to see us aboard his vessel on its return.'

A knock on the door halted his narrative. 'Yes?'

A female voice said in Urdu, 'I have brought yours and the *missahib*'s dinner, *sahib*.'

Craig strode to the door and opened it to let in a small, sari-clad woman carrying two brass trays holding piles of chapattis and small bowls of food. And though the

smell was appetising it had little power to promote
Leonora's hunger. Although Craig had conducted the
interview with a creditable amount of civility, Leonora
harboured no illusions of gaining her freedom easily
from him. She still laboured under the miasma of fear;
hatred had flowed too long in his veins for him to surrender his overwhelming aim to avenge his father's
murder by any means he could—and she was one of
them.

He thanked the servant—which surprised her, since
she'd imagined that she was the only one among the
Europeans in India who did—lifted out a wicker stool
from a dark corner of the room and stood it at the table
on which the trays had been placed. With a gracious
wave of his hand he invited Leonora to eat and, when
she rose, he carried her stool to the table.

To hide her growing uneasiness of what this man
planned for her future, knowing that Angus Grant would
pay out nothing to restore her to her mother, Leonora
nibbled at the flat bread and spooned small quantities
of lentil puree and tasty vegetables into her mouth. Craig
had no such qualms, apparent from the gusto with which
he ate.

'But why does my stepfather deserve your vengeance?' Leonora queried, anxious to know the full story
and so be able to think up plans for her own escape.

He poured out water into a tumbler from an earthenware carafe brought in on a tray, and took a drink.
Setting the glass down with a decisive thump, he said,
'The betrayer in our midst. While we waited for my
father's vessel to return from France and take us to that
country and safety, the Judas Angus Grant slipped out
at dead of night and brought in the dragoons.'

Leonora laid down her spoon carefully. 'I see. And your father died in the skirmish? How is it you escaped?'

'We had been warned by the Sassenach swine that if we tried to resist we would be killed. But my father, who had probably heard from some other source that the dragoons were raiding his warehouse, dashed in waving his claymore—and...and was cut down. Bayoneted to death.' He emptied his glass. 'I was too stunned to offer the dragoons any resistance. Else I would not be here today, and you would be free.' Craig poured out another tumblerful of water and swallowed half. He grimaced, muttering, 'Wish I'd thought to bring some whisky.'

'And your mother, sir—where was she?' Leonora asked gently.

Pushing away from the table, he resumed his restless pacing. 'My mother? I never knew her. She died when I was a baby. My father brought me up, had me educated and taught me his trade, which has stood me in good stead here in Bengal.'

'Did you manage to escape the dragoons and set sail for India?'

He laughed derisively and came to stand near the table, his thickly lashed gold eyes looking down at her. 'No, lady. One can't run far tethered in chains to one's fellow prisoners. I learned from the Sassenach that Grant had betrayed us, that the Mackintosh property and assets had been confiscated, and that Grant had been pardoned and given a share of the loot. I was separated from my fellow convicts and taken to the Tower of London through Traitors' Gate. They mistook me for an aristocrat.' He gave a smile of disbelief. 'But then the error was discovered and, still in chains, I was dragged off to the Deptford docks and marched on to an East Indiaman.

Before being thrust below I saw Angus Grant swaggering on deck, watching the activity on the docks. So he didn't see me.'

He did not mention the night the ship had pulled away from England, with somewhere in the stinking dark a lone voice singing a haunting Highland song. He had imagined the skirl of bagpipes in accompaniment. His heart had cried for Scotland, her brave sons, his fugitive prince and, above all, his beloved father. He had dropped his head on his drawn-up knees and wept.

'The hour is late, ma'am,' he said gruffly. 'Try and get some sleep. Tomorrow we have much to discuss. I'll send Rumi in with some hot water and also a brazier, as the night is cold.'

Leonora said nothing; she felt very tired—not that she would be able to sleep, she reflected, yet she needed to be alone and think over this bizarre night.

He sketched her a deep bow as if apologising for her present circumstances. 'Goodnight, ma'am.' Abruptly he swivelled around and left. She watched him go with mixed feelings. His figure was tall and imposing—he stooped to pass through the doorway and then closed the door softly behind him. Immediately after Leonora heard the crunch of his booted footfalls fade on the gravel path outside, she straightened up off the stool and, lifting the earthenware lamp from the table, tiptoed to the entrance. In the dim light she examined the portal but to her surprise saw no bolt or latch. The door obviously locked from the outside.

She felt the panic rise in her again, and knew that, although Angus Grant did lust after her, he held no tender feelings of love for her. For him to pay ransom for her was laughable—he would rather see her dead.

Her mother would be the one to suffer. She would pay the money without quibble, but her business and finances now belonged to Angus Grant and therefore she had no freedom to use her fortune as she pleased.

A sudden idea struck Leonora. If there was some way she could bribe one of the servants here—and she had seen several loitering on the premises every time the door had opened—he might take a message to old Pedro Fernandez, her potential betrothed. Whatever his designs on her, he at least had offered the respectability of marriage. Considering his vast wealth, she hoped he would not shy away from paying the ransom in Angus Grant's name, since Craig would not accept money from anyone else.

She moved silently back to the table, replaced the lamp and picked up the purse of jewels she had offered Craig. Carefully she pushed it to the bottom of her bag, which she would use as a pillow. She lay on the bed and stared up at the flaking ceiling, wondering if her mother had discovered by now that she was missing.

A little later the Indian woman named Rumi entered, bearing a basin and ewer of hot water, followed by a man carrying in a small brazier filled with glowing charcoal. He left immediately after he had deposited his burden, and Rumi began gathering up the trays. 'You are not hungry, *missahib*?'

Leonora jumped a little and glanced up at the servant. Rumi had pushed back the headpiece of her dark green sari, and her black eyes gazed unhappily at Leonora's almost untouched tray.

'No. I'm sorry, but I'm not hungry,' Leonora said politely, studying this woman and wondering if she was susceptible to bribes.

The servant clicked her tongue distractedly. 'Hira Nag Sahib will not be pleased.'

Leonora raised herself on one elbow and stared with interest at Rumi. 'What did you call him?'

'Hira Nag Sahib. We servants call him so.'

'The Diamond Cobra? Is it because of his ring?'

'*Ji, missahib,*' she said conversationally, clattering all the bowls on to one tray and stacking them. 'He is clever artist. He is painting many pictures of great *sahibs* such as Sabat Jung Sahib.'

Leonora understood that Rumi meant Lord Clive, who was known by the indigenous population as Sabat Jung, the Daring Commander.

Rumi chattered on, 'He is painting pictures of battles he fought in his own country, Belait, and the battles in Hindustan. His cleverness spread and the rajas and *nawabs* wanted him to paint them.'

'The ring was a present?'

Rumi's thin lips parted with a grin of admiration. '*Ji!* The Mogul governor, Nawab Sahib Mir Jaffar, he asked the *sahib* to paint his picture and found it much pleasing, so he paid him handsomely and gave him the Hira Nag ring for luck.'

Secretly, Leonora felt heartened that Rumi was friendly and so obvious an inveterate gossip. She could learn much from the woman. I must build up a rapport with Rumi, and, if I am subtle about it, she might help me when the time is ripe, she told herself.

'I must be gone, *missahib*, or the *sahib* may wonder what I am doing. *Namasta.*' Rumi raised heavily bangled arms, steepled her hands, gathered up the trays and departed. Leonora heard the bolt slot into place and with a groan she dropped back on the bed. There was certainly no chance of escape tonight.

The grating of the bolt and sharp raps woke her abruptly from a fitful sleep. She shot up in bed and just for a moment felt totally disorientated. She blinked at the patchy, once whitewashed walls. Seconds later she recalled her predicament, and recognised her surroundings. When she heard the sturdy door creak she swung her legs off the bed and arranged her skirts modestly about her.

In walked Craig Mackintosh, looking immaculate. No doubt he had washed, while she sat dishevelled, trying to compose herself in a semblance of dignity.

He nodded agreeably to her. 'Good morning, Senhorinha Leonora.'

She pondered that a man with enough daring to kidnap someone who came from an influential, well-known family, while caring nothing for the consequences, needed to be treated with tactful wariness and not antagonism if she intended to safeguard herself. Yet she refused to mortify herself by pleading with him to let her go free. She decided that her days of entreaty had ended. And her mistrust of men had evolved since her mother had married the hateful Angus Grant. 'Good morning, Mr Mackintosh,' she returned, inclining her head with studied politeness, gazing at him from under her thick, long, straight lashes.

His amber eyes sparked with amusement and a faint smile lifted a corner of his mouth. 'I won't ask whether you slept well, ma'am, because even if you did you would deny doing so. A servant will be in shortly with the necessities for you to wash. And before we start on our journey tonight a tub will be brought in and filled with warm water for you to bathe.'

Leonora's deep blue eyes widened in alarm. 'What journey, Mr Mackintosh? Where are you taking me?' In the ray of sunshine piercing the morning mist and pouring through the barred window she saw him more clearly. His thick, neat brows and meshed lashes were an attractive dark brown that went well with his golden eyes, fiery hair and copper tan. But his masculine beauty affected Leonora not at all, because he plotted all manner of trouble for her.

'It all depends on you.' He spotted the stray black curls dangling on her magnolia-fair forehead and slender neck in attractive dishevelment, and felt a mystifying urge to touch them.

'Mr Mackintosh, I'm afraid I do not have the ability to solve riddles. Please be specific.'

'I have written out a ransom note and addressed it to your stepfather, Angus Grant, and to prove you are with me I need your signature.'

'I don't think you paid attention to what I said last night, Mr Mackintosh. Or perhaps you have forgotten. I fear you are wasting your time.'

He bowed a little stiffly and stared woodenly at her. 'Indeed?'

'Indeed! He knows I mistrust him—and all men, for that matter. He will not pay a single *pice* for me.'

Craig moved to one side when a servant asked permission to enter, and waited for the man to deposit a basin and an ewer of water on a table tucked away in one corner of the room. The man salaamed briefly, and looked a little surprised when Leonora thanked him.

After he had gone Craig shut the door and leaned against it, crossing his long legs, which were encased in tightly fitting trews. A slow and, dare she admit it, stunning smile curved his mouth. 'You mistrust all men, do you?'

Leonora felt annoyed with herself for the inadvertent slip. She lifted her slightly indented chin and a slim eyebrow. 'Yes. I have every reason to. But that has nothing——'

'Why? Tell me why you mistrust men, *senhorinha*?'

'That has nothing to do with the present circumstances. It's enough for me to say that my stepfather will pay no ransom for me. Why don't you accept what I offered you last night? I'm sure your needs will be amply satisfied.'

He laughed deeply, softly, with genuine humour, and too late she realised her unfortunate choice of words. 'Really? But if you mistrust and dislike men, that's a wasted proposition.'

She could feel her cheeks burning and cursed herself for a fool. 'I...I meant I can pay you with the jewels. I'm sure you will be happy with them, sir. Perhaps if you see them you'll change your mind.' She reached for the bag, but he stayed her with the raising of his finger.

'Sorry, lady. I've already made it clear that it's Angus Grant's money I want. I mean to make him destitute.'

Leonora sighed. 'If he does pay, it will not be his money but my mother's. She has done you no wrong, so why do you wish to harm her?'

'Neither have you, but in matters such as this one the innocent too are obliged to suffer.'

'No, not if you abandon your cause. After all, you still have your life, and by your own lips have proclaimed your affluence. Vengeance, sir, will not bring back your dead father.'

Craig nailed her with his glare. 'You haven't deceived me in the least, ma'am. I am aware that you are trying to protect Angus Grant because he is your lover!'

CHAPTER THREE

LEONORA came slowly erect, every part of her quivering with outrage. Her voice throbbed as she spoke. 'How dare you slander me so? Using mere conjecture!'

He put his head to one side and let his gaze wander over her, disconcerting her with his frank and mocking appraisal. For a while he watched the high and full curves of her breasts and faint colour sweep up from her neck to her cheeks. He had never seen a woman look so vividly agitated. 'Then tell me what you are doing with a bag packed for travelling? Why are you leaving home? You are going to a lover and that lover is Angus Grant!'

Leonora had difficulty controlling her anger and her rapid breathing. She refused to admit that she was absconding from home—it had nothing to do with him. Slowly she let out her breath. 'I would have you know, Mr Mackintosh, that I love my mother dearly. In no circumstances would I do anything to hurt or humiliate her!'

'No?'

'No, Mr Mackintosh.'

He shook his head, pinched the bridge of his nose and sighed out a laugh of disbelief.

'You have no right to judge me when you have no proof,' she said, glaring at him.

'My eyes did not deceive me, I assure you, lady.'

'I don't know what you're talking about, sir. I don't recall behaving in an unseemly manner with my stepfather.'

He uncrossed his legs, pushed away from the door and slowly advanced towards her. 'Do you remember the New Year's ball given by Lord Clive?'

It had been a glittering affair, she recalled, held in the quadrangle of Fort William in a marquee draped with satin and with a polished platform for the band and dancers. All the settlers who had attended had turned out in their decorative best: company officers in blue uniforms with gold frogging and epaulettes; wealthy merchants in periwigs and watered silk frock-coats in an assortment of colours, all enhanced with falls of fine lace at throat and sleeves. The women far outshone the men in their wide, wired, flounced skirts of silks, velvets and satins, liberally embroidered and ruched with lace, bodices low and waists gathered into laced stomachers. Leonora had worn lemon taffeta and she had received the most glances: admiration from the men and envy from fan-fluttering and perfumed women. 'I remember.'

'You will also recollect Angus Grant leaning close to you, gazing into your eyes and ignoring your mother, whose face was torn with anguish. On the other hand your cheeks were flushed with—love?' He came to stand in front of her, his golden eyes viewing her through the thick meshes of his dark lashes, and lifted her chin with a single finger. 'I thought at that time Grant was displaying the pure love of a father for his beautiful daughter—but I was mistaken.'

Leonora could not speak—the finger under her chin seemed to anchor her so that she felt unable to move or look away from the magnetism of his eyes, their splintered brilliance flecked with brown.

'Did he do this to you, Leonora darling?' he asked, his voice deep and husky.

She watched his face lower, saw the clean-cut angle of his jaw, a pulse beating in the ridged muscles. His breath, warm and clean, touched her face. 'No,' she whispered. For a brief second his mouth came down on hers. She felt a jolt pass through her body. They both jerked apart, and for a moment stared at each other. He stepped away from her as if she had stung him. Leonora hastily dropped her eyes and looked absently down at her hands, linked loosely in front of her. Santa Maria! What had happened then? She was dazed at her reaction to this man, who had erupted into her life like a freak storm to wreak devastation.

'I'll be back in a moment,' he said, and abruptly left. Once outside the dwelling, he shot the bolt and leaned against the door. He passed his hand over his brow and brought it away full of sweat. He swore silently in Gaelic. What the devil had come over him? He was involved in the serious and dangerous game of extracting ransom, not in stealing kisses. They were definitely *not* on the agenda.

Leonora felt bemused and shaken by what had occurred. She berated herself for meekly succumbing to his kiss instead of offering some resistance. Her behaviour would embed more firmly in his mind that she was a wanton. She felt astonished that she should be disturbed by his opinion.

Rumi came in then, bearing an ewer of warm water to replace the empty one. *'Salaam, missahib,'* she greeted Leonora. 'You had good sleep?'

No, she had not—most of the night had passed in her worrying, knowing that her mother would be distraught as soon as she discovered Leonora's disappearance. But she smiled faintly and nodded her head. She was in no mood to talk so soon after the upheaval which had gone before. Firmly she thrust Craig's alarming kiss from her mind.

'I will bring in your breakfast after you have washed, *missahib*.'

Leonora thanked her, and Rumi left bearing the empty ewer and the now cool brazier. Feeling refreshed after her wash, Leonora fetched a brush and comb from her bag and tidied her hair. Then she straightened the quilt on the bed, sat on it and drew the large bag, holding her possessions, next to her.

By now her mother must have had her bedroom door broken open and discovered her missing, she pondered in distress. Foolishly she had left a note addressed to Dona Julia, explaining that she could not marry Pedro Fernandez and as a result had absconded, and begging that no one be sent to search for her, but promising that she would be safe and that she would be in contact as soon as possible.

I must get away from here, she told herself—I cannot cause Mother so much anguish...oh, why was I so reckless? She prayed to God that her mother would go to Father Dominic for solace. But that good priest was bound under the Seal of Confession not to divulge Leonora's plans. Even so, he would be wondering what had become of her, considering he had trusted her to go straight home.

A discreet tap at the door startled her out of her thoughts. The bolts were pulled back and Rumi entered, carrying a tray. 'There! I have brought you good breakfast, *missahib*.'

At first Leonora wanted to say she wasn't hungry, but that would alienate the servant and she needed an ally if she was to make a bid for freedom. She settled herself at the table where she had shared supper with Craig last night. The servant put down the tray, on which were a pot of tea, cup and saucer and pink slices of papaya. As Rumi turned to leave, Leonora stopped her with, 'What place is this, Rumi?'

The servant hesitated and glanced warily at the door. 'Hira Nag Sahib has forbidden us to tell you, *missahib*. My husband is the cook here and the *sahib* may well sack us if we go against his wishes. He is our mother and father and pays us well. You are understanding, *missahib*?'

Leonora smiled. 'Yes, I understand. I'll ask the *sahib* myself.' He had earned the loyalty of his servants and she would find it a hard task trying to win them over with bribes. Still, she had to try. But not yet—she had to build up a rapport with Rumi first.

The servant left, and Leonora was surprised to discover that she enjoyed the simple breakfast. Shortly after, Craig entered, and just for a brief second her heart lurched. Worse, she felt colour wash into her face. She was thankful he was not looking at her, but busying himself removing her breakfast tray to the floor and placing an inkstand and a sheet of worded paper on the table.

She knew that it was the ransom note before he mentioned it. So that brief moment of tenderness he had displayed in touching her lips with his own had not made the slightest difference to him—he still intended to hold her hostage.

He turned the paper round to her, dipped the quill in the inkwell and said soberly, 'Please put your signature on the sheet, ma'am.'

Leonora read the note with concentration. It was brief and to the point, informing Angus Grant that she had been taken hostage and that on production of one *lakh* of rupees she would be free to return to wherever she had been heading before the abduction. She knew that he imagined she and Grant had a hide-out where they carried on an illicit affair. It surprised her to feel a little hurt that he should think so lowly of her.

'One *lakh* of rupees is an enormous amount of money, Mr Mackintosh,' she said, her cobalt-blue eyes widening, the thick, black lashes almost reaching her arched eyebrows. The nostrils of her thin, small nose flared and her breath came fast. 'And—and you give an ultimatum. The money must be left at a venue you've mapped out, and if it isn't forthcoming by seven o'clock tonight—or some assurance that it will be paid—then you fear for me. What exactly do you mean by that?'

'I'll leave that to your intelligence. Now if you please——'

She laughed cynically. 'I can tell you Angus Grant is going to be highly amused with this note. He'll think it a jest. I advise you to abandon this ridiculous——'

Craig cut his hand through the air in a gesture of extreme impatience. 'Look, ma'am, I realise you are trying to save your lover from an empty purse which, of course, will eventually affect you. Strewth! I can't visualise you living in rags, begging on the streets of Calcutta.' He tapped the paper. 'Please sign this, lady, and let's hear no more objections.'

Giving him a sidelong glance of scorn, she poised the quill above the paper. 'If I sign, it will look as if this note came from me. Where is your signature?'

He looked steadily at her and stretched his lips in exasperation. 'It is obvious that I can't sign and give myself away. All right, just add a few words that you will be safe—unless no ransom arrives—and then sign. But sign you must, else Grant will not believe you have been kidnapped.'

She continued to stall. 'What will you do to me if the note is ignored?'

'Then I have other plans for you. But if it's any consolation, I shall not harm you physically.'

'And if I refuse?' she asked with mock sweetness, placing the quill neatly at the side of the paper and looking innocently up at him. If he should know how fearful she felt, he would apply more pressure on her, she was certain.

Mackintosh's handsome face grew iron-hard. 'If you refuse, then I very much fear that I will have to send him a lock of your hair and clothing.'

'You wouldn't dare!'

He smiled disarmingly and bowed. 'Try me.'

Despite his show of courtesy, she knew that he meant what he said, and she had no intention of giving him that pleasure. Leonora took up the pen and wrote a few lines to her mother, stating that she was safe and apologising for the distress her abduction was no doubt causing. She wrote how much she loved Dona Julia, and signed herself simply 'Leonora'.

'I thank you, ma'am,' he said with mock graciousness, and strode out.

She hoped he had forgotten to shoot the bolt, but immediately after heard it slot home. Groaning her frustration, she pushed away from the table and crossed the brick floor to stand in the beam of sunlight that poured through the window and warmed the room. The chilly morning mist had cleared and beyond the gravel path towered the forest above lush undergrowth. She only fleetingly noticed the scene, her mind engrossed with thoughts of Craig.

Suddenly she was filled with a desire to know more about him. So far all she had grasped was that he had a grudge against Angus Grant, that he was an accomplished artist and that he had learned the lessons of trade from his father. Apparently he operated some sort of business. And where did he live? If he resided in or around Fort William in Calcutta she would surely have seen and heard about him. And though her mother had married Angus Grant thirteen years ago, and they all lived on the estate comprising a sprawling bungalow and acres of mango plantation left to Dona Julia by her father Dom Aviz, it seemed strange that Craig Mackintosh had only just heard of his enemy dwelling in these parts. And why had she not noticed Mackintosh at the New Year's ball? Perhaps she had been too preoccupied thinking up plans on how to avoid a betrothal with ancient Pedro Fernandez.

As the day wore on and grew warmer, Leonora paced about the room wondering if the ransom note had been sent off. She saw no one except Rumi, who brought in delicious-looking meals which Leonora, in her anxiety, left mainly untouched.

Then, after darkness fell, and her partly eaten dinner had been cleared away by a disgruntled Rumi—whom she did not heed—Leonora stood near the window gripping the bars. Suddenly the door opened and in strode Craig. Leonora released the grille and spun round to face him, her heart increasing its rhythm. In the light of the feeble lamp, her deep blue eyes regarded him stiffly, defiantly.

Craig shut the door and moved towards her, his action one of studied deliberation. His golden gaze roamed her delicate features and beautiful figure, which he could see had not been forcibly squeezed into stays.

'There was no answer to the ransom note,' he said with deadly quietness.

Leonora disliked the look on his face. A silent rage reddened it, the line of his jaw ridged with tension. She swallowed to relieve the fear lodged in her throat. 'I— I did warn you, sir, that my stepfather would have no intention whatsoever of paying ransom for me. You wouldn't heed what I said, and wasted your time and mine. And now, pray, what do you intend to do?'

'Naturally, I'll try again, but not from here. It is doubtful that he'll be able to trace us to this place— nevertheless, it would be safer if I brought our departure forward.' He lowered himself on the bed and lounged back on the bolster, his angry gaze raking her with contempt. 'Did you write some code in your brief message to your mother?'

'Really, sir, I'm not versed in any codes!'

'It's a ruse, lady. He thinks that, if he ignores the note, I'll feel tempted to return you. Not so! We're leaving— now!'

'Then let us be gone, Mr Mackintosh. You are the one who is wasting time. Alas, you have a predilection for doing so!' she accused vehemently. 'You seem to enjoy using your idle hours in futile kidnappings. What are you trying to prove, sir? That you are some kind of rogue hero? I assure you, Mr Mackintosh, that you are playing a dangerous game.' But her threats seemed of little avail.

A thick, well-shaped eyebrow rose and he smiled in faint mockery. 'You appear anxious to be gone. I wonder why? If you imagine you can escape from me while we are on the move, I fear you have miscalculated my intentions and underrated me. As for the futility of kidnapping you, that is not what *I* think.'

Leonora delved into the embroidered canvas bag and drew out her mantilla which she draped over her head, then, collecting the holdall, she seated herself on the wicker stool and affected an air of patience. 'I await your command, lord and master.'

He laughed softly and, taking his time, straightened his tall frame off the bed. For a while he stood staring down at her. Then, cupping her attractive chin, he said, 'I'll say this for you, lovely *senhorinha*, you do not lack courage.'

Leonora jerked her chin out of his hold, wholly disconcerted. 'I—I'm ready, sir,' she said, stumbling over her words.

'You can't go dressed like that, ma'am. You might be recognised.'

'I assure you, Mr Mackintosh,' she said with soft irony, 'I didn't come prepared to be kidnapped, least of all for a masquerade. So I suppose you'll offer me a suit of your clothes?'

'Now that, ma'am, is an excellent suggestion!' And Leonora could have bitten her tongue. He appeared not to notice her flush and went on, 'I fear, however, they would never fit you. A better idea is for you to wear a *bourka*. Do you know what that is?'

She looked at him loftily, which was a bit difficult considering her low perch. 'I have been in this country for nigh on thirteen years. Father Dominic, who educated me, saw to it that I learned all the customs of the place.'

'Good,' he said with a satisfied smile. Then he asked casually, 'Why did your mother decide to leave Portugal, lady?'

She saw no point in deceiving him. 'A few months after my grandfather's death, Senhor Pinto, his property agent in India, informed my mother that Bengal was in turmoil and that unless she came out to occupy her estate it might well be taken over. Because of the diminishing Portuguese power, many of the Portuguese settlers were selling up and either returning to Portugal or sailing to other settlements in Macau or Penang, in the east, or Brazil in the west.' She said this agreeably enough, yet maintained a hint of aloofness.

'I see—and she liked what she saw, or she too might have sold up and returned to Portugal.'

'She met Angus Grant.'

'Ah!'

Leonora bit her bottom lip. How could she tell this abductor that she had disapproved of her mother's marrying an impoverished trader who coveted her fortune? Child though she had been, Leonora had seen through Angus Grant.

'I must make arrangements for our departure, lady,' Craig said.

After he had gone, Leonora fell to deliberating that she could not blame him entirely for her predicament. If she had not ventured out on her own without her mother's knowledge, she might not be here. She knew a guilty thrust of conscience when she realised that, had Father Dominic not persuaded her otherwise, she too would have caused her mother deep hurt by her wilful absconding—which, paradoxically, had rebounded on her through the medium of Craig Mackintosh.

Rumi entered the room a little later. Not only did she bring the *bourka*, tossed over her shoulder, but also carried in a tray with some chapattis and a small bowl of vegetable curry. Instead of hurrying out after Leonora thanked her, she hesitated. *'Missahib,'* she began in a soft voice. 'You have eaten little all day. Hira Nag Sahib says we will make long journey. You will need your strength.'

'Did the *sahib* tell you to say that, Rumi?'

The servant shook her head. *'Nahin, missahib.* I do not wish you to be ill. You are the only foreign lady I am knowing who has thought to thank us servants. Do not worry too much. *Huzoor*, Hira Nag is a good *sahib*. He will not harm you.' And, before Leonora could say any more, Rumi departed.

No brazier had been brought in to combat the chilliness of the room, and Leonora shivered. In the dim light of the primitive earthenware lamp, its wick soaking in oil, she examined the contents on the brass tray. The appetising aroma of the food made her stomach growl. There was no point in starving herself, she mused, and sat down to eat every morsel.

By the time Craig Mackintosh entered she had slipped on the voluminous *bourka*, which made her feel like a grey ghost; it covered her from head to toe and had two netted holes at eye level to enable her to see. An odd excitement assailed her and she ascribed it to the fact that she would soon be out of this dreary room.

He held out his hand. 'Give me that bag.'

She pushed her arms through side slits in the robe and snatched up the holdall. 'Thank you, but I'm quite able to carry it, sir.'

He drew in a weary breath. 'Look, ma'am, we might come across *dacoits*, and, since at one time you yourself offered me valuables which you have in a purse tucked in there, they'll be safer with me. I shall be armed.'

She reluctantly surrendered the bag, and in the exchange his hand accidentally brushed hers. Immediately she recoiled, as if he had bitten her like the cobra he had been named after and of which he undoubtedly approved.

'Good lass,' he remarked quietly, unaffected by her reaction. 'I'll see you in a while. Seat yourself in the cart outside.'

She felt that it was useless to argue with him. If he wanted her jewellery he was welcome to it, though she favoured the Vasco da Gama ruby cross and chain, given to her by her grandfather whom she had loved. She wished she had taken the piece out and hung it round her neck.

Opening the door he ushered her outside with a sweep of his hand. 'I'll be with you in a trice.'

The brightness of stars and a half-moon in an indigo sky illuminated the cold night, and Leonora was thankful for the enveloping warmth of her shapeless garment as she walked, escorted by two guards, to the vehicle silhouetted a short way from the building. Rumi waited by the bullock cart with two large white bulls yoked to it. Underneath was a glowing lantern suspended between the rear wheels.

Rumi approached and guided Leonora to the back of the cart, lifted the flap so that she could enter and followed her in. Leonora saw that the vehicle was clean, arranged with bolsters for seating, and space where boxes were stored that would probably hold bedding and eating utensils. A single oil-lamp threw enough light to see by. And the odour of oxen failed to overpower the smell of newness which denoted that the cart had been specifically made for the kidnapping. She felt her heart slide, wondering if she would ever set eyes on her mother again.

In the dim interior of the oscillating cart, Leonora occupied part of the time observing her companion. Rumi, clad in a dark sari, a thick blanket thrown round her shoulders, sat cross-legged opposite, her thin arms covered in tattoos and silver bangles, hennaed hands relaxed in her lap. She appeared to be oblivious of all, eyes closed, thin face vacant. Leonora assumed the woman to be in her late thirties, and at present in the throes of some kind of meditation. Instinctively she wondered if the ideal moment had arrived for her to attempt an escape. She reflected, her spirits lifting, that the cart seemed quite low enough to jump from. All she needed to do was quietly lift the back flap, leap out, and run as fast as she could to—to...she would think of that later. First, however, she must test the woman's alertness.

As softly as possible she rose on her knees, ready to creep to the bottom of the cart—when the Indian startled her.

'What is it you want, *missahib*?' Rumi's low voice proved as effective as the restriction of a ball and chain.

With a silent moan Leonora sank down again. 'I—I fear I'm exceedingly uncomfortable. I feel grimy and need a bath. The *sahib* promised that I would have one before leaving that lodge. I suppose there was no time. It has been my custom to bathe daily, hence my restlessness,' she improvised, although she did yearn for a bath.

Rumi's disbelieving gaze from close-set black eyes seemed to penetrate Leonora's *bourka*; the ruby studs on the nostrils of her squat nose glittered like malevolent drops of blood. 'When we have travelled out of the jungle then we will stop at a *serai* where we can bathe and eat.'

'*Serai?* Is that a traveller's rest?'

'*Ji, missahib.*'

Leonora felt sure that her mother had organised a search for her, and assumed that those appointed to the task would look in the resting halts first. Or would it be too obvious for them? She sincerely hoped not; she desperately wanted to be found, if only to relieve her mother's anxiety. Word must have swept through the settlement and the East India Company Writers' building in Calcutta of her disappearance, despite Mackintosh's warning in the ransom note against informing the authorities. Did he not know how servants talked? 'Where is the *sahib*?' she asked.

'He rides with us, *missahib*. He is behind the cart. Would you speak with him?'

She grimaced to herself. Faith, if I had jumped down I would have landed right in front of the man. 'No—no, I don't.' She lounged on the bolsters and let her imagination run wild. His gentlemanly behaviour could be a front, a method of keeping her relaxed and quiet. He had promised not to harm her physically, but what was to prevent him and his henchmen from strangling her here in the jungle and leaving her body as a banquet for hyenas, jackals and other predators? And as if to confirm it, a laugh from a hyena permeated the night and made Leonora shudder. Time lapsed and she toyed with the idea of discarding the stifling *bourka*. Then she froze.

The sound of terrified yelling as if a man was being attacked erupted in the silence. Cart and riders came to a sudden halt. The yells changed to high-pitched screams. Santa Maria! Someone was being tortured, Leonora suspected in horror.

At precisely the same time, the flap of the cart was lifted and a turbaned head with a cloth covering the mouth materialised. Leonora felt too petrified to utter a sound, sure that they had been ambushed.

'Now, very quietly, both of you get down. We have to push this cart off the path and into the jungle.' Mackintosh's urgent whisper, in Urdu for the servant's sake, sent a ripple of relief through Leonora. She could not imagine why. 'Douse the lamp, Rumi,' he added. The Indian woman did as she was told. Odour of the smoking wick filled the cart and total blackness descended. Then, gradually, Leonora's eyes grew accustomed to the surroundings. She saw Craig's hand held out to help her down and rose to take it. As she moved forward, he caught her round the waist and swung her to the ground. The chilliness outside made her thankful that she had not discarded the cumbersome *bourka*—or so she tried to convince herself, yet could not quite dismiss her appreciation of the garment for concealing her confused expression. She had decidedly experienced an odd pleasure from the touch of his hands. How could she entertain such feelings for a man who stooped to kidnapping an innocent person, and cared nothing for those who suffered? No reasonable answer surfaced.

Even as he ordered the two men with him to shove the cart out of sight, Leonora swept her curious gaze over him. He had disguised himself in the garb of an Afghan warrior: hip-length coat secured with a wide sash which supported a gleaming pistol, full pyjamas tucked into felt boots. The whole outfit was black, giving him a sinister yet rakish appearance.

'Get behind that tree with Rumi and wait until we've finished with the cart,' he ordered.

The screaming had stopped. Leonora saw her chance for freedom, though she felt very much afraid. She must make the effort, she thought, and act while everyone was occupied camouflaging the cart, bullocks and Craig's black steed. But her kidnapper appeared to be well ahead of her. 'And don't try any derring-do or you'll be hurt. That screaming you heard is the work of *thuggees*. They'll show less mercy for a woman. Understand my meaning? Now do as I say.'

Her mouth went dry. *Thuggees!* Madonna! She swallowed and stared at the vast jungle, visible in the brightness of the moon casting dappled shadows of foliage from soaring trees.

He did not wait for her to move, but swept her up in his arms, strode through the undergrowth and deposited her at the bole of a vast sal tree. Amazing how secure she felt in his strong arms. Shortly after, Rumi arrived, a little breathless from trying to keep abreast of her master. 'These individuals roam in gangs,' he enlarged painstakingly, as if Leonora were a dull child, 'so it's best we remain out of their sight.'

'And if it hadn't been for this harebrained scheme of yours, sir, none of us would be in peril. Pray, turn back now and those *thuggees* will be none the wiser. Why tempt fate?' she said, finding difficulty in keeping her voice a whisper.

He looked disdainfully down at her. 'Oh? And allow you and your lover to enjoy an ecstatic reunion? Can't you get it into that beautiful head of yours that what I'm doing is no whim but a well thought out plan?'

'And how many times am I to repeat that the man is not my lover?'

'As many times as you wish—you'll not convince me, woman.' He gave her no opportunity to reply, turning away and vanishing into the undergrowth.

Angrily she let out her breath and sat stiffly against the trunk. She could hear the men heaving the cart and leading the animals into hiding. Thereafter a profound silence descended. Nothing stirred, as Leonora stared down to see in the dappled moonlight a layer of mist covering the forest floor which gave it an eerie appearance. She was vaguely aware of the smell of foliage wafting around—and deeply conscious of an unknown danger.

A twig cracked. Hairs on her nape rose. Her skin erupted in goose bumps. A strong premonition prevailed of an unseen yet tangible presence close by. She felt an overwhelming compulsion to run—when suddenly a strong arm grabbed her from behind and a hand closed over her face.

CHAPTER FOUR

BECAUSE of the *bourka* covering Leonora's face, the attacker, whom she could not see since he was behind her, failed to locate her mouth. Her numb brain somehow assimilated this fact and instinctively she let out a piercing screech. She struggled with her foe and received a clout over her head which dazed her into silence—yet left her still conscious. The man now found the position of her mouth and clamped hard fingers over it. Despite the thickness of her garment his smell of earth, sweat and wood smoke reached her nostrils. Next to her, she heard Rumi putting up a fight. No screams issued from her; presumably her assailant had had no trouble finding *her* mouth to silence it.

The blow to her head had rendered Leonora helpless, so with ease her attacker dragged her along backwards, her heels scraping in the leaf-strewn earth. Several sets of feet padded behind and with a sick feeling of horror she realised that she and Rumi had been captured by *thuggees*. Santa Maria! Was the rest of her life destined to be spent taken hostage by one group or another? But with these fanatics there would be no escape, no mercy. Unless, that was, Craig Mackintosh's desire for revenge against Angus Grant proved obsessional enough for him to rescue her to enable him to effect his own brand of punishment—if he himself had escaped capture.

Her head began to ache just as she was dragged into a clearing where a small fire burned. Around it squatted several men in grey turbans and long robes fitted to the waist and flaring to the ankles. The flickering flames cast eerie light and shadow on their dark faces. The men rose to their bare feet and headed for Rumi, who was still struggling and needed to be dealt with first, Leonora surmised through the veil of pain and terror enshrouding her brain. They roughly gagged Rumi, bound and trussed her up against a tree. Her eyes had grown enormous and fear-crazed, her thin frame trembled.

Now the men turned and slowly crept towards Leonora, their bodies half bent, scarves with knots in the centre held taut between their hands. Evil grins and the sign of the God Shiva—horizontal lines chalked across their dark foreheads—filled her with alarm and made her quake violently. She cringed, tried to break away from the creature who held her fast. But her resistance was feeble to the degree of being non-existent. Santa Maria! They were about to strangle her!

'Take off the Muslim's *bourka*,' the man leading the others ordered. How can we see what we are doing?' Leonora was aware that only Muslim women wore *bourkas*, hence they suspected her of being one. A forest of hands reached out to grab the garment, and her heart drummed in a torment of horror. But her mouth had been released and with all her might she let out scream upon scream.

Suddenly pandemonium reigned, and hands fell away from her, as all eyes riveted on the apparition that came thrashing through the undergrowth.

Craig Mackintosh, in full Highland attire of tartan kilt, sporran, stockings, black jacket, his fiery hair flowing, wild and loose beneath a tartan cap complete with white cockade set at a rakish angle, his amber eyes

ablaze, galloped into the clearing astride his huge black
steed and yelled something in Gaelic at the top of his
voice which resounded through the forest. Simultaneously he wielded a deadly claymore, flashing with
ominous threat in the firelight. To Leonora he looked
like a fearsome sun god. She felt astounded to see that
he bore the trident of the God Vishnu in the centre of
his forehead. He held up his hand specifically to show
the cobra ring, its diamonds throwing out iridescent
flares, its ruby eyes and forked tongue shedding red fires.
It soon became apparent that the *thuggees*, unlike her,
thought of him not as a likeness to a god but as the deity
itself. She suddenly grasped that this was exactly the
effect Craig wished to convey. From her studies of the
two main religions of India, Leonora recalled that in
Hinduism the cobra was believed to be the pet of the
God Vishnu. Craig had utilised this concept by displaying the ring.

It worked.

All the *thuggees* immediately dropped to their knees
and prostrated before his rearing horse, calling on the
god to spare them. No doubt they had never seen anyone
of so fearsome a countenance and so bizarre an outfit
and, because of the sign on his brow and the diamond
cobra, believed him to be a reincarnation of Vishnu
himself.

In spite of Leonora's abiding by the conviction that
he posed as great a threat to her safety as the *thuggees*,
she felt beyond all logic great relief at seeing him, and
was forced to admire his ingenuity.

In his deep, resonant voice, speaking fluent Bengali,
he ordered the fanatics, 'Give those women to me.' He
pointed his claymore at Leonora. 'That one is mine!'

He lunged down, swept her on to the front of his saddle, hoisted the bound Rumi to the back of it and away he galloped, leaving the men still prostrated.

The rumpus Craig had created disturbed the creatures of the forest. Birds flapped and squawked, langur monkeys whooped discordantly and owls hooted. Meanwhile, Leonora wondered how long the *thuggees* would take to discover that Craig was no god but a human who had successfully hoodwinked them.

It was some time before the trio on horseback came upon the hidden cart and the two frightened men left to guard it and the muzzled oxen.

'Motilal, take your wife and comfort her,' Craig said to the man who caught the stallion's reins. 'I'll see to the *missahib*. Please, all of you keep as quiet as possible. This might just be a respite. There is no time to lose. Come, let us hurry on our way.'

Motilal carried Rumi down from the back of Craig's saddle and hastened with her to the cart.

Leonora still felt shaken from her ordeal, but recovered a little to argue, 'I—I think, Mr Mackintosh, you must be—be jesting. How is it possible to hurry in a slow-moving cart?'

Craig's strong arm still held her hard against him, stirring within strange, disturbing emotions which she had no wish to analyse. She could feel the vibration in his chest as he laughed. 'You're right, lass. Nevertheless, there is a short cut to the nearest *serai* at the edge of the forest and near the banks of the Hooghly. It is also close to Chinsura.' And he went on to explain, 'The Dutch East India Company there are preparing for battle with the English, who are marching to meet them now. We should reach the *serai* before the night is out and hope all is quiet till we're ready to leave again.' He appeared to muse aloud, and only the perturbing pressure of his hand lightly massaging her midriff, which seemed to burn her through the thickness of the *bourka* and her dress, indicated that he was sensually alive to her.

She could not fathom how in her present state of fear, exacerbated by a headache, she was able to react with sensitive awareness to this man who boded no good. The sinister power he operated over her proved to be born of eroticism, a sensation she was now beginning to understand, and which she must ignore at all cost.

Without revealing by word or action the effect he unwittingly forced on her, she said, 'I would like to return to the cart, sir. I fear I am much overwrought from— er—from the rough treatment I received at the hands of the *thuggees*. It has resulted in a severe headache.'

'Are you sure it's that, Leonora, and not me?' He spoke in a voice so soft, so steeped in allure, that it added to her confused state of mind.

'Why, certainly it's you, sir. You are the axle of my present predicament. Now please put me down. I—I need to go to bed.'

And then he shocked her by saying, under his breath, close to her ear, 'So do I—with you.'

She stiffened away from him, leaning forward in the saddle. 'I resent being spoken to in so loose a manner, sir!'

Craig gave a low laugh, dismounted and swung her down. He held her under the armpits. 'False prudery! What are you keeping it for? I wager I can give you as much pleasure as, if not more than your ageing lover.'

She struggled, but in her present condition felt too weak to put up much opposition. He drew her closer till she felt her nipples burgeon and throb against his hard chest. 'Really, sir!'

'He wouldn't know of our liaison even if I did decide to return you to him. But it seems unlikely he'll have you back, since the second ransom note was ignored. I should have known he'd use the bazaar whores to compensate for your loss. And you could replace him by taking me as a lover. I'll do my best to thaw you, beautiful frozen madonna.'

'Is this the payment you want for saving me from the *thuggees*, Mr Mackintosh?' He abruptly released her, causing her to stumble back, but she quickly regained her balance. In the moon's radiance she could see his mocking face and superb physique, displaying a wild magnificence in the Highland outfit. Be that as it might, it had no romantic effect on her, she desperately tried to convince herself.

'I want a great deal more than that, ma'am,' he said lightly, sketching her a deep bow followed by a soft chuckle. Moving aside, he swept a hand in the direction of the cart. 'If you please.'

Mackintosh had succeeded in upsetting her by deriding, mocking, laughing at her as if she were a dolt, she thought, feeling oddly hurt. She controlled her trembling body and perforce climbed into the cart, and knew her efforts looked ungainly, affording another reason for him to have fun at her expense.

Inside the dim interior, Rumi lay curled up in deep slumber. Leonora took a long breath and slowly exhaled. She turned her gaze on the servant and envied her her ability to sleep despite their recent turmoil. With a weary moan she lay her aching head on the bolster and knew no more.

*   *   *

As the cart trundled forward on well-oiled wheels, Craig unfastened a bundle tied behind his steed's saddle, changed back into his Afghan clothes and carefully packed away his Highland ones.

He recalled that, while he had been a prisoner with a few of his compatriots, they had been told by the Sassenach, following the débâcle of Culloden, that the Duke of Cumberland had decreed that henceforth kilts and tartans were prohibited, and clans made non-existent. However, he had kept the ragged trews he had worn throughout the harrowing and grief-stricken voyage to India. At Bombay he had been impressed into the British army and supplied with the redcoat uniform. He had carefully hidden the trews and, when the opportunity arose, had washed and packed them away. Years later he had managed to find a weaver who could copy the tartan and a tailor who had eventually succeeded in sewing up a complete Highland outfit.

Now Craig returned the holdall to its original position. He secured the sheathed claymore to a strap slung across his shoulder and back and made sure the pistol was firmly holstered and tucked into his sash. Within minutes he had caught up with the cart. After giving Rumi's husband, Motilal, and the cart driver, Ram Das, instructions to take it in turns to sleep, he decided to make plans for the future.

Mackintosh's mind refused to settle to work—instead his thoughts wandered off to Leonora. Just for a moment he felt a pang of remorse for his treatment of her. There had been no need for him to needle her with all that obscenity worthy of a whore reluctant to sell her favours. Especially in her present state of exhaustion, brought about by her recent trauma with the *thuggees*. Except that she riled him with her icy control and frozen image. So beautiful, so unattainable. He wanted to pierce that cold exterior and find a warm, approachable lass and, yes, a sensual one. He could not understand himself; not only did he harbour the hatred of vengeance against Angus Grant, but also jealousy. The bastard had captured the heart and body of the woman he supposedly hated—yet desired with a burning zeal he had not encountered before. By a strange twist of fate effected by the misunderstanding that she was Grant's daughter, Leonora was his prisoner and—he shook his head in wonder—he did not want to let her go. What happens now, Mackintosh? he asked himself. There's bonnie Fiona waiting for you. But he did not want to think about Fiona.

It was Rumi's soft voice which brought Leonora awake. 'What is it? Where——?'

'We have arrived at the *serai*, *missahib*. Keep your *bourka* on till we are in one of the rooms. Come.'

Before getting down Leonora enquired with concern, 'Did those *thuggees* hurt you, Rumi?'

The servant looked touched and Leonora thought she spotted the glint of tears in her eyes.

Rumi wagged her head. 'You are a kind lady, *missahib*, to ask. *Nahin*, those devils did not hurt me. I am thinking I hurt one of them with my kicking!'

'But after the frightening time they put us through, do you feel better now?'

'*Ji hah*, *missahib*, I thank you. The sleep, it makes one well. And you? How does it go with you?'

'Like you, I feel better after the sleep, Rumi.'

The servant smiled and raised the back flap for Leonora to descend. The moment she alighted she smelled the fishy odour of the river, and through the eye netting of her garment observed that it was still night. In the moonlit radiance she saw that it was slightly misty and that the cart had arrived in a large courtyard around which apartments were built. So this was the wayfarers' rest known as a *serai*. Tents had been erected in a wide area circling the central well and camels, horses and elephants were tethered to posts. Here and there a fire burned and men sat huddled round them smoking hookahs and gossiping.

No one paid much attention to the party—other vehicles were arriving or leaving. Motilal and Ram Das busied themselves unyoking the oxen and placing bundles of grass in front of them. Her gaze strayed to Craig Mackintosh. He had dismounted and was in the act of placing a nose-bag over Kala Khan's head. Then, as if sensing her eyes on him, he looked straight across at her. Her face burned and hastily she turned to follow Rumi into a small room. Shortly after, a servant attached to the *serai* asked if they required food and baths.

Behind a curtain of split bamboo dividing part of the room, Leonora tossed warm smoke-scented water over herself from two buckets. A primitive affair, but oh, so refreshing. Since Craig had her canvas bag, which held a change of clothes, she decided to wear only her camisole and ankle-length cotton petticoat till Rumi arrived. She would ask the servant to fetch the bag. Folding up her dress, which she intended to wash when she reached her destination, Leonora stepped out of the bathing area and into the small bedchamber.

She gasped and held the dress against her breast in a protective attitude—Craig Mackintosh lounged on the low string bed. 'What are you doing here, sir? I thought this was the women's area.'

'Not at all, *senhorinha*. It is in fact the communal part of the *serai* where families and married couples stay,' he said blandly, smiling up at her, his hands behind his head.

'Then I must ask you to install me in an apartment for unwed women. I resent this intrusion. As you see, I am only partly dressed.'

'I did knock, but received no reply so thought I'd investigate whether you had absconded. As for being partly dressed——' his voice grew husky and he lifted himself on one elbow '—you look modest enough to me—and bonny.'

He drank in her beauty as she stood hesitantly before him, and thought her the most stunning woman in the world. Her cheeks were flushed after her bath; tendrils hung in front of her ears. The rest of her black tresses were swept back from the enchanting widow's peak and caught in a large knot on the crown of her head. He observed her long, slim neck on perfectly moulded shoulders and shapely bare arms. He wondered whether her skin was as smooth and silky as it looked, and yearned to touch her.

'I—I need some clothes, Mr Mackintosh, and you have my bag.'

He swung his long legs off the bed and rose. 'So I do. I'll be back in a moment.'

It was not the bag he returned with but a beautiful peacock-blue caftan with a broad sash. The sleeves were wide, the neckline slashed to the waist and fastened with two jewelled clasps.

He held it out to her and Leonora drew in her breath, taking the garment from him, feeling the purity of silk. 'It's beautiful,' she whispered, and smiled up at him, her cheeks dimpling, her parted lips revealing small white teeth. 'Where did you get this?'

'From a shop a few doors away.'

'Oh, but I cannot accept——'

'Go and put it on, Leonora,' he cut in softly, his eyes growing dark as they looked deep into hers.

Leonora vanished behind the bamboo curtain just as a knock sounded on the door. She heard Rumi call out that she had brought dinner, and Craig's invitation to enter. Her hands trembling a little, Leonora donned the caftan. It felt smooth and sensual against her skin.

Craig said nothing when she stepped into the room, but the open admiration in his eyes spoke eloquently enough and brought a flood of colour to her cheeks.

The food had been placed on a low table. Craig pointed to cushions surrounding it and they seated themselves. 'We'll talk after we've eaten,' he said.

Leonora tucked into the fare. Her headache had vanished after her deep sleep, the bath had refreshed her and she felt light-hearted and fit to face whatever Craig had contrived. She could feel his eyes on her while he ate, but she chose to ignore him and enjoy the delicious repast. Scooping up the last spoonful of stewed guava, she drank some sherbet and then washed her hands in a small brass finger-bowl and dried them in a square of towelling provided.

They both finished together, and though neither had spoken she had to admit that the atmosphere was relaxed enough for her to have enjoyed the food.

'Mr Mackintosh, I would be obliged if you could kindly let me know what you intend doing with me now that you are convinced my stepfather has no intention of paying the ransom.'

He dabbed his mouth with the towel and turned to her. 'We are going to Murshidabad. It's farther north, on the right bank of the Hooghly.'

She looked at him in surprise. 'But why? It's so far away.'

'It is where I conduct my business from. I happen to own jute and cotton fields and factories there. We send the commodities downriver to my agents in Calcutta and then export to other countries.'

'I see,' she said, her indigo eyes widening with understanding. 'I wondered where you had been that you should take so many years to make up your mind about avenging your father's death. You have never lived in Calcutta?'

'Oh, I have, but only in the fort for a short time before we marched to Plassey to fight Siraj-ud-daula. I have not put foot in the civil area. Therefore I knew nothing of Angus Grant's whereabouts or that he had a family till I spotted him at the New Year's ball.'

Leonora swallowed and looked squarely at him. 'Mr Mackintosh, why do you want to take me to Murshidabad? Wouldn't it be a lot easier to return me to my mother?'

He stood up slowly and stared down at her, his amber eyes relentless. 'You are coming with me to Murshidabad, lady. No more arguments on that score.'

Leonora drew herself up straight and looked steadily up at him. 'You should by now realise, sir, that your original plans for ransom have failed. It would be in your own interest to return me to my mother, who must be distraught at my disappearance. Unlike you, I feel it is a waste of time and energy plotting vengeance. As you can see, it has brought you and me nothing but trouble. I harbour no ill will against you, and you can rest assured that I will not set the police on your trail.'

His expression grew remote, indifferent, the eyes opaque. He smiled and clapped slowly. 'Bravo. Well done, lady. What do you expect me to do? Drop to my knees and kiss the hem of your robe in gratitude for protecting me against the authorities? Sorry, I'm not prone to such extremes of gallantry. If your mother was blind enough to marry a renegade and murderer, then she has to endure whatever that entails. And if you, being her daughter, must suffer also—so be it. It all contributes to Angus Grant's downfall.'

'How?'

'You'll see.'

In a choking voice she rasped, 'You, sir, have been aptly named.'

A faint ironic smile curved his well-formed lips. 'I have?'

'Yes, you do carry the venom of the cobra!'

He laughed softly. 'Thank you, ma'am.'

She watched him stroll languidly to the door and assumed that he intended to leave. Instead, he shot the bolt and leaned against the rough wood, folded his arms across his chest and gazed through his thick lashes at her. 'But you are wrong. I am not known as a venomous cobra, *senhorinha*, but a *diamond* one. Tell me, how do you account for that?'

A faint pink coloured her face—she chided herself for losing the control Father Dominic had so admired in her. She could not understand how she had allowed Craig Mackintosh to penetrate and destroy her reserve in a single sweep that left her breathless with grudging wonder. Even so, she had no trouble retorting, 'The "diamond" is easily explained, and I certainly don't consider it flattering. The jewel may be beautiful, but it carries the curse of being too valuable.' Her gaze dropped to his ring. 'It strikes me as hard, cruel. Men kill to possess it, women yearn to decorate themselves with it. Rumi told me that you acquired the title because of the ring. Is this true?'

It came as no surprise to her when she heard his amused laugh. 'So, you're not as indifferent as your attitude proclaims, hmm?' He pushed away from the door and sauntered to stand in front of Leonora. It took an effort of will to remain where she was and not succumb to the urge to back away from him. As if to make sure that she did not, he caught her shoulders and drew her to him so that she could feel, with unnerving awareness, his muscled length skimming her soft curves.

He had discarded all the weapons he had carried on the journey, and wore a black woollen shirt over ballooning trousers tucked into calf-length, tooled leather boots. And as she glanced up at him she observed, in the lamplight, the fiery sheen of his wavy hair. He too must have bathed—she could smell the clean tang of soap and smoky water. Perfectly ordinary. No reason why her heart should behave erratically. It must be fear, she assumed.

'Aye, I'm known as Hira Nag, because of the ring. Also for another simple reason. Indians create their own sobriquets for Europeans, merely because the majority of them are unable to pronounce some western names just as we sometimes find difficulty speaking theirs. I'm afraid they make a terrible mess of saying "Mackintosh".'

She automatically burst out laughing, and he joined her. Then they both grew serious. She watched the darkening of his amber eyes, and the single muscle hammering in his tightened jaw. 'You have dimples when you laugh and your eyes are so deeply blue. As bottomless as the ocean, and as mysterious.' A spell-inducing nuance feathered the softness of his tone. Gliding his hands from her shoulders up her slender neck, he cradled her head for a moment, undid the heavy knot of hair. Her tresses tumbled in a blue-black waterfall down her back and he swept his hands through its thick silkiness. As she stood staring helplessly up at him, he caught her in his arms, lifting her on to her toes till her lips were just under his. Slowly, triumphantly, he smiled. 'Goddess,' he murmured, then his mouth came down on hers.

In his strong arms, Leonora felt like a pliant puppet whom he manipulated according to his will. The warmth of his mouth moving over hers, persuading a response, sent a surge of pleasure pervading her body. The growing elation she experienced and the pressure of his embrace rendered her powerless to resist if she wanted—and Leonora did not want to, lost in the pleasure of his kiss. He continued to kiss her while holding her a little away from him, then, removing his right hand, unclasped the front of the caftan and slipped the garment off her shoulder.

Leonora floated in a world of languorous ecstasy. She sighed in disappointment when his mouth left hers to explore her neck, her bare shoulder. Suddenly she was shaken by an exquisite eruption, alive to his hand pushing away the material to bare her full breast. He held her fullness and his mouth closed over it, his tongue caressing the jutting peak. She shook her head as if waking from an erotic dream. The spell he had woven over her broke and she struggled to be free of him. But he refused to let her go, appearing to be excited by her writhing. He caught her pushing hand and twisted it behind her, gripping the wrist. Again he bent to kiss and caress her breast and drink from the swollen nipple.

'Leave me alone, Mr Mackintosh!' she panted, appalled by her wantonness.

He lifted his head, but his fingers replaced his mouth, they played, fondled, aroused, till her body pulsed with heat and promoted an ache for fulfilment. Yet this passion he evoked was wrong. Santa Maria! How could she have permitted such intimate liberties? She who wished to be a nun! She could not account for her reckless behaviour.

Craig glared down at her, his amber eyes afire. He appeared as ferocious as a tiger deprived of its prey. 'You are enjoying this as much as I am. Don't tell me it's virtue that prompted you to stop.'

Leonora was trembling. 'All I ask is that you let me go, sir! Else I'll scream and create a scene! You—you wouldn't want that, would you?'

He released her abruptly and pushed her on to the bed. 'I know what stopped you! The thought of your lover finding out. Or did you have that bastard in mind when I was kissing you? Guilt, was it?' He lunged, grabbed her shoulders and shook her till she felt as if her head would fall off. 'Was it?'

'No!' she cried. He let her go and stood glowering down at her. Leonora pulled the front of the caftan together and, trying to stifle her sobs, said, 'Whatever I say, you wouldn't believe me. I behaved wrongly, but not for the reason you give. Please do not repeat what you did tonight.'

He nodded in angry understanding. 'You ached so much for your lover that you were willing to submit to me—till your conscience smote you!'

With an effort Leonora collected herself and resumed her cold façade. She looked through him and calmly said, 'Will you kindly leave, Mr Mackintosh? I am very tired.'

For a moment she thought he would hit her, then with a contemptuous curl of his lips he turned and strode from the room.

CHAPTER FIVE

ON CRAIG'S departure, Leonora took off the caftan carefully and lay down in her shift. She could not sleep; her whole body squirmed with guilt remembering Craig Mackintosh's sensual kisses. Too late she berated herself for not resisting him from the start. Now it was inevitable that she abscond. No use lying here regretting what could not be changed. She had to act. If only an opportunity arose—which did not seem likely for the rest of the night.

Urgent banging on the door had Leonora swinging out of bed. '*Missahib!* Get up! Let me in!'

She recognised Rumi's agitated voice and quickly flung the *bourka* cloak-wise round her shoulders, in preference to slipping into the elaborate caftan. Only after Craig had left her last night had she realised that the door could be locked from the inside. Drawing back the bolt, she allowed Rumi to enter. 'What's the trouble? Why, it's still dark! Have the *thuggees* attacked the *serai*?'

'*Nahin, missahib.* There are many soldiers riding in. I am thinking they are sepoys wanting to rest in *serai*. Hira Nag Sahib has gone to hear what talk he can.'

Excitement grew in Leonora's veins. If these were the British-trained sepoys of the Bengal Army then there must be a British officer commanding them, she deduced. Here was her chance to escape. 'Why all the anxiety, Rumi? This is a public *serai*, anyone can use it.

Why have you come to tell me so common an occurrence in the middle of the night?'

Rumi waggled her head, lifted her shoulders and waved her hands about. 'The *sahib* says we must make ready to go when he comes back, *missahib.*'

The servant had left the door open and stood in the entrance. Beyond her, Leonora could see in the light from lamps and torches what looked like a cavalry battalion of uniformed sepoys and, as she had correctly assumed, riding ahead of them was a European officer. He shouted an order to halt. With a flame of hope flickering in her heart she recognised the young Irishman who had partnered her in a dance at Lord Clive's New Year's ball. She watched him dismount while a reckless plan developed in her brain.

She eyed the frail form of Rumi, which could be shoved aside with the least effort, and although she liked the Indian woman she could not allow sentiment to obstruct her bid for freedom.

'You're too late, ma'am.' Craig Mackintosh's silhouette loomed forbiddingly in the doorway.

'How did you know what was in my mind?' she asked in surprised tones. Was the man a mind-reader?

'I could see you tensing, ready for action. And don't attempt to scream. Because, if you do, you'll be responsible for the deaths of at least four people and perhaps more. I shall not stand passively by and allow myself to be arrested.' He spoke so softly, almost a whisper, yet it carried the intonation of intimidation.

Except Leonora's aim to escape proved stronger than her fear. 'Mr Mackintosh, if you let me go now, I swear I shall not betray you. I-I'll explain to the officer that

I ran away from home and—and that you found me here.'

Craig smiled incredulously and shook his head. 'No, lady, that won't wash. *I* know you're courageous enough to leave home, but Captain Kelly would not believe you. As a rule, beautiful, wealthy European women do not run away on their own, not in India. So, now——' he glanced at the bed where the caftan had been discarded and the neatly folded dress she had travelled in '—get into your gown and *bourka* and we'll leave without much ado.' He closed the door quietly behind him.

Earlier in the night Craig had sat with the other male travellers round one of the camp fires and had listened to the gossip. He had learnt about the battalion of British sepoys riding towards the *serai*. From here the army was pushing on to Chinsura to prevent the Dutch from occupying the town. Something else he had learnt: one of the Indians squatting round the fire had seemed bent on making enquiries about a foreign woman who had been kidnapped. Had anyone seen her? There had been much ribald laughter and bawdy jokes. Where was this *feringhi* woman?

'If I knew,' the enquirer had said drily, 'would I ask?'

'They are all in the foreign settlements, brother, with armed guards parading in their compounds. Who will take the risk of kidnapping them?' Craig had asked in his fluent Urdu.

The man who had been carrying out the investigation had been a thick-set individual capable of physical violence. 'There are some who will risk anything for money. I have been asked by *sahibs* of the East India Company at Calcutta to find this *missahib* who, it is rumoured, has been abducted for a large ransom. A reward has been offered by the lady's people. So if anyone here finds out where she is, I'll share the money with you.'

'Would her abductor bring her to so obvious a place?'

'He might, brother,' the investigator had answered Craig. 'We *kotwals* are well trained in the tricks of rogues. They come to obvious places thinking we will not look there.'

Mackintosh had felt distinctly uneasy. Despite his warning to Angus Grant, the bastard had brought in the police. Damn him to hell! He had feigned boredom and yawned. 'Let's get some sleep. It's late, brothers, and I have a long journey to make tomorrow.' The others had assented with grunts, covered themselves with coarse blankets and curled up round the fire. But Craig had not been able to sleep. His thoughts had see-sawed between the pleasure and frustration he had experienced with Leonora, and apprehension of what the police officer had stated.

He had received a worse shock when, before dawn, his former colleague Captain Patrick Kelly, who had fought with him at the Battle of Plassey commanded by Lord Clive, had ridden in with his battalion of sepoys. Craig had felt certain that the young officer would not recognise him in his Afghan clothes, yet Kelly's appearance on the scene had augured ill. Fate was catching up with him. He knew the consequences if he was caught: there would be no reprieve. Grant would see to it that he was deported, possibly to hang. But he could not abandon his commitment to keep Leonora captive till he had ruined the traitor. He owed it to his father and fellow Jacobites who had died so needlessly.

Now he could see that Leonora intended taking advantage of the situation to make her escape. And who could blame her? He stood guard outside her room till the door opened and she followed Rumi out. He hoped to goodness she would heed his threat and keep quiet. He exhaled with relief when she made no sound.

Once the cart trundled on, he ordered Motilal and Ram Das to keep a strict eye on Leonora, to see that she did not leave the vehicle, and headed back to the *serai*.

As he rode in he saw in the light of camp fires the sepoys tethering their horses to hitching posts and feeding the animals. Captain Kelly stood apart, talking to one of his Indian officers. Craig dismounted and waited till the two men finished speaking, saluted each other and parted. He watched as Kelly headed alone for one of the rooms. Mackintosh strode briskly till he was abreast of the captain, then said in a quiet voice, 'I never thought to meet you here, Patrick. Chance plays some strange tricks.'

The Irishman stopped abruptly and gaped at his friend. 'Strewth! Craig! Craig Mackintosh? Sure it is!'

'The very same, but not so loudly.'

Kelly lowered his voice. 'What the hell are you doing here, and in that rig-out? On a spying mission, I dare swear. I thought you'd left the accursed army.'

They had reached Patrick's apartment and Craig smote his friend on the back, all the while laughing. 'No, I'm travelling alone and don't wish to draw attention to myself. A European undoubtedly arouses too much interest.'

'Then, pray, what are you doing here?'

'Thought that was obvious, Patrick. I'm on my way to my place at Murshidabad. I spotted you and your men riding in and decided to catch up on some gossip. How is Calcutta?'

Kelly swept off his cocked hat and indicated a divan against a whitewashed wall. 'Have dinner with me, and a tot of brandy, perhaps?'

'I'll have some brandy, but I can't stay long.'

Ensconced on divans laden with cotton cushions in the most comfortable apartment the *serai* had to offer, the two men sipped brandies. Patrick remarked that he couldn't divulge where his battalion was headed. 'Top secret, sir! Sure it is!'

Craig already knew that they were marching to Chinsura to head off the Dutch. He refrained from mentioning it to his friend lest he should embarrass him. Instead he probed for news of Calcutta.

'All hell has broken loose in the colony. Remember the frozen madonna? I pointed her out to you and partnered her at Lord Clive's ball.'

Craig had to restrain himself from manifesting too much eagerness. 'Aye, sure I remember the lass.'

'You'll think I'm jesting when I tell you she's been kidnapped and held for ransom!'

Craig affected shock. He opened his eyes wide. 'Ach! I wouldnae believe that.'

'You're as sceptical as her stepfather——'

'You told me he was her *father*.'

'No, Craig, I was wrong. If he were her father he would perhaps pay the ransom, but he refuses.'

'Why?'

Kelly shrugged his wide shoulders and thoughtfully scratched his pale sideburns. 'Said the girl had arranged her own disappearance to extract money from him. Sounds plausible.'

Craig grudgingly admired his adversary. Grant hoped to get his stepdaughter back without having to pay a penny for her. 'So what happened?'

'He has a whore in the bazaar, and she set spies on the man who arrived at the stated venue to collect the ransom.'

Craig could feel his stomach tightening. Faith! He could have sworn that Ram Das had covered his tracks thoroughly. Evidently not, since the blasted *kotwal* had followed them here. One consolation—he had not quite traced them. Or had he? And was using a ruse to cast his net once they were on their way and only four of them to contend with?

'I believe the girl and her supposed kidnapper are headed this way. So if you come across any suspicious-looking individuals—someone got up like you, for instance!' Kelly joked. 'Well, if you suspect any individual, report it to the *kotwal*. He's here, I think.'

Craig certainly did not think it amusing, yet he laughed along with Patrick in a bid to allay suspicion from himself. 'I hope he doesn't suspect me.'

The Irishman took a gulp of his brandy. 'But you'll not credit this. Sure you'll not.'

Putting down his empty glass, Craig said casually, 'Not credit what?'

'Grant's Portuguese wife is dead.'

Mackintosh felt thankful that he no longer held his glass, or he would have crushed it to smithereens.

Through the pounding in his head he heard Patrick saying, 'At first Grant was suspected of murdering her, but cholera was raging in the bazaar and the doctor declared that the disease had killed her. Last I heard was that Grant had disappeared. Gossip had it that he had gone to his courtesan, Kamila.'

Mackintosh did not pay much attention to Patrick when he changed the subject, but to cover his own shock he made the right responses. He felt sure that Grant was involved with his wife's death.

Outside, music had started up and hand-drums beat out a resonant rhythm in tune with his disturbed heart. When a sepoy brought in a tray of food, Craig said his goodbyes, wrung Patrick's hand and took his leave.

He was scarcely aware of mounting Kala Khan and riding out of the *serai*. How the hell was he going to tell Leonora about her mother's death? There was no question of holding the girl any longer, if what Kelly had told him was fact. Once they reached Murshidabad, he would fly his carrier pigeons to Calcutta and find out for certain whether her mother had died.

A short while later he came across the cart at a standstill on one side of the dusty road. His servants stood in a group outside the vehicle, shouting accusations at each other. My God, it could not be. But it was. 'What's wrong?' he asked, knowing well what the answer would be.

The three servants spun round to face him. 'Forgive me, *sahib*,' Rumi entreated, steepling her hands and wagging her head. 'The *missahib*, she told that she has call of nature. What could I do? I go with her little way in jungle. She is telling me to turn my back. But when I look round for her she is . . . she is . . .' Rumi pulled the edge of her sari across her mouth to stifle a sob.

'She'd gone.'

'*Ji, sahib*. I found only her *bourka*.'

Craig felt towering rage against his servants and especially Leonora, and it showed in the devilish set of his jaw.

'She cannot have gone far, *sahib*, I am thinking there is too much jungle,' Motilal chipped in, no doubt to protect his wife. 'We will set out now and find the *missahib*.' He waved a hand to the thick forest that lined the rutted road.

'Do not move from here,' Craig enunciated, his burr pronounced. '*I'll* look for the *missahib*.' And God help her when I do find her, he added in silent fury.

Leonora already regretted her impetuosity while she struggled through the undergrowth. She had hoped to find a footpath that would lead her back to the road but not the cart, then keeping to the shadows she intended returning to the *serai*, demanding to see Captain Kelly and asking for his assistance. It had seemed so easy to persuade Rumi that she had to obey the call of nature, and while the poor trusting servant had obliged, led her into the forest and modestly turned her back, Leonora had seen her longed-for opportunity to escape.

Except now, hours later, she was lost. She dared not risk shouting for help lest she should disturb another gang of *thuggees* or ferocious wild animals.

The deeper she staggered into the forest, the more she rued leaving the cart. After all, Mackintosh had not harmed her in any way. True, he had kissed her passionately, but partly with her consent. And his three servants had been models of respectfulness. She had nothing to fear from any of them. Why, oh, why...?

Then she heard it. Leonora froze. The sound came again. A vibrating growl.

The animal must be some distance off, she assumed with a growing sense of despair and terror. The creature could either be a leopard, black panther or tiger. She knew exactly what they looked like—her stepfather had several skins in his study. What to do? Where to go? Wildly she looked about and above her. The trees were too straight, with no footholds for her to climb. Oh, Santa Maria! How could she have been so foolish? If she had had to escape she could have waited till they reached a village or town. As it was, she now had no choice but to remain perfectly still—almost impossible with her trembling body, limbs and rustling skirt. She hoped the beast could not catch her scent. She had learned something about wild animals that inhabited the subcontinent. Tigers had been blessed with a keen sense of smell. But since it was a windless night ... Except— was the animal a tiger?

The roar erupted louder, closer. She felt a great weakness attacking her legs, as if they were about to dissolve. Then she spotted a tiny flame flitting between the trees ahead, like a will-o'-the-wisp. She prayed that it wasn't a *thuggee* but Craig Mackintosh looking for her.

It was not Craig who bounded out from the jungle to confront her but a huge, striped animal, magnificent, terrifying, visible in the faintly dappled moonlit night.

She opened her mouth to scream. No sound came. Backing away dizzily, she was brought up perforce by the unyielding hardness of a trunk. She sagged against it, her stricken eyes staring at the enormous tiger just yards in front. It stood in a half-crouch, one vast front paw lifted, head thrust forward, glaring at her with brilliant eyes which showed no mercy.

'Rajkumar! Rajkumar!' a male voice called. The tiger looked away from her, blinked, screwed up his face, revealing long, lethal fangs and let out a roar that caused the earth to tremble and the birds and other animals to shrill and cry out in alarm. As for Leonora, she believed her hour of death had approached and closed her eyes in resigned prayer.

'What are you doing here, Rajkumar? Have I not told you to stay near me at night?' The male voice drew closer now. The man admonished the animal in Hindustani, which Leonora understood. Her eyes flew wide open to perceive a Biblical figure with long white hair, his slim body enshrouded in a flowing, seamless garment. He could pass for Noah, she thought imaginatively, the only distinction being that in the centre of his forehead he bore the white trident of the God Vishnu—which reminded her wistfully of Craig's masquerade. She could see the man distinctly in the flame of the lamp he held.

'*Arre Bap!*' he exclaimed, stepping backwards. 'Oh, father! What brings you to the jungle, *missahib*?'

Totally tongue-tied, she had just enough strength to lift a trembling hand and point to the tiger, who was pushing his nose against the stately old man's veined hand, the fierce eyes closed in bliss. In more congenial circumstances—that was, if the animal were behaving in this uncharacteristic manner behind the safety of bars—she might have softened to see the affection between the frail man and the powerful beast.

The man glanced down at his pet in some surprise, as if he could not believe her fear. 'Do not be afraid of Rajkumar, he will not harm you while I am here,' he said, smiling and stroking the fearsome, magnificent head. 'But what are you doing in this place, *missahib*?

No white ladies ever roam the forest. Not even with their *sahibs*.'

Leonora swallowed and managed to croak, 'I—I am lost. I left the cart I was travelling in and——' She gulped in a shuddering breath.

He held up a hand and nodded in sympathy. '*Ji*, I understand. You could not find your way back again, is it not? Did you not have a woman with you?'

'I did, but I—I lost her. Who are you, pray?'

He petted Rajkumar and spoke. 'I am Ajuna the yogi. I brought Rajkumar up from a cub. His mother was shot by a hunter. Now he looks after me at night. In the day he roams the forest, but at my call will come to my aid. I must warn you, *missahib*, that there is a gang of *thuggees* living in the forest. They do not harm me because I am a holy man. Come, I know the way back to the road. I will lead you there.'

Leonora hesitated. 'Er—how do I address you, good man?'

His kindly dark eyes twinkled, though the flames from his flickering oil-lamp cast macabre shadows on his thin, bony face. 'Call me Sri Ajuna.'

'Sri Ajuna, I must tell you the truth. I—I am a victim of kidnapping. And I wonder if you can help me. I promise to make it worth your while if you return me to Calcutta. I haven't any money on me at present, but I'll reward you handsomely.'

Rajkumar growled, switched his tail from side to side. The yogi looked about, as if expecting to see someone or something materialise. He stroked the animal and spoke soothingly to him.

The old man turned his gaze back to Leonora. '*Missahib*, I am a hermit. I seldom visit cities or villages. I

devote my life to the glory of God and need no money—
the forest yields enough food. Former pupils sometimes
visit me and give me simple clothes and flour. You see,
I am pledged not to live outside the forest. But I will
take you back to the road.'

'Then, Sri Ajuna, can you give me instructions of how
to return to the *serai*? I promise not to trouble you any
more.'

The hermit looked unhappy. 'It is dangerous travelling
alone to the *serai*. As I have said, there are *thuggees* who
might chance upon you. I think it is best that you return
to the cart. When it stops at a village you can try to
attract the attention of the people there.' He was clearly
trying his best to be rid of her, Leonora thought with a
sinking heart.

Rajkumar let out a roar and Leonora shrank back
against the tree.

Sri Ajuna lifted up his lamp and swept it round him.
'There is someone here. Do not move, Rajkumar.' The
tiger obeyed, twitching his tail and staring into the
darkness behind Leonora.

Suddenly into the opening stepped Craig Mackintosh,
startling her. 'You're right, Sri Ajuna, not to assist this
woman. She's my wife and wants to return to her people
in Calcutta.' He ignored Leonora's gasp of protest and
swept on, 'You'll agree, her place is with her husband.'
And to Leonora's astonishment he approached the tiger
and tweaked its ears. The animal made a low 'Arooum!'
of affection and brushed its immense body against Craig,
almost unbalancing his strong frame.

She took a few paces towards the yogi. 'Sri Ajuna,
this man lies. I am not his wife!' Rajkumar pricked up

his small ears and growled a warning at her. She squealed and leapt back against the trunk.

Sri Ajuna was not convinced by Leonora's words. He wagged his head in disbelief and disapproval. 'It is always the same,' he complained. 'Runaway wives give the usual story.' And Craig glanced over his shoulder to send her a smile of mockery. 'Why do you want to leave Hira Nag Sahib? He is a very good man to our people and all like him. Hence he must be a good husband. Go, *memsahib*, go with him.' He raised his hands in a *namasta*, wished them both happiness in their life together, turned and called to Rajkumar, and the animal meekly followed him.

Craig did not expect Leonora to be as obedient as the tiger. He swung her up, tossed her over his shoulder and, before she had time to protest, said sternly, 'Keep quiet, woman, or you'll have all the damned *thuggees* and animals on our track!'

Leonora paid scant notice of his irritation, impatience and rough handling of her. She was too preoccupied marvelling over how relieved and safe she felt to be with him again.

CHAPTER SIX

CRAIG deposited Leonora none too gently inside the cart. 'Now listen, lass—if you continue to harass me by trying to escape, you shall not see Calcutta again.'

Leonora studied him for a while but could read nothing in his hard expression. 'Does that mean, Mr Mackintosh, that you intend to return me to my home?' she asked breathlessly.

'Aye, it might be sooner than you think.'

'Then why are you continuing the journey to Murshidabad? Isn't that a waste of time?'

'No, lady. It is imperative that we get to Murshidabad; there is something of grave importance I need to find out.'

'About me?'

'It involves you. Once you reach Murshidabad, you'll meet friends of mine, and if you wish to return to Calcutta safely it would be to your advantage to refrain from mentioning that you are my hostage.'

She raised her slim brows. 'Really? And, pray, what am I supposed to say, sir? Will not your friends wonder what an unmarried girl is doing alone in your company without a chaperon? I can scarce claim to be your sister!'

He smiled faintly. 'An excellent idea. Alas, my friends happen to know my history. However, I could say your people have entrusted you to my care till I deliver you to your uncle who lives at Jangipur, a day's journey from Murshidabad.'

'You've planned it well, Mr Mackintosh,' Leonora said with cynical admiration as she settled herself in the cart. 'What if your friends don't believe you? And are you not afraid I will tell them the truth?'

He gave the signal for the cart to move, swiftly mounted and edged his horse close to the vehicle. 'If you do, then, as I have stated before, you will not see Calcutta again.'

She believed him. 'And what am I supposed to be doing visiting my uncle?'

'He's ill and wishes to see his favourite niece. By the way, he is Portuguese, Senhor Fonseca. Memorise the name.'

'And how long are we to remain in Murshidabad before you take me to see this fictional uncle?' she enquired sweetly.

'Plenty of time to think of that,' Craig replied with finality, and cantered his horse to the front of the cart.

For the remainder of the long journey, Leonora noticed that he became distant and withdrawn. A frown almost constantly marred his forehead. Even so, she was surprised to discover that she missed hearing his deep laughter, albeit that it was often filled with mockery.

The party stopped at a couple of villages to stock up with food and to allow the animals some rest.

She felt uneasy, sensed that something was amiss. Since her escapade in the jungle he had not taken his meals with her—he had deliberately sought to avoid her. Leonora could not imagine why. She had planned to cultivate a friendly rapport with him in the hopes of appealing to him to somehow send a message to her mother stating that she was well, but he wore an aloof, unapproachable air; consequently she herself adopted a remote attitude. Meanwhile, she worried about Dona Julia.

So did Craig. Yet he retained a spark of hope. Kelly might have misheard the information about Leonora's mother, considering how wrong he had been in believing that Angus Grant was Leonora's father. Craig knew how distorted gossip could prove. Only after verifying the truth via carrier pigeon from his residence would he tell Leonora.

To Leonora, Murshidabad seemed enormous compared with Calcutta. It lay in a sprawl as if basking in the late afternoon sun on the bank of the shimmering River Hooghly, on which garlanded barges and boats with large single sails drifted along. Soon the party came to the outskirts of the city.

The back flap of the cart had been pushed to one side, enabling her to watch the bazaar lining the wide, dusty road leading to the interior of the town. She had never been allowed near a bazaar, and now momentarily forgot her predicament to enjoy the exotic scene.

As the vehicle trundled along, she gazed through the anonymity of her *bourka* in fascination at the canvas-covered stalls selling every kind of merchandise: eastern fruit, gunny sacks of grain, leather and velvet shoes and slippers, jewels set in heavy gold and silver and bolts of fine cotton, rich silks and velvets. Crowds in colourful turbans and saris wafted back and forth, haggling over prices, laughing and shouting, chewing the ubiquitous betel-nut stuffed in triangles of glossy *pan* leaves. Adding to the cheerful confusion were the transport animals:

camels, elephants, bullocks, buffaloes and a few horses carrying produce or dragging carts full of people. The air hung heavy with strong perfume wafting from the distilleries and mingling with the stench of animals and filthy drains.

The travellers were out of the bazaar now and nearing the town. Rumi drew Leonora's attention to the Nawab's palace, typically Indo-Mogul in design, with golden domes and spires topped with the crescent of Islam.

The servant motioned Leonora to the front of the cart and pulled back the flap. She pointed ahead, beyond the driver. 'That is the *sahib's* house.'

Leonora's indigo eyes widened in surprise—it was no extraordinary sight. A good-sized bungalow with a flat roof to sit out on during summer evenings. 'Is this the Diamond Cobra Palace?' she enquired with a hint of incredulity. She had expected an ornate building like the Nawab's.

But it was Craig, riding alongside, who startled her by breaking his reticence to reply, 'No, ma'am. The Palace of the Diamond Cobra is a two-month journey away near the Himalayan foothills.' His explanation he conveyed with affable formality. 'This is the residence I work from. The warehouses are along the waterfront, where I supervise the loading of jute on my barges that sail to Calcutta. I have excellent agents here and in Calcutta who handle my business in my absence.'

He still wore his Afghan outfit, the flowing end of his turban covering his nose and mouth, obviously to keep out the dust which rose at the least disturbance. Only his amber eyes were visible, narrowed against the glare.

'It is the prerogative of the rich and idle to push work on to other people's shoulders.' She derived satisfaction from needling him for his indifferent manner.

He laughed softly. It fell pleasantly on her ears. 'You forget that honest people with money can and do help impoverished folk to earn their living, provided they're willing to work. And, talking of the idle rich, you cannot exonerate yourself from that category.'

'I certainly didn't waste my time, sir!' she retorted. 'I worked as a teacher in Father Dominic's day school, and taught the younger children of converts the rudiments of English and Portuguese. And I did it voluntarily.'

'Very charitable,' he said drily. 'And after school you fooled everyone, including your mother, by carrying on an affair with Angus Grant.'

Leonora bit down on her lower lip. She did not want Craig to think so ill of her; oddly, it hurt. She yearned for his approval, and suddenly realised that she had grown to like him, despite his recent aloofness. In fact, she had adversely found him more attractive because of his reserve. But there was no point in denying his accusation, since he would not believe her. Instead she gave an exasperated sigh and kept quiet.

The cart rumbled to a halt on the gravel driveway in front of the bungalow, and servants in white liveries with red tartan cummerbunds came dashing out. They were not the only ones who appeared.

As Leonora was helped from the cart, a young, beautiful woman with auburn hair came tripping down the veranda steps. 'Craig! Oh, Craig!' she called in delight, lifting the voluminous skirt of her blue dress and running to him.

Eagerly he dismounted, threw off his turban and swept the girl into his arms. 'Fiona, my love!' he greeted, and kissed her warmly.

Leonora was appalled by such behaviour. Public demonstrations of affection between men and women in India were frowned on by both Europeans and, more so, Indians. Be that as it might, she could not suppress another hitherto unknown emotion akin to resentment which she experienced against the girl, which had nothing to do with breach of convention. It disturbed her to see the two locked in each other's arms. And, from the deep, throaty laughter Craig emitted, he was thoroughly enjoying himself, oblivious of everyone else.

Quickly she turned her back on the couple, her heart thumping, and followed Rumi up the steps. Not for the first time was she grateful for the haven of her enveloping garment. Shame burned in her face as she recalled the night at the *serai* when he had kissed her, and—her heated response. She felt used, besmirched. Thank heaven she had eventually summoned control and warded him off.

'*Senhorinha*, I'll send your bag along,' he announced. She marvelled that he could drag himself away from his paramour to speak mundane words to her, or to remember that she existed.

Leonora nodded to indicate that she had heard, and hurried behind the servant; she did not relish drawing attention to herself.

The chamber Rumi led her to was high-ceilinged and spacious. Absently she noticed beautiful paintings of Scottish and Indian landscapes hanging on the white-washed walls, her mind still reeling from the shock of witnessing the love scene. Moving across thick rugs in bright colours covering the red, glazed floor, she approached a four-poster which stood beside a large window. Through it, the fading light from the sinking sun streamed. In different circumstances she would have appreciated this pleasant evening in February, but her distracted state of mind precluded any enjoyment. She threw off the dusty *bourka* and sank on to the comfortable bed spread with a yellow silk coverlet. Rumi had left the room to bring in her mistress's bag and, with a sigh of tiredness, Leonora leaned back against the pile of plump bolsters.

The next thing she knew was that someone was shaking her shoulder. '*Missahib*, I have brought your bag. The *bhisti* has poured warm water in the tub. The bathroom is over there.' Rumi pointed to an open door.

'Thank you, Rumi. I am in dire need of a proper bath and grateful to the water-carrier for filling the tub. Where did you say my bag is?'

'I have put it on the sandalwood table near the dressing-table. Do you want me to help you bathe and dress, *missahib*?'

'No, Rumi. You know I can manage. You must be very tired yourself and in need of a bath. Go now and relax.'

The servant thanked her.

As soon as Rumi had left, Leonora bolted the door. She did not want Craig Mackintosh marching in and out at will, nor did she wish to give him the opportunity of trying to seduce her again. Not that he would make the effort now that he was reunited with his lady love, she thought sourly. Why sourly? She could not work out the mechanics of her brain. Firmly she thrust him from her mind.

First, she checked in her bag and felt satisfied that all her jewellery was intact. Second, she took out the only other dress she had packed away, a plain beige silk, and clean underclothes, and made for the bathroom. It was fully tiled in blue and had a large copper tub from which steam rose. Before undressing she bolted the back door and felt secure in the knowledge that whoever wished to enter, back or front, would have to knock.

And knock they did. No sooner had she dressed, slipped on the ruby cross which had once belonged to Vasco da Gama, and brushed her hair into a shining knot, than she heard the peremptory series of raps on the front door. She knew who it was before she asked.

'Mackintosh,' he replied in answer to her enquiry.

She tried to sound calm. 'Is anything the matter?'

'Open the door and I'll tell you.'

She thought it best to do what he said. From the impatience in his voice, she feared he might break his way in. As soon as she drew back the bolt he pulled the door wide. Her quick glance swept over him taking in his clean suit of clothes, which were in the Scottish mode: his full-sleeved silk shirt, jabot with masses of fine lace, and velvet waistcoat to match the scarlet background of his tartan trews.

She should have known that a man as handsome and dashing as he would definitely be attractive to beautiful women, and spared herself unnecessary—what? Hurt? Shock? Knowing full well she was his hostage, she should not have allowed herself to become emotionally involved with him. Really! She must be going insane to entertain such a ridiculous notion. Of course she was not emotionally entangled with him or anyone else.

Craig bowed slightly and offered her his arm. She saw the diamond cobra sparkling on his finger and it made her shudder.

He followed the direction of her gaze and smiled derisively. 'It won't bite.'

Raising her eyebrows she looked pointedly at his arm. 'Pray, where are you taking me, Mr Mackintosh?'

'To dinner, lady. I hope you're as hungry as I am. I assure you, the cook has excelled himself. But first we must join my guests. They're anxious to meet you.'

She wanted to ask him how many guests he had, but he was already guiding her into a large room she vaguely recognised as a parlour. Her attention focused on the auburn-haired girl whom Craig had kissed earlier, and the elderly man seated by her side on a maroon velvet-upholstered settee. The couple rose as Craig propelled Leonora towards them.

She felt drab in her plain dress compared with the beautifully groomed girl in a green taffeta gown laced at the bodice, the full skirt parting in front to reveal a cream, brocaded petticoat. The girl's shining ringlets fell beneath a green bow and in her hand she held a feathered fan.

'Leonora, this is Miss Fiona Mcintyre,' he introduced. 'Fiona, this is Senhorinha Leonora Maclean.'

'How do you do?' both girls said together, and gave each other polite nods and smiles. It seemed so hypocritical on her part, Leonora thought, pretending to find pleasure in the introduction, but it would be ill-bred of her to ignore the demands of etiquette.

Craig caught Leonora's elbow and turned her towards the old gentleman, who wore a dark blue frock-coat.

'And this is my good friend, Ian Mcintyre, Fiona's father.'

Ian's pale grey eyes lit up as he took Leonora's hand and bent his wigged head over it. 'Ach! Pleasure to meet so bonny a lass.'

She liked him instantly. 'A pleasure to meet you too, sir,' she returned, giving him a radiant smile.

Ian Mcintyre reluctantly released her hand when Craig guided her to a wing-backed chair. 'What would you like to drink?' He looked deep into her eyes. Was he warning her? she wondered, averting her glance and settling her skirt as she sat down.

She rarely drank anything stronger than fresh fruit juice, except on special occasions when she would accept a drop of wine. 'I'll have a little Madeira, please.'

'Most certainly, ma'am.' He gave her a stunning smile, and Leonora without thinking smiled back. Her expression soon grew serious as he spoke. 'And you, bonny Fiona, what will you have, lass?'

She looked at him archly. 'You know what I have, my love. Same as you and Father. No less than whisky!'

The three of them burst out laughing, while Leonora felt excluded and yearned to slip away unnoticed to her room.

Craig moved to the polished ebony drinks cabinet and took out crystal glasses and decanters. Leonora watched his long fingers as he poured out a drink and brought it to her. 'I hope you enjoy it, lady.'

'I'm sure I shall, Craig.' That should shake him, she thought mischievously.

It did. He looked taken aback, his amber eyes staring at her quizzically. 'Er...good, Leonora.'

He served his guests, then stood in front of them, discussing matters and people Leonora knew nothing about.

Ian Mcintyre glanced anxiously at her from time to time. But she gave him a sweet smile, indicating that she had no objection to the conversation. In reality Leonora objected very much. She felt excluded, unwanted and something more. This fierce emotion that swept through her she at last recognised as the fiend jealousy. It was totally illogical; she had in the past convinced herself that she despised Craig Mackintosh for taking her hostage, though time had mellowed her feelings enough for her to acknowledge silently that she actually liked him. Apart from that, nothing had changed—she still remained his prisoner. So why did she experience jealousy? She should be thankful that Fiona had captured his heart, drawn his interest away from her. To divert her mind from those two laughing together, she forced herself to admire the workmanship of the long clock in a corner of the room, and jumped a little when it suddenly chimed the half-hour after eight o'clock. She decided that her best move was to excuse herself on the pretext of tiredness after the long journey and escape to her room. That way she could conquer this feeling of humiliation. Leonora drained her glass, set it firmly on the fretted table beside her and was about to speak when a gong sounded.

'Ah! Dinner at last!' Craig tossed back his drink and offered Fiona his arm. 'Come, my love.' He smiled into her eyes.

The girl laughed and tapped him playfully with her fan. 'I dare say you were ever a flirtatious rogue!'

'May I, *senhorinha*?' the old gentleman said, his hand on Leonora's elbow assisting her to her feet.

She laughed softly. 'Certainly, sir. I thank you.'

It might have been her imagination, but she could have sworn she saw Craig hesitate and his body stiffen as he and Fiona led the way into the dining-room.

The smell of food stimulated her appetite. Craig and Fiona sat in straight-backed chairs at the long, polished table lit with candelabra, and Ian Mcintyre and Leonora sat opposite.

It was a sumptuous and well-cooked meal: clear soup, followed by baked river fish and sliced limes. The main course consisted of finely minced mutton packed into envelopes of thin pancakes and served with a variety of lightly boiled vegetables. The dessert was a choice of transparent halva embedded with nuts or baked rice pudding. But Leonora could not fully enjoy the meal. She felt alarmed at the amount of liquor Craig and his guests imbibed. Fiona had a fit of the giggles every time anyone spoke, and Craig looked on with amusement. Ian Mcintyre carried on an animated conversation with himself entirely in Gaelic. It was time she made her exit and left this lot to the mercy of the sober servants standing patiently near the ebony sideboard and staring impassively ahead.

Slipping silently out of her chair, she quietly thanked the servants and asked them to convey her compliments to the cook. They bowed low, bringing their right hands to their foreheads. One of the men rapidly preceded her and opened the door.

Craig's deep voice, stone-cold sober, halted her with 'Where are you going, *senhorinha*?'

Fiona chuckled. The old man started singing an unrecognisable tune—if it could be called a tune.

Leonora sighed, turned in the doorway and passed a weary hand across her brow. 'I'm tired. I'm going to bed.'

Fiona gave a high-pitched laugh. Her father stopped singing, put his head down on the table and promptly started snoring.

Craig, pushing back his chair, rose. 'I'll see you to your room.'

'I'm quite capable of finding my way there alone.' Then, as an afterthought, she added, 'Pray, do not worry. I'm too tired to try and escape.'

Fiona suddenly burst into tears and yelled, 'Rob! Oh, Rob! It's all your fault! Rob Murray, do ye ken?'

Craig stared at her in astonishment. 'What?'

'I think Miss Mcintyre is more in need of your escort than I am, Mr Mackintosh,' Leonora chipped in drily.

He swung his golden gaze on her and frowned. 'Earlier, you called me Craig.'

She arched her brow provocatively. 'I know. But I believe it's a lady's prerogative to change her mind. Goodnight, Mr Mackintosh.' She held her head high and glided out of the room.

Once inside her chamber, Leonora shot the bolt and strolled towards the large four-poster, its mosquito net lowered from the canopy and tucked under the mattress. She thoughtfully and slowly began undressing. Was Craig in love with Fiona? But what about the girl—did she return his feelings? And who was Rob Murray?

Leonora lifted the net and climbed into bed. She should not be concerning herself with other people and their problems, and this included Craig Mackintosh. If he did not return her to Calcutta within the next few days, she would seek yet again to find a means of escaping and freeing herself mentally and physically from his power.

She woke early and was dressed when the knock came. Fully expecting the caller to be Rumi, who had promised yesterday to have the clothes she had travelled in washed and delivered this morning, Leonora opened the door and was surprised to see Fiona.

The girl looked pale and nervous. 'May I come in?'

'Good morning, Miss Mcintyre,' Leonora greeted politely, standing to one side. 'Please do enter.'

'I came to apologise for my behaviour last night——'

'Miss Mcintyre,' Leonora interrupted quickly, 'it is not for me to object. I am merely here on sufferance till Craig is ready to deliver me to my kin.' It was the truth. She felt relief knowing that, however Fiona interpreted her words, she had not lied.

'Aye, Craig mentioned he was escorting you to your uncle's place. However, I can see you are a lady born and bred, and perhaps you were appalled by my behaviour. You see, *senhorinha*, I do not wish you to have a poor opinion of me. If I behaved disgracefully, it is because I am troubled.'

Leonora found herself liking this girl. The jealousy she had harboured against her last night she blamed on her extreme tiredness, and the fact that she had been isolated with Craig for over a month. Without being conscious of it she had grown used to having him around, which had no doubt led to possessiveness. But now, after a refreshing sleep in a comfortable bed, she could dismiss her spate of resentment as irrational.

'I'm sorry,' Leonora said sympathetically. 'Is there anything I can do?'

The girl sighed. 'I fear not.'

'Have you spoken to Mr Mackintosh? He might be able to help you.'

Fiona's green eyes showed a hint of amusement. Her lips quivered in a tremulous smile. 'I can scarce confide in Craig.'

Leonora ignored the sudden twist in her abdomen. 'What about your father? I am sure he will do his best to assist you.'

Fiona gave a heavy sigh and dropped her hands to her sides in an expression of hopelessness. 'It doesn't matter. Talking of Father, he was intrigued with the ruby cross you're wearing. He says it's extremely old and valuable.'

Leonora lifted the jewel and stared at the rounded stones. 'Yes, it is. It belonged to the first European and Portuguese explorer, Vasco da Gama, who arrived in India by sea.'

'Really?' Fiona took the rood from Leonora and examined it in awe.

'Yes. It came into the possession of one of his contemporaries, my ancestor who helped finance his expedition. Da Gama gave him the cross in gratitude.'

'It's beautiful. You wouldn't consider selling it to Father? You see, he is a jeweller and made his fortune from buying and cutting gems to sell to the numerous rajas. He'd give you a good price for this.'

Leonora thought rapidly. Here was her chance to make enough money to bribe her way out of this house, hire a barge or horse-drawn cart and get home. She did prize the cross—it had been given to her by her adored grandfather. But her desperate circumstances dispensed with sentimentality. The remaining drawback was that Fiona's father might tell Craig he had bought the piece from Leonora and he would immediately come to the right conclusion.

She shook her head. 'I regret it's not for sale. But thank you for offering to buy it.'

Fiona shrugged and let go of the jewel. 'I'm about to have breakfast. Care to join me?'

They ate their fruit in amicable silence and were sipping China tea from delicate porcelain cups in the dining-room when Craig strode in. He looked shaken, all colour gone from his face.

'Why, Craig, what plagues you? I thought you were enjoying yourself among the pigeons.'

He ignored Fiona's flippancy and addressed her, 'Do you mind if I have a word alone with Leonora? I assure you it is of the greatest importance.'

'Not at all,' Fiona said, eyeing him curiously. She picked up her cup and left the room.

A premonition that Craig was about to impart unpleasant news assailed Leonora. She watched him open doors, making sure that no one lurked outside. Her anxiety mounted as he drew a chair close to hers and took her hand. His eyes grew dark and troubled.

'Leonora, I . . .'

He hesitated for so long that she felt compelled to prompt him. 'Tell me.'

He let go of her hand and abruptly stood up, staring down at her. 'I can't bring myself to say it.'

Leonora slid back her chair and rose slowly, her body shivering. 'It's about my mother, isn't it?'

He nodded.

'Wh-what has happened to Dona Julia?' she asked in a hoarse whisper.

'She's dead.'

CHAPTER SEVEN

THE faint tinge in Leonora's cheeks and lips vanished; her indigo eyes were huge and stricken. Indeed, she looked like a frozen madonna. Dead? Dona Julia, dead? She could not speak the words but they tolled in her brain like a funeral dirge. She swayed forward and Craig's arms came round her. He cradled her head against his wide chest, his heart thudding like muffled drumbeats in her ear.

He felt torn in half when he heard her soft, pathetic moans. 'I'm sorry, Leonora. I wish I could have spared you pain. You had better lie down. I'll fetch some hot tea.'

She eased herself out of his embrace and shook her head. 'I...don't want to lie down.' She struggled to control her ragged breathing. 'How do you know she...she is...' Leonora could not bear to utter the word.

'I confess I have known for some time. Since we rested at the *serai*.'

Her legs felt boneless. Abruptly she slumped down on the chair she had recently vacated and stared up at him. 'That's about three weeks ago. Why did you keep it from me till now?'

Craig lowered his tall frame into the seat opposite and tried to take her hand, but she lifted it away from him. She saw his jaw harden. 'Because Captain Kelly told me, and I wasn't sure how much of the truth he spoke. He's been wrong before. I decided to wait and find out from here, where I possess a cote of trained carrier pigeons. I couldnae chance telling you, lest the news should be rumours.'

'How do you know it's true now?' she asked, desperately hoping he had received the information from an unreliable source.

'I sent the message to my agent——'

'How would he know?'

'Let me finish, lass. I enjoined him to enquire from Father Dominic. He's friend and Confessor of your family and would know the truth.'

Her beautiful deep blue eyes filled with tears and he felt like a swine for subjecting her to so much misery. But at least he had not been guilty of her mother's death.

Therefore he was taken aback when she burst out, 'You killed her!'

Her words were like a whiplash across his face. He shot up from the chair, kicked it away, his eyes wide, the pupils enlarged. 'What the devil do you mean? I have nae been near your mother.' A knowing gleam appeared in his eyes. 'Ah! I might have guessed. You're compelled to use me as a scapegoat to exonerate your wretch of a lover from blame. I feel certain that he very cleverly got rid of Dona Julia. And now you'll return to him.'

'I don't think you're speaking with sense, Mr Mackintosh. How can I return while you hold me hostage? I have always wanted to go home to my mother and no one else. And by your ruthless actions you have killed her. I dare say she died of heartbreak over my kidnapping, and you are responsible! If you had accepted my jewellery and sent me back, this tragedy need never have occurred.' It took all the stamina she could muster to reinforce her self-control to prevent herself from breaking down in front of him.

His mouth turned down at the corners and his eyes swept over her contemptuously. 'One thing you have forgotten, ma'am. You were the one who ran away. Else why pack a bag? You hoped that by going to the priest you could enlist his help. Instead he persuaded you to change your mind. I heard him tell you to go straight home.'

She felt guilty colour sweep into her face and, averting her gaze, stared absently at her hands moving restlessly in her lap. Abruptly she looked up. 'If I had not gone out that evening, you would have thought up another plan to kidnap me. But we waste time with talk, sir.'

He drew himself up tall and proud, then sketched her a stiff bow. 'I'll take you back within the hour,' he said and strode out.

The knock on the door of her chamber came from Rumi, and in a daze Leonora let her in. Silently the servant laid out on the bed a pale pink muslin dress lined with floral cotton and amply gathered underskirts. It was an exquisite day-gown, the stomacher laced in front with pink ribbon, totally unsuitable for travelling and ridiculous for someone in mourning.

Leonora frowned. 'Where did you get this?'

Rumi looked hurt. 'I told the *sahib* that you had no pretty frocks and could I have one made for you? So I took the dress you gave me for washing to my brother, who is very good tailor.'

'It's sweet of you, Rumi, and I do appreciate your thoughtfulness.' Leonora smiled apologetically. 'But the *sahib* is taking me back to Calcutta, and that gown is too dainty to wear for the long journey. Who paid for it?'

'The *sahib*.'

'I fear I cannot accept it. Where is my burgundy dress? Has it been washed?'

Rumi's dark gaze slid guiltily away from Leonora. '*Nahin, missahib*, it had many tears in it and . . .' She hesitated.

'And?'

'I threw it away, *missahib*.'

Leonora sighed, feeling too drained to argue over the triviality of a mere dress when her mother's death shadowed her life. She nodded apathetically and moved to the bathroom to bathe, and weep copious tears of grief. On her return to the bedroom she saw that Rumi was still there tidying up. Her holdall and another bag had been packed, but the pink dress still lay spread on the bed.

'Wear it, *missahib*. I would like to see you look your best before you go.'

'But I thought you and Motilal were travelling with the *sahib* and me,' Leonora said, looking puzzled.

Rumi wagged her head. 'My man and I are to stay here till the other *missahib* and the *sahib*, her father, return to Patna where he does trade. After they have left then we will travel to the Hira Nag Palace in the mountains.'

To please the servant, Leonora discarded the creased beige dress and slipped into the muslin creation. She smiled woefully when she heard Rumi's praise. 'Thank you, Rumi. But I shall have to wear my black mantilla as a shawl over this.' She could not bring herself to mention the tragic death of her mother.

Without demur, Rumi unpacked the large triangle of heavy black lace and draped it over Leonora's shoulders. 'I know, *missahib*. We all know of your grief.'

They probably knew about Dona Julia's death before I did, she thought with bitter pain.

'*Missahib*, I beg you, do not report Hira Nag Sahib to the police. He has done you no harm, has he?'

Leonora smiled sadly, admiring Rumi's loyalty. 'Of course I will not tell on him. I promised not to do so if he delivered me home safely.' She paused, then thoughtfully went to the holdall and took out the purse. 'I would like to show my appreciation to you for looking after me so well.' She drew out a few rupees. 'Take them, Rumi.'

'*Missahib*, *baksheesh* is not needed. I will remember you as a good, kind lady.' She refused to accept the money. Steepling her hands, she raised them to her forehead. '*Namasta*, *missahib*, the gods go with you.'

Leonora hugged the little woman and pressed the coins into her palm. Her throat hurt as she whispered, 'Goodbye.'

Rumi did not come to the carriage to see them off, but all the other household staff were there and so was Fiona. She and Craig stood some distance away, conversing earnestly in low voices.

While servants roped luggage on the roof of the handsome carriage, Leonora slipped unobtrusively into the vehicle. She tore her gaze from Craig and Fiona and abstractedly looked at the shrubs lining the gravel drive. Her heart ached with every beat; she yearned to be alone to give vent to the terrible grief that ravaged her mind and body. She had no mother to return to, only—a lustful stepfather. Cold sweat of fear broke out on her brow at the sudden realisation of what her homecoming would entail. Santa Maria! No, she could not return to that bungalow while Angus Grant was there. Never! Where could she go?

At that moment, Fiona appeared by the window. 'I'm so sorry to learn about your mother, Leonora,' she said sympathetically. 'I know exactly how you feel. I lost my mother five years past. Accept my sincere condolences.'

Touched by the girl's sympathy, Leonora put her hand out and squeezed Fiona's. 'Thank you, Fiona. Goodbye.'

She heard Craig get in beside her and give the driver an order to proceed. The carriage rolled forward and a roar of farewells from the large collection of servants went up.

As the sturdy horses pulled the vehicle along at a steady pace, Leonora could feel Craig's piercing gaze on her, but she steadfastly stared out of the window and absently noted that they were passing through the same bazaar they had encountered on their arrival.

Her mind crowded with thoughts of her mother, her love, devotion and care. Her throat ached with the effort of holding back her tears. Oh, *mãe amor*, how will I survive without you?

'We've arrived.'

His abrupt announcement jerked her back to the present. She saw that they were parked near the wharves. From the strong fishy odour she should have known they were near the river. Refraction from the water forced her to shade her eyes. Coolies shouting and bickering as they heaved crates of gunny sacks on to large barges, moored to the wooden jetty, jarred on her ears.

'You're taking me back by boat?' she asked in dismay as he handed her down. Several people stopped work to stare at her and now she wished for the concealment of the *bourka*. In her dainty muslin creation she must seem as incongruous as a ship in a desert.

'Naturally,' he said drily.

His sarcasm made her glance at him. He was soberly dressed in a black frock-coat, white shirt, plain cravat and cream breeches. His head was bare, the fiery mane swept back and secured with a large bow. 'I'm surprised you didn't insist I wear some disguise, sir.'

'There's absolutely no need, since Grant is not interested in paying a ransom and I'm merely escorting you back to Calcutta.'

'Aren't you afraid that you might be suspected of kidnapping me?'

He took her elbow and guided her towards an elegant barge. 'You'll no doubt inform the police,' he said coldly. 'I'm prepared for the worst, so nothing will surprise me.'

She did not answer, concentrating on keeping her balance on the narrow gangplank. The weather was warming fast—she could feel the noonday sun boring into her scalp the short distance she walked from the carriage to the cool interior of the barge.

Glancing round the cabin he conducted her to, Leonora saw that it was airy and comfortable. She crossed the thick rugs covering polished boards to sit on the large divan spread with an embroidered coverlet, beside a window, the curtains of which were looped back with silk cords that gave a European touch to the cabin.

He bowed stiffly and was about to leave when she said, 'Mr Mackintosh.' He halted, lifted a dark eyebrow in query. 'Why—why do you not inform the police that I'm safe here and then make your escape? India is a large country——'

'I know, Leonora, except my days for running away ended after Culloden.' And added with scorn, 'I don't need your sympathy, either.' He gave a mocking bow and abruptly left.

Alone and dejected, the full impact of her mother's death overwhelmed Leonora, and with a loud groan of agony she threw herself across the divan and sobbed out her heartbreak.

Craig entered his cabin, adjoining Leonora's. Unlike hers, it was stark. He strode over the palm-leaf mat, stood near the narrow divan beneath the window and stared out on the wide, mud-coloured river crowded with all shapes and sizes of craft. The barge sailed from the jetty amid much shouting of orders, and chanting, and started its voyage downstream. A breeze wafted through the window, cooling his heated brow. Throwing off his coat, he lay back on the divan.

His thoughts churned in turmoil. He ranted at himself for the failure to extract ransom from Angus Grant. The old bastard had got away with it again. It reminded Craig of the terrible fiasco of Culloden. But this was the first time in India that his plans had gone awry. Leonora, he felt certain, hated him and would do her utmost to effect his ruin. He cared little about that since he had resigned himself to the fact when Patrick Kelly informed him of Dona Julia's death. What Craig feared was his emotional state. He had kidnapped Leonora with the intention of hating her, and now to his deep consternation his involvement with the lass could well be that he had fallen in love with her! He shifted restlessly. No! It could not be, he tried to convince himself. He rationalised that they had been alone together for weeks, he had appointed himself Leonora's guardian and had unconsciously developed an invisible link with her. So why did he yearn to make love to her? Ah, well, she was a beautiful woman, and being a red-blooded male he felt this way about any attractive young woman. Craig frowned. This explanation satisfied him not at all. Why did he not feel the same way about the lovely Fiona? He could find no answer.

For the first few days, Leonora kept to her cabin and took solitary meals there. She felt grateful to Craig for leaving her undisturbed, allowing her to grieve alone. The isolation had helped her to come to terms with her mother's death and accept it. She knew the pain of loss would be there for a long time, but now she believed she could cope with life, and face others without dissolving into tears. One man she had no intention of meeting again was Angus Grant. Paradoxically, the only person who could help her was Craig Mackintosh.

When the servant brought in the evening meal, she asked him, 'Can you tell me where the *sahib* is? I would like to speak to him.'

'The *sahib* is on deck, *missahib*. He eats up there. I will take you to him when you have eaten.'

A few minutes later he led the way up the hatch. The moment she stepped on the deck she inhaled deeply, relieved to be out in the fresh air. Before the servant pointed him out, Leonora spotted Craig. He was seated in front of an easel busily painting. She assumed that he intended to capture the spectacular sunset on canvas before it vanished into the rapidly approaching dusk. He probably heard her step, as she saw him cover his work and lay the palette on a table, which also held brushes in containers. Craig dismissed the servant, rose and advanced to meet Leonora.

'I-i-it's hot in the cabin. I need some fresh air,' she stammered in embarrassment, feeling like an intruder. 'I hope I haven't interrupted your work.'

'Not at all, lady,' he said with an affability she had not expected. 'I welcome the diversion.' Taking her elbow, he guided her to a bench fixed beneath a canopy at the centre of the deck.

For some unknown reason Leonora felt thankful she had taken trouble with her appearance. She had been pleasantly surprised to discover more new dresses which Rumi had slyly packed, and had chosen a pale blue creation with falls of lace at the elbows and wide neck. Over her shoulders she had draped the black mantilla.

Once they were seated a silence fell, which Craig made no attempt to break. She stole a glance at him. He gazed ahead, his handsome face set in serious lines. The dipping sun changed the river to liquid gold and touched his hair with a flaming halo.

Leonora dismissed her fanciful thoughts and concentrated on what she planned to say to Craig. 'Mr Mackintosh.'

Craig switched his gaze to her, a single eyebrow rising in a hook shape.

She hunted for the correct words while awkwardly smoothing the heavy knot of hair at her nape. At last she blurted out, 'I do not wish to return to my home.'

His astonished stare came as no surprise to her. 'What? Why not?'

'With my mother dead, it will no longer be my home.'

His eyes narrowed suspiciously. 'And Angus Grant?'

She deliberately sought to misunderstand him. 'He is the rightful owner of my mother's property—what is left of it.'

'I know. And are you not anxious to be with him?'

Leonora met his gaze squarely. 'No. I have always abhorred him.' She had never seen Craig look so dumbfounded. Shifting uncomfortably under the penetration of those golden eyes, she murmured into the stillness, 'It's true, sir.'

He recovered enough to emit a sharp whistle of amazement and followed it with, 'The devil you do!'

'The devil I do!' she echoed boldly.

If she had expected Craig to respond with his customary laughter, she was disappointed. Instead he glowered at her, his eyes glittering with anger. 'And you let me believe that you were in love with him.'

'No, I did not,' she denied, regarding him coldly. 'It was you who chose to believe that.'

'But you soon stopped denying it. Why?'

She sighed and idly watched the bargee to the fore who periodically called out the depth of the river as he plumbed it.

'Why the deception, Leonora?'

'I believed my mother was alive. She knew of my dislike for Grant, but, because he was her husband, she made me promise out of loyalty to her never to reveal my true feelings to anyone outside the family. But now she is dead,' Leonora whispered sadly, 'loyalty does not signify. I refuse to return to my stepfather, Mr Mackintosh.'

'Aye. I understand now.' Relief and joy surged in Craig's heart. Here on deck, the air balmy in the gathering dusk and rising river mist, he ached to sweep this beautiful girl into his arms and kiss her breathless. Though this was the ideal place, it was not the occasion for such demonstrations. He forced himself to remember that Leonora was still in the throes of grief. Every night since they had boarded the barge he had heard her sobs through the thin panelling that divided their cabins and felt helpless to comfort her, knowing that she blamed him for her mother's death.

'He is not at the bungalow, Leonora. After your mother died, foul play was suspected——'

'You mean he killed her?'

'Perhaps. But the doctor pronounced that she died from cholera, which was raging in the bazaar at that time. Shortly after her death your stepfather left the bungalow. Kelly told me he has taken up residence with his Indian mistress, Kamila.'

'What if it's rumours? You yourself have stated that Captain Kelly has been mistaken before. Grant may still live at the bungalow. I cannot risk returning there.'

'There is an alternative. I could take you to Father Dominic. He'll make suitable provisions for you. You trust him, I hope?'

In the dusk he saw her eyes light up with pleasure, making his pulse leap. 'Oh, yes! It is singularly remiss of me to have forgotten the good Father. Oh, thank you, Craig.' Impulsively she leaned forward and pecked him on the cheek. He looked nonplussed and Leonora felt the heat of confusion rush to her face. Santa Maria! He must think me a brazen wench, she admonished herself, I cannot conceive of what prompted me to kiss him. Grief for Mama has surely turned my brain. And he is betrothed to Miss Mcintyre.

'Don't look so alarmed.' He appeared to regain control of himself enough to bestow on her an indulgent smile. 'I quite enjoyed that, although I am not deserving of your kiss. It is through me that you are suffering today.'

She smiled ruefully. 'I harbour no grudges, sir. In a short while we shall part, perhaps never to meet again.' She stood up. 'The hour is late and I have taken up too much of your time.'

He caught her hand and drew her down again to sit beside him. 'A moment, lass. Tell me what you intend to do in the future.'

The gentle stroking of his thumb along the back of her hand sent disturbing flurries of sensation down her spine. 'I hope to return to Portugal.'

The words made Leonora alive to the fact that she was an heiress. She could not claim her mother's estate in India, which automatically belonged to Angus Grant. But her grandfather had willed his villas, vineyards in Portugal, vast property in Brazil and coffers of gold to Leonora, at present under the protection of guardians and trustees. All this wealth would be hers in two years' time whether her mother had died or not. She could occupy the villa in Lisbon whenever she liked, but it would not be officially hers till the stated time. If she married tomorrow, she and her husband could claim her property immediately. Except she had not yet found a man to wed—a paradox indeed. She could have laughed, she could have wept. What use were riches when there was no loved one to share them with? She had no alternative but to return to Portugal. A daunting prospect, since she knew nobody there. It would be equivalent to venturing into alien territory, she alone among strangers and with the enormous responsibility of administering vast estates. Moreover, she would have to undergo a constant stream of suitors in Lisbon, for the Aviz wealth was well known there.

'Portugal?' His sharp enquiry startled her out of contemplation.

'Yes. I own nothing in this country. My mother's property in India became Grant's possession when she married him. Besides, I have no relations here who would take me in for a while.'

'And you have relatives in Portugal?'

'No. But my grandfather left me a house there.' She didn't enlarge on that; it seemed pointless to do so considering that she and Craig would soon part, she pondered with an odd poignancy.

A servant appeared out of the gloom carrying a couple of lanterns, hooked them on each end of the canopy and departed. In the artificial light Leonora looked up at Craig and was appalled to see his stunned and ravaged face. 'Craig! Pray, what troubles you?'

'You do, Leonora.'

'Why, sir?'

For answer he squeezed her hand so hard that she winced. 'Sorry, lady.' He kissed her palm and, rising, drew her to her feet. 'As you say, the hour is late. Let us to bed—separately.'

Craig came to collect her once the barge had docked opposite the East India Company's warehouses at Calcutta. 'I hope you had a comfortable voyage lady,' he asked politely.

Leonora gave him a wan smile. 'Yes, thank you.'

Then followed a busy time as coolies fought to take the luggage to one of the carriages for hire, grouped with others in the shade of a tall neem tree beside the dusty road. Inside the vehicle a tense silence reigned. It was not long before the bone-rattling conveyance arrived at the church.

Craig handed her down and for a moment they stared at each other. Leonora could find nothing to say. Her natural reaction had been to thank him, but in these unusual circumstances it was totally illogical. No sane person thanked their kidnapper unless they were in collusion with him. Even so, she was troubled with the thought that she would never see him again, despite the pain he had caused her. And yet... She held out her hand. 'Goodbye—Craig.'

He took her small hand in the vastness of his and raised it to his lips. 'Goodbye, beautiful Leonora. It is a pity we could never be...er...friends.'

She stayed till his tall figure entered the carriage, and watched the vehicle rumble away. It was a mystery to her why she experienced this sense of desolation and a sudden desire to see him again. With a sigh of resignation she picked up her bags and drifted to the rectory.

It was Daniel, Father Dominic's Christian servant, who answered Leonora's knock. He beamed his welcome, saw her comfortably seated in the small sitting-room and departed to fetch the priest.

She had lost all count of the months but assumed that it was past Eastertide from the debilitating onset of the hot weather. The heat of midday brought beads of perspiration out on her smooth forehead, and from her reticule she extracted an embroidered handkerchief to mop her face. Perhaps it was nervousness that also contributed to her condition.

'Leonora, *menina*!' Father Dominic breezed into the room, his cassock flapping and rosary clacking. She darted from her chair and caught his outstretched, veined hands. Grief-stricken misery came to the fore and Leonora's tears flowed afresh, despite her assumption that she was strong enough not to weep when she encountered the first person she knew. 'Oh, Father Dominic...' She could not go on as sobs racked her body.

The priest put his arms around her. His voice shook as he spoke. 'I know, my child, what you have suffered. If only I could have been at your mother's side while she was conscious before she died. But be assured, I gave her the last rites.'

He patted Leonora and led her back to the chair. 'I think you need a cup of tea, *menina*.' He called to Daniel and gave his order. From an old bureau the priest took out a large fan woven from palm fronds and handed it to Leonora. 'Here you are, *senhorinha*, keep yourself cool. And do not say a word till you have drunk your tea and feel composed.'

She dried her tears and began fluttering the fan. By the time Daniel brought in a tray she had herself under control. But Father Dominic refused to let her speak until she had eaten bread and butter and drunk the hot, sweet tea.

Some time later, when Daniel had removed the tray and she and the priest were alone, she said, 'Before I tell you what happened, I would like to see my mother's grave. Pay my respects.'

'Of course, *menina*. We shall go at once.' He was about to pick up umbrellas, which doubled as sunshades, from a stand near the back door when Daniel came in to say that a *sahib* wished to speak to the priest.

He would not be long. Father Dominic excused himself and told Leonora to stroll in the garden.

The heat blasted her as she stepped out into the bright sunlight, and she was thankful for the shade of the umbrella. Father Dominic joined her shortly after, and they walked along a flagstoned path bisecting the rectory garden, already seared brown in the heat.

He led her through a gate into the graveyard and steered her to where her mother lay buried beneath a marble slab. Carved on it were the dates of her birth and death and nothing else. Leonora knelt down on the hot earth and lost herself in prayer. At last she stood up, anger bubbling inside her. 'Angus Grant didn't even commemorate her with an epitaph.'

'Do you remember Senhor Pedro Fernandez?'

'The man Dona Julia would have me marry, Father?'

'*Sim*. The *senhor* has ordered a headstone for the grave and asked me to think up a prayer for it. He was determined to pay the ransom for you, but when he sent the money it was returned. I find that very mystifying.'

She felt too stunned to comment, and the priest went on, 'This is for your ears alone. He made much profits from Dona Julia's business and she begged him not to reveal it to your stepfather. If anything happened to her, she asked that the money be given to you.'

Blood went out of Leonora's face. 'And—and I suppose, Father, that in return Dona Julia's wish is that I marry him?' How could she refuse her dead mother's request?

CHAPTER EIGHT

FATHER DOMINIC shook his grey-streaked head. 'No, Leonora, he is a kindly man and has accepted that you find him too old for a husband. What is more, he agrees. Even so, the good *senhor* was fond of both you and Dona Julia, and believed Angus Grant to be a rogue. Now, before we go back, let us say the *"De Profundis"* for your dear mother's soul.' The two people bowed their heads while the priest intoned the prayer for the dead.

Back at the rectory, he tried to persuade Leonora to give details of her kidnapping. She stared up at the screen punkah, attached to ropes passed through openings in the wall and manipulated by a servant sitting out in the veranda.

'I'm not prepared to talk about that yet, father. I'll just say Craig Mackintosh found me and offered to bring me to you.' She squirmed at having to deceive her Confessor, but that could not at present be helped.

'Ah, yes, the new breed of nabob. I understand the Indians call him Hira Nag Sahib.'

'Er—yes.'

And from the knowing smile on the priest's face, she had the uncanny feeling that he knew that Craig had been her kidnapper.

The great fiery orb of the sun sank below the horizon, leaving an aftermath of fading scarlet merging into a deep purple sky. Father Dominic and Leonora set out for the Grant bungalow in a gaudily-painted, hired *ghari*. The box-like vehicle, pulled by two ponies decorated with beads and feathers, eventually arrived at its destination and rumbled along the horse-shoe drive.

Father Dominic had convinced Leonora that Angus Grant had left the bungalow, and that she would be safe in the care of the servants who still resided in their whitewashed quarters at the bottom of the back garden.

'Are you sure you do not want some refreshment and a drink, Father?' Leonora asked after the priest had assisted her to alight and placed the travel bag at her feet.

'Quite sure,' he returned, climbing back again. 'As I have explained, Leonora, I am expecting an important visitor.'

She did not watch the carriage depart, but picked up the bag, crossed the gravel drive and mounted the veranda steps. The place looked deserted, neglected, which augured ill. Glancing across at the front garden, she observed in the twilight that the once tidy beds now abounded with dried stalks, which the gardener in the past had painstakingly removed, but there was no sign of the *mallee* who at this time usually watered the plants. She gazed at the veranda floor and saw with consternation that it was covered in dust. Where were the servants? An ominous silence prevailed.

Tiptoeing to the door leading to the house, she saw that there was no lock. Someone must be inside, she thought with a gnawing sense of unease. Perhaps the night-watchman was preparing for sleep in one of the spare rooms. Placing her bag on the floor she knocked timidly.

No answer.

Leonora drank in a deep breath and started rapping harder. Under the fresh onslaught, the door gave. Why had it not been bolted? she puzzled. A little apprehensively and slowly she pushed it wide and stepped into the large parlour. Mounted high on the walls were the familiar and, to her, the sickening display of skins and heads of wild animals shot by Grant. Lower down was an array of crossed swords and daggers. Leonora's gaze swept over the heavy furniture, noticing the layer of dust. Her mouth felt dry and her heart increased its tempo. Perhaps Grant had dismissed the servants and sold the bungalow. But why had it been left open? Prompted by instinct she silently traversed the rapidly darkening room and entered the pitch-black corridor that divided the rest of the building in half. For a while she waited till her eyes grew accustomed to the darkness. Hardly breathing, she stole along the passage to her bedroom. Its doors were wide open and she placed her bag just inside. But on further reflection she decided to hold on to the bag to use as a weapon lest her premonition of danger should prove correct. Then she continued her inspection through the rest of the house. It appeared to be empty, but in the dark she could not be sure. Something else troubled her: a faint smell of alcohol pervaded the air. It could well be her imagination, she mused, in view of the fact that Grant was more often drunk than sober. Perhaps the stench of liquor had become ingrained in the house and remained after his departure.

Overwrought with tiredness, Leonora groped her way back to her room. After a short nap, she promised herself she would go to the servants' quarters and find out what was happening. But, as she rested her weary body on the cool coverlet, Dona Julia's perfume rose from the

bed to overwhelm, haunt and once again trigger off the
deep pain of her grief. Her beloved mother had undoubtedly lain here and fretted, Leonora reflected
poignantly, her heart bursting with sorrow, and she
pressed her head deeper into the scented pillow which
had surely absorbed her mother's tears. And now hers
joined to mingle in torment till in utter exhaustion she
succumbed to the mercy of deep slumber.

Craig was restlessly pacing the sitting-room of the rectory
when Father Dominic returned from taking Leonora to
the Grant bungalow.

'Ah, Senhor Mackintosh, you wished to speak to me?
I am most grateful to you for bringing Leonora back.
You seemed anxious when you made that appointment
this afternoon. Pray, what can I do for you?'

'Where have you taken Leonora?' Craig asked
abruptly, coming to stand squarely in front of the priest.

'Calm down, *senhor*, and be seated. I have taken
Leonora home, to the late Dona Julia's bungalow. She
is quite safe there.'

Craig did not move. 'Is she?'

The priest looked up startled. 'What do you mean?'

'I have just come back from the courtesan, Kamila.'
A hint of amusement gleamed in Craig's golden eyes as
he watched Father Dominic stiffening with disapproval.
'She tells me that Grant left her an hour ago to collect
some valuable items from the bungalow. Apparently he
owes her a great deal of money, and little by little is
slowly stripping the house to pay her off. Also, he be-
lieves that Leonora is dead and intends to claim her
property.'

The priest's dark eyes narrowed suspiciously. 'Why would the courtesan tell you that, *senhor*?'

Craig shrugged. 'Out of spite or disillusionment, I presume, possibly stemming from the fact that Grant hadn't paid her what he'd promised. She's probably blackmailing him.'

Father Dominic's olive complexion paled. 'And if he discovers Leonora is alive——'

'There's no need for me to tell you what he will do.'

'We have no time to lose, *senhor*!'

'My sentiments exactly. You stay here, I'll take the *ghari* to the bungalow.'

'Bring her back safely, *senhor*.'

'I promise, Padre.'

'God bless you, my son.'

A sound filtered through Leonora's sleep-fogged brain, yet she could not find strength to open her lids. She groaned, twisted on to her side and settled down to continue her disturbed repose. Something trailing on her cheek brought her wide awake. Slowly she opened her eyes but remained lying in the same position, her body petrifying with terror. A cold hand seemed to grip her heart. Dull light glowed from behind her, and with an effort she recalled that she was occupying her own room and that someone standing at the back of her, near the bed, probably held a candle or small lamp. The sleep had refreshed Leonora and enabled her brain to function with alertness. This person in the room had woken her by passing the tip of a finger down her face, she calculated. Just for a split second she wondered if her mother's spirit had returned to haunt this house of ill omen, but soon dismissed the idea as fanciful. Dona

Julia would never frighten her. Besides, this phenomenon breathed harshly like a living being.

Leonora heaved herself off the bed and spun round. Her indigo eyes grew large with shock as she spotted Angus Grant, grotesque in the candle-light, his shadow huge and wavering on the whitewashed wall. Her delicate nostrils quivered from the stench of liquor emitting from him. In horror she watched an evil grin spreading across his mouth, revealing broken brown teeth, and saw the leer lurking in his pale green eyes beneath shaggy grey brows that overhung almost to his meagre lashes.

He carefully placed the candle on the bedside table. 'I knew ye'd come back to yer Angus.' His voice burred and slurred as he tried to stagger round to join her, but the effort proved too much and he let his gross body fall across the bed.

Leonora backed away. The window of her chamber opened on to the veranda, and it would take her no more than a few moments to jump out as she had done on that memorable evening of her kidnapping, but she conquered the urge for the time being—she needed information from Grant. In his present state he did not seem capable of coherency, nor was he in any condition to harm her. Sober, he could and would violate her and there was no sweet *mãe* to come to the rescue. She resolved to question Grant and hoped that in his befuddled frame of mind he would not have the artfulness to lie, and would in a muddled manner reveal the truth.

She drew herself up tall, proud, the stance lending her courage. 'You killed my mother, Angus Grant, didn't you?' It was a wild guess and she hoped it would take him unawares.

'It wasn't I who poisoned her. She complained of feeling ill and the woman, Kamila, gave me the *datura* saying it would make Dona Julia well. How was I to know the stuff was poison?'

'You dare to confess to this perfidious crime to my very face! I swear that you shall not escape justice.' She knew now how Craig had felt.

'Who will believe you? The doctor has already certified her dead from cholera.'

'I am convinced that you deliberately killed her. Why? She gave you everything in worldly goods. What did you wish to achieve from her death?'

With a grunt and a snort, Grant propped himself on his elbows. His bleary gaze tried to focus on Leonora and travel her length. 'Ach! It was ye, lass, who killed her. Not me. If ye'd been here to nurse the stupid bitch, she'd be alive.'

She felt her heart lurch with guilt and remorse. What Grant had said was perfectly true. Both he and Craig Mackintosh had been right. 'Do not dare abuse my mother! You will speak of her with respect in my presence.'

Not sparing her, Grant went on, 'Ye didnae think of her when you staged your own kidnapping and demanded a ransom from me, knowing full well that it was her money. Ye're no saint, lass. And now here you are, returned to your beloved Angus. Hey?' He bellowed with coarse laughter, struggling to sit against the headboard. Choking and spluttering, he wagged a dirty finger at her. 'I could make it hard for ye, lass. Aye, hard for ye. But seeing I have a generous turn of mind, I'll offer to marry ye.'

Shock transfixed Leonora. She could do little except stare at him in horror until he finished his obscene proposal with a vulgar chortle. 'What? Marry you?' she choked in fury. 'What kind of fool do you imagine me to be? I declare, Angus Grant, that you are quite insane. I would never defile the memory of my beloved mother nor deprave myself by marrying her murderer. Never! You do not deceive me in the least; I know it is my possessions you covet, and you are aware that you can claim them if you should marry me. But I prefer to remain unwed and inherit my legacy in two years' time.'

'In truth, I intend to marry you not only for your wealth but also for your body. I have hungered to possess it for years. After I have done with you, bonny lass, you'll have no choice but to marry me. If you do not, then I fear you will have to go the way of your mother.' Grant appeared to have sobered up with alarming rapidity—he rose from the bed, went steadily to the door, shot the bolt and advanced towards her. He must have learnt of her arrival in Calcutta, assumed she would come here and lain in wait for her, hidden in a dark spot somewhere in the house. The man knew that she did not fear him when he was drunk. Now he was coldly, deadly sober. Light from the flickering candle flame cast shadows on his puffy face, stressing its oldness, its hideousness. His triumphant expression had the power to swamp her with a chilling sweat of terror.

Her mouth now as dry as kindling, Leonora inched towards the low window facing the veranda and prayed it was not bolted. She had not taken the trouble to ascertain this, and cursed herself for the negligence. Keep talking. Keep his mind occupied and at the same time look for some avenue of escape, she repeated to herself.

'What will your mistress say to all this?' It was the first thing that entered her head and it appeared to have the desired effect.

Grant came to an abrupt halt, looking startled. 'What do you know about her?' he growled.

'I have known about the courtesan, Kamila, for a long, long time, Angus Grant. You have lavished all my mother's fortune on this woman and perhaps others to satisfy your carnal pleasures.'

'Your mother's fault for not giving me what they did. But I'll take my pleasure with you, whether you're willing or not.'

Suddenly he lunged and grabbed her upper arms. He lifted her bodily and fell with her on the bed, amazing her by his physical power. 'Help!' she screamed at the top of her voice. Next instant she felt his hand strike her full across the mouth and repeatedly across her face. She tasted the salt of blood on her tongue.

Her head and the ceiling reeled. Leonora's voice choked when she tried to cry out through bleeding lips. Yet she gathered what strength she could to fight him. She raked her nails down his cheek, heard his shout of pain and whimpered when she felt as if her jaw had cracked with the impact from his closed fist. 'Now lie still, woman!' For a few moments she could not move, until she felt him tugging at her bodice while he ground out obscenities in her ear. Rage and hatred refused to let her succumb to the blackness threatening to obscure her mind. Despite her fading strength, Leonora pushed at him, strove to twist away from his hands, hot and sweaty, squeezing the bare flesh above her breasts. Her skin crawled with revulsion. Santa Maria! Save me from this spawn of Satan, she prayed in angry desperation.

Then, adding to her terror, she felt him flinging up her skirts and his hands fumbling with her legs. 'I've dreamed about this, proud bitch,' he growled in lustful glee. 'Now I've got ye!'

'No, you vile wretch!' she gasped hoarsely. 'I was not born to be defiled by you!'

His coarse laughter fell cruelly on her ears. 'Were ye not? Stupid wench, all women were born for this. Now do not delay, lass, spread yer legs for Angus,' he hissed, 'Don't be frigid like yer ma was.'

His hands gripped her legs and tried to force them apart. He raised himself a little, one hand releasing her to loosen his breeches. Then from out of nowhere came the advice her old ayah had once given should she ever need to defend herself from a man. At that time she had laughed. Now the wisdom of the old woman's words loomed in capital letters across her brain. Leonora saw her chance. With every measure of strength she could summon, she brought her knees up sharply and at the same time heaved, till at last she was free. He let out a yell of pain and dropped with an almighty thump to the stone floor. Even so, she forced herself from the bed and attempted to stumble towards the window. Too late. His hot, moist hand closed round her ankle. Leonora fought to kick free, but the dizziness she had warded off by sheer rage threatened to engulf her.

As Grant grabbed her other ankle, attempting to drag her to the floor, the window burst wide and in the opening a tall figure stood framed. She recognised Craig Mackintosh and cried out in relief. Next instant, a curtain of oblivion descended behind her eyes.

*　*　*

Craig saw Grant let go of Leonora and stagger towards the door, but the older man was hindered by his fumbling to draw back the bolt. Mackintosh swung him round and slammed his fist into Grant's face, and with satisfaction watched him slide with a grunt to the floor. He returned to Leonora, lifted her gently in his arms and carried her to the bed. His mouth stretched in a grim line when he spotted the cut on her lip and purple bruise on her jaw. It would soon start to swell. He felt along her jawbone and knew it had not been broken. For the time being she was safe enough, and from her regular breathing he judged that her faintness would merge into sleep. Meanwhile he had this bastard to deal with.

Clenching his teeth, Craig gripped Grant by the neck of his crimson brocaded waistcoat and dragged him out of Leonora's room and into the parlour. Hoisting him on to an upholstered sofa, he stared down at his obese foe whom he had hated for years—that hatred had not abated one iota. Craig knew a strong temptation to grab one of the swords on the wall and run the bastard through. Except that he deemed it cowardly to kill a defenceless man—though this brute had sought to violate Leonora. Nevertheless, Craig swore that he would make Grant pay one way or another. First he would have to bring him round. Craig took pleasure in reviving his enemy with a succession of sharp, rapid slaps across both cheeks.

Grant soon regained consciousness and held up his arms to ward off the blows. 'What the devil are ye up to, fool?'

'What indeed, wretch!' Craig straightened up and looked down his straight nose at Grant with all the contempt at his disposal.

'Who the devil are you and what are you doing in my house? I'll have you thrown out and horsewhipped. Do yer hear?' Grant snarled, glaring up at Craig, but in his eyes the younger man spotted a hint of fear.

'You will? By whom?'

Grant's eyes wavered. 'You're a trespasser, sir. Get you gone from here and leave me and my stepdaughter alone. We have a right to live in this bungalow.'

'You have no right to assault Leonora. I am here to save her from your vile hands. I have a mind to report you to the East India Council. You could be flogged and thrown to languish for years in the dungeons at Fort William.'

'What is she to you?' Grant asked, his voice laced with suspicion, though the blustering bravado had left him. 'Ach, I know!' he said, pushing himself to his feet and standing with his hands on his hips. A knowing smile spread over his florid face. 'It's that old priest, meddling and sending his henchmen to save his seemingly pure churchgoers. He came here poking his nose into my affairs, listening to Dona Julia's lies about me. Now he's trying the same tricks with Leonora. But I'll tell you this, sir, my stepdaughter is not the innocent you think she is. No, the lass is a strumpet. Perhaps she's tried her wiles on you.' He grinned triumphantly when he saw the colour wash out of Craig's face.

'I intend taking her away from here, Grant, make no mistake.'

Angry male voices brought Leonora back from the abyss of unconsciousness. After a while she recollected that she lay across her own bed in the darkness of her room. The candle must have been snuffed out. Her throbbing jaw and aching lip reminded her of her recent ordeal. Craig Mackintosh had saved her from Angus Grant, the very devil himself. She suddenly realised that the raised voices belonged to the two men in question. Where were they?

Thrusting aside her pain, she listened. The altercation appeared to be taking place in the parlour. Leonora could not bear to lie there idly lest her stepfather should persuade Craig that she was at fault. Mackintosh did not trust her and might well believe Grant. No, she could not allow him to leave her here at Angus Grant's mercy. The thought propelled Leonora into action. She carefully rose from the bed and was appalled at the state of her clothes, torn in the struggle with her stepfather. Quietly she moved to the *almirah*, a wide, intricately carved cupboard where her gowns lay flat on shelves. Blindly feeling around, she touched a redingote, dragged it out and quickly donned it. The material was of indigo cotton velvet and was surprisingly cool.

It occurred to her to leave the two men to argue and escape on her own to the church. Yet, for some unaccountable reason, she wanted to see Craig Mackintosh. It could not possibly be from any sense of gratitude to him for saving her from assault; if it had not been for him she would not be in her present predicament and her beloved mother might well be alive, she deliberated with cool logic. Leonora therefore ascribed her present frame of mind to curiosity in that she yearned to know what had prompted Craig Mackintosh to come to her rescue.

She tiptoed to the entrance of the parlour. The door stood open but a brocade curtain concealed the aperture and hid her from view.

TAKE 4 MEDICAL ROMANCES *FREE*

Mills & Boon Medical Romances capture the excitement, intrigue and emotion of the busy medical world. A world often interrupted by love and romance...

We will send you 4 Brand New Medical Romances absolutely Free plus a cuddly teddy bear and a surprise mystery gift, as your introduction to this superb series.

At the same time we'll reserve a subscription for you to our Reader Service. Every two months you could receive the 6 latest Medical Romances delivered direct to your door Post and Packing Free, plus a free Newsletter packed with competitions, author news and much, much more.

What's more there's no obligation, you can cancel or suspend your subscription at any time. So you've nothing to lose and a whole world of romance to gain!

Your Free Gifts!

We'll send you this cute little tan and white teddy bear plus a surprise mystery gift when you return this card. So don't delay.

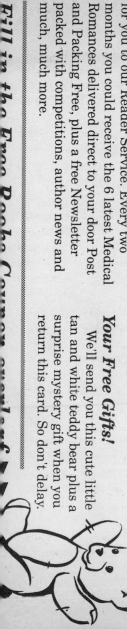

Fill in the Free Books Coupon overleaf NOW

Free Books Certificate

Yes! Please send me my 4 Free Medical Romances, together with my Free Teddy and Mystery gift. Please also reserve a special Reader Service subscription for me. If I decide to subscribe, I shall receive 6 superb new books every two months for just £8.10, post and packaging free. If I decide not to subscribe, I shall write you within 10 days. The free books and gifts will be mine to keep in any case.

I understand that I am under no obligation whatsoever - I can cancel or suspend my subscription at any time simply by writing to you.

I am over 18 years of age.

Extra Bonus

We all love surprises, so as well as the Free books and Teddy, here's an intriguing mystery gift especially for you. No clues - send off today!

Mrs/Miss/Ms _____
(BLOCK CAPITALS PLEASE)

Address _____

_____ Postcode _____ 5AOD

Signature _____

NO STAMP
NEEDED

Reader Service
FREEPOST
PO Box 236
Croydon
Surrey
CR9 9EL

'Ye'll not take the lass from me!' Angus Grant yelled. 'She and I are to be married, I tell you. What business have you breaking in here—I'll have the police on you!'

Craig sighed wearily. 'We've been over all this before. When Leonora recovers, I'll question her. I can hardly credit that a woman whom you have beaten up would wish to be your wife. I'm not budging till the lass wakes. Then I'm taking her away.'

'You haven't yet told me who you are. I have an idea we have met.' Grant peered curiously at him.

A short, bitter laugh escaped from Craig. 'Well might you ask, sir. I knew you fourteen years past—the traitor of Drummossie Moor.' His voice, though soft, conveyed intense hatred.

Leonora could almost feel her stepfather's fear in the silence that followed. 'I—I do not understand what yer talkin' about. I was ne'er at Drummossie Moor.'

'Perhaps my name will jog your memory. Ever heard of Craig Mackintosh—fought with the Duke of Perth? You were there battling along with me and the lads you betrayed to the Hanoverian butcher and his Sassenach soldiers. But that was not all: my father and some of those he sheltered were murdered as a result of your betrayal. And I swore that if ever I found you I'd avenge their deaths. Except that to kill you will be too easy a way out for you, and you're not worth risking my life over. But I vowed to make you suffer where it will hurt most. Leonora and her riches are what you crave, and to deprive you of them is ample retribution!'

'And what will ye do with her, ye bastard?' Grant's voice was thick with wrath.

'Certainly not what you tried to do.'

'Yer after her fortune, I dare swear!'

'Dare swear all you like. Leonora comes with me.'

Oblivious of the stream of abuse Grant spat out, Leonora swished the curtain aside and swept in. She stopped before the two antagonists, her face white, her body trembling with shock and rage. A silence descended and both men stared at her. She glared from one to the other. 'You dare to quarrel over me and have the effrontery to discuss what you both intend doing about me with or without my consent. Who do you think you are, treating me as if I were an inanimate piece of merchandise? I have no intention of marrying you, Angus Grant, and I refuse to go with you, Craig Mackintosh. I am done with both of you!' She flounced back into her room, collected her bag and reticule and climbed out of the window on to the veranda.

Craig Mackintosh was waiting for her at the bottom of the steps. In the brightness of the moonlit night she saw him distinctly. Brushing past, she crunched along the gravel path towards the double wrought-iron gates.

Seconds later he snatched the bag from her and, gripping her elbow, swept her along. 'The carriage awaits us in the road.'

'I think I can find my own way to the church, Mr Mackintosh,' she said, trying to speak haughtily.

'I'll take you there, *senhorinha*.'

'What have you done with him?'

'Grant? I'm afraid it will break your wee heart to know he is enjoying a spate of oblivion on the parlour floor—at my hands.'

'You've murdered him?' she gasped, attempting to pull away.

He hauled her along, almost lifting her off her feet, and pushed her into the carriage. 'Nay, I refuse to hang for that bastard. He pulled a dagger on me, snatched it from the wall before I knew what was happening, and in warding him off I dealt him a blow on the chin. He will come round any moment now.'

She felt relieved to know that Grant was still alive. Although he did not enjoy popularity in the colony or as an East India trader, he did wield some power and could not be ignored. Craig could well hang for his murder.

'You are taking me to Father Dominic, Mr Mackintosh?'

'If that's where you wish to go, lady. Else you can stay at the hunting lodge.' He tapped the panel, signalling the driver to proceed.

She focused her gaze on the slats of the window. Closeted with him in the hunting lodge was an eventuality she did not wish to repeat. She had been alone with him long enough and found the experience emotionally dangerous. 'I would prefer to go to Father Dominic.'

Craig immediately commanded the driver to return to the church.

'I cannot stay at the rectory, of course,' she said, 'but perhaps he can ask some parishioner to accept me as a paying guest till I can arrange my passage back to Portugal.'

In the light of the lamp swaying from the ceiling of the carriage she saw his amber eyes narrow on her thoughtfully. Leonora returned his stare squarely. 'How did you know where to find me, sir?'

He let out a soft, cynical laugh which made her think irrelevantly how attractive he was. 'Where else would you go?'

'But how did you know I—he would...?'

'Try to violate you? I am aware of what manner of man he is. I saw Father Dominic after he returned from taking you home. He asked me to keep an eye on the bungalow. Which I did, and returned to hear your scream.'

She passed a nervous hand from the attractive widow's peak on her forehead to the gleaming blackness of her swept-back hair. 'So it was you Father Dominic had an appointment with.' He nodded and she went on, 'Mr Mackintosh—er—why did you do that? Come to my rescue, I mean?'

He shrugged non-committally and then winced, holding on to his left arm. Leonora stared at him and noticed how pale he had become. 'You're hurt?' She looked down and saw with horror that the back of his hand was covered in blood which dripped from the tips of his fingers.

CHAPTER NINE

SINCE his capture following the Battle of Culloden, Craig had taken advantage of any ethical opportunity he had encountered, provided that it had not entailed obsequiousness, or loss of pride and integrity. However, seeing the consternation over his wound on Leonora's face delighted him. He decided to test just how far her concern for his well-being stretched. The cut Grant had inflicted was superficial, Craig owned, but to practise a little deception on this lovely woman and enjoy her attention would hurt nobody and would prove a pleasurable experience for him.

'I'm no newcomer to wounds, lady,' he said, smiling faintly. 'I've fought in some battles in this country.' True. He recalled that a few months after his arrival in Bombay his regiment, the ill-trained Bombay Fusiliers, had been despatched to Fort St George, Madras, to swell Major Stringer Lawrence's army. But the regiment had proved more of a handicap than an asset and had been compelled to undergo the Major's harsh training programme to bring it up to the excellence achieved by his rivals, the French. In the fort Craig had befriended the young officer, Lord Robert Clive. They had fought several campaigns in which Craig had sustained a few wounds, the worst being when a musket ball had scraped his hip during the battle for Arcot...

Craig forced his mind back to the present. He still wore the dark coat he had donned for the river journey, and it made the bloodstain invisible. As a result, Leonora had no idea where the wound had been inflicted. 'I have a kerchief here,' she said, pulling out a wisp of fragile cotton and lace from her reticule.

He shook his head. 'Look to your own hurts, lady. He didn't spare you either, the swine.' Craig lightly touched the cut on her lip and the bruise on her swollen jaw.

She had almost forgotten her agony but, now that he drew attention to it, she became conscious of the dull throb. 'I'll survive till we arrive at the rectory,' she said with a shrug. 'I'm sure Father Dominic will find a panacea for our wounds. He appears to be learned in the matter of medicines.'

Craig closed his eyes and rested back with a sigh. She took the cue from his silence that his injury was serious, and was startled at how concerned she felt watching the increasing pallor of his face and the line of pain etched round his mouth.

Leonora checked her cut lip: it felt sore but a clot had formed, preventing bleeding. She used her handker-chief, absently mopping the beads of sweat clinging to her brow, her interest absorbed in his condition. He looked so ghastly that for a moment she panicked, won-dering if he had died. Her troubled gaze fell to his wide chest. Tentatively she placed her hand on it, experi-encing pleasurable tingles travelling up her arm. She sighed with relief when she felt and observed the steady rise and fall of his breathing.

The carriage came to a halt and, peering out between the slats of the window, Leonora saw that they had arrived at the steps of the church. To her anxiety Craig had not stirred. 'Mr Mackintosh, we are here.' He failed to respond. She touched his arm and immediately his eyes flew open. 'We've arrived at the church, sir,' she repeated gently. 'I'll help you down.'

He gave a courteous nod and smiled. 'I thank ye kindly, lass, but I think I can manage. After you.' He indicated the door with his hand dripping blood.

Leonora looked at it in alarm. 'Mr Mack——'

'Madam, if you please.'

'Yes, yes,' she said and hurried out. Automatically she held out her arm, inviting him to lean on it to aid his descent. Craig alighted clumsily, caught her proffered arm and wrapped it round him, placing his own hand on her slender waist and hugging her to his side. He rested heavily on her as they staggered up the church steps. Glancing back over his shoulder, he called to the driver, asking him to bring the baggage.

From his laboured breathing, Leonora knew that Craig suffered much pain. Her own aches started up again from the slight jarring of each step she climbed. Yet she felt secure, held close to him, and enjoyed the heaviness of his weight. Absurd, she reflected, to permit herself to enjoy the thrill of his nearness when shortly they would part and he would return to his Fiona. The thought provoked a twinge of jealousy. Her musing came to an end when he fumbled with the vast double doors of the church which usually remained opened—but tonight they did not budge. Craig rapped impatiently on the solid wood. 'Why the devil did Father Dominic bolt them?'

'We'll have to go to the rectory, sir. We should have gone there direct.'

'Aye, but it's easier getting there through the church.'

'Then send the *ghari* driver to rouse Father at the rectory and tell him to let us in,' Leonora suggested, beginning to sag under her burden. She would not be able to sustain her upright position for much longer.

But before Craig could issue his order, she heard the large bolts being drawn back. Man and woman tensed as one of the doors opened a little. In the dimness of candle-light they spotted Father Dominic in his black cassock. Silently he pulled the door ajar, enough to let the couple slip through, and pointed to the nearest pew. Leonora passed the priest her purse to pay the *ghari* driver, which he did, and then he dragged the luggage inside and shot the bolts.

'Tomorrow starts the Hindu festival of Holi,' he explained, 'in which participants throw coloured water or powder on anything and anyone they perceive. I have taken the precaution of locking the church at night when the local brew flows freely. One can never be too cautious during festivities.'

Leonora nodded absently and carefully lowered Craig on to the polished pew. She turned to the priest. 'Father, I fear Mr Mackintosh is gravely injured. He has a stab wound which needs immediate attention, and has lost much blood already.'

Father Dominic hastened from his task of securing the door. His dark eyes stared in horror at Leonora's swollen and bruised face, looking worse in the flickering light. 'From what I can perceive, Leonora, you are in a sorry state yourself,' he remarked with a faint gasp. 'Stay here a moment, I will fetch water and clean cloths.'

She watched his thin, dark figure hurry along the aisle and genuflect before the altar, his soutane rustling and rosary clicking. Once he had disappeared into the vestry, she turned to Craig.

Despite her own pain she witnessed his with deepening concern. He rested back against the hard wood of the pew, but his head lolled forward as if he was unconscious. To verify his state, she curled her fingers round his broad wrist and gave it a slight shake. 'Mr Mackintosh... Craig,' she whispered. But he did not respond. In a fit of panic, she faced the tabernacle far ahead with its red oil-lamp suspended above it. Many times she had prayed in the peace and quiet of this incense-scented church and found consolation. Now she dropped to her knees and begged that Craig might live.

She rose when she saw the priest returning balancing a basin, an ewer and carrying several pieces of clean cloth draped over his arms.

'He's unconscious, Father,' she said a little desperately, as he placed the utensils on the pew in front.

Between them, they eased off Craig's coat. She emitted an appalled gasp at the sight of his brocaded white waistcoat and fine lawn shirt soaked in blood. When eventually they peeled off his clothes to the waist, she gaped at the slash across his arm.

But she was grateful to see that Father Dominic proved equal to the task; from his deft actions it was apparent that he had ministered to similar wounds. Quickly and thoroughly he stanched the flow, cleaned and applied an unguent to the gash, and wadded and bandaged it.

'It is best that we move him to a safer place,' the priest commented thoughtfully. 'Undoubtedly Senhor Mackintosh has an enemy who will endeavour to complete his murderous act. Therefore, I have decided on placing him in the crypt below the altar. It is not a true crypt, in that no burial has taken place in it. I am the only person who ventures there; it holds records and files

of baptism and marriage certificates. And now to attend
to you, *menina*. No, do not speak as yet. You can tell
me what happened once we have made both you and
Senhor Mackintosh comfortable.'

It did not take Father Dominic long to clean up the
cut on Leonora's lip. Then she told him briefly of what
had occurred. 'Yes, I expected something of that nature,'
he said on a doleful sigh. 'Now let us remove the patient
to the crypt.'

He tried to bear most of Craig's weight as he and
Leonora propped him between them and slowly, carefully, took him below. Dankness and mustiness greeted
her nostrils as they stepped into the underground room.
In the feeble rays of an oil-lamp she saw a row of dusty
ledgers on a low shelf above a large, ancient escritoire.
Against the opposite wall stood a wide settle. The priest
transferred Craig's weight on to Leonora and disappeared briefly to return with a cheap cotton quilt which
he spread on the bench to act as a mattress.

'Where do I sleep, Father?' Leonora asked, once they
had laid Craig on the settle.

'Here, with him.'

She started in disbelief. 'I do not understand.'

His tired eyes showed a faint spark of humour. 'Come,
menina,' he said, leading the way to a curtained area.
He drew back the maroon drape and revealed a chamber
a little larger than a deep recess. All it could accom-
modate was a rattan sofa complete with upholstery. 'Wait
here a while. I will fetch someone who is anxious to speak
with you.' He slipped out through a back door.

Leonora wished she had prevented the priest from
going; she felt too tired to talk any more, but she
supposed that Father Dominic considered the matter

urgent. She slumped down on the sofa and let out a loud
sigh.

'*Menina*, wake up. See whom I have brought.' The
priest's voice pulled her back from the brink of sleep.

Leonora blinked several times and peered in the gloom
at the old woman squatting at her feet. 'Ayah! Oh, Ayah!
What happened to you?'

Without thought, Leonora knelt down beside the crone
and hugged her. 'Oh! I'm so happy to see you. I thought
Grant Sahib had got rid of all the servants.'

The old ayah caught Leonora's hands and kissed them.
'He has, *missybaba*. He dismissed us when the *memsahib* became ill. But, before I left, the *memsahib* told
me much to tell you if you should be found and returned
to Calcutta.'

Vaguely Leonora heard the priest say that he would
fetch the baggage left in the church.

'First tell me where you are living. Have you any
money?'

'*Ji, missybaba*. The *memsahib* gave me some rupees
and Fernandez Sahib pays me money. The *padre sahib*
offered me a room in the servants' quarters here in the
church grounds, but I did not want that gossip-monger,
Daniel, to know where I lived, so I am now staying in
Fernandez Sahib's compound.'

'How did you know I was here, in the church?'

'Through the restless tongue of Daniel. He spread it
about that first you came to see Padre Sahib and then
you went to your good mother's house.' The old woman
wagged her oiled head in distress and placed both her
brown gnarled hands on her brow. 'What will I say,
missybaba, I have been much aggrieved by the *memsahib*'s death and your disappearance. Then, this little

while past when Padre Sahib came to bring me here, he tells of how your evil stepfather was at the house and tried his wickedness on you, but a good *sahib* saved your virtue and life. Is this so?'

Leonora's heart swelled with love for this wise old woman who had been with her since her arrival in Calcutta from Portugal. Through a haze of tears she scanned the beloved face, brown and seamed with wrinkles. A silver nostril-stud drew attention to the long, thin nose and brought a glitter to the dark eyes, once large and luminous but now appearing narrower from the fold of loose skin on the upper lids and the web of lines around the lower lids, the sparkle dimmer with age. 'Why have you taken the risk to come here, old one? Grant Sahib may track you down and perhaps harm you.'

'*Ji.* That he may. I hear he is trying to trace me, for he knows that your mother told me he was poisoning her. Alas, I can prove nothing. Be that as it may, *he* is not knowing that! I told the doctor *sahib* at the Fort, but he did not believe. He said the *memsahib* had a pestilence, at that time spreading through the bazaar.' Tears appeared in the old ayah's eyes and Leonora hugged her, and smoothed the blue and white bordered sari over her small, oiled head. 'I then came to the *padre sahib* and told him, and he reported the matter to the police *sahibs*, but that devil, Grant Sahib, said the *memsahib* was raving in a fever as all who have the sickness do. None would believe he had killed her.'

'I do, because he confessed to me that he had dosed her with *datura*, or at least that his mistress had.'

'Ah, but with his consent, *missybaba*.'

'I must, therefore, see that justice is done, even if I have to do so through my own hand,' Leonora vowed, her face hardening.

'*Nahin, missybaba!* You must get away from here as soon as you can. Padre Sahib has promised that he will see that you do. I came to warn you that the courtesan Kamila plans to have you killed—she has strange ties with the *thuggees*—so that Grant Sahib will inherit your fortune. I beg of you, *missybaba*, for the sake of the happiness and love we shared, leave Calcutta.' The old lady straightened to her full height, which reached Leonora's shoulder. 'May Vishnu and Shiva guard you, my child.' She kissed the girl's hand and slipped out.

Leonora stumbled to her feet. 'Ayah, wait!' She staggered outside, but came face to face with Father Dominic. 'Did you see my ayah? I want her to stay with me. She's like a member of my family.'

'No, *menina*. She cannot go with you. Come, get inside.'

She eyed the priest with defiance. 'Cannot go with me? I am going nowhere, Father Dominic. I mean to stay here and find a lawyer who will bring Angus Grant to justice. My mother's death must be avenged.'

'You have no idea what you are up against, my child.'

'Yes, I do. Ayah has told me. But I mean to remain here and fight.'

'No, you must leave Calcutta with Senhor Mackintosh, first thing in the morning.' He put up his hands to prevent further argument. 'You will be comfortable on the sofa. The *senhor* is close by and may need your attention. After all, who can be more suited to the task than his—future wife?'

CHAPTER TEN

LEONORA'S expression showed utter incredulity. 'I am amazed to hear you make so rash a statement, Father Dominic. Please be assured that I have no intention of marrying Mr Mackintosh. Moreover, I had rather remain unwed! I fear I am none too trustful of men.' Hastily she amended. 'Except, of course, you.'

The priest shook his head in weary despondency. '*Sim, menina*, I know you see me as the father figure you yearn for, and I appreciate that very much. Your good mother, *Deus* rest her soul, once told me how attached to your real father you were, and how your heart was broken when he returned to his country and died in battle. But I beg you not to allow this experience, tragic though it is, to destroy your young life.'

'You are much mistaken, Father Dominic—my life is in no danger of destruction. But it will be if I am forced to marry. Whether my father's decision and death has influenced my attitude is of little consequence. We are dealing in practicalities and realities of life.' She stopped for breath and dashed on, 'And why are you so keen that I should marry Craig Mackintosh? Why him? Has he mentioned that he wishes to wed me?'

'Look, *senhorinha*,' he said sternly. 'It is for your safety that you should marry Senhor Mackintosh. I see the signs that you are both in love with each other.'

Her head jerked backwards in astonishment. 'What? In truth, Father Dominic, have you added matchmaking to your duties?'

'There is no need for sarcasm, *senhorinha*,' he reproved mildly. 'But I feel it is essential for you to marry, and Senhor Mackintosh is the ideal suitor——'

'Really? Why?'

'He is not interested in your money, he has accrued much wealth of his own and is in a position to safeguard your property. I fear Senhor Grant will do all in his power to try and trace you, Leonora, either to force you to marry him or to stage your accidental death. Not only I but also the ayah have impressed upon you that he is bent on availing himself of your fortune.'

Leonora passed an unsteady hand across her brow in a disturbed gesture, and lowered herself on to the rattan sofa. 'My beloved mother did tell me about my fortune, but at that time I wasn't interested since it would be years before I could inherit it. Now circumstances have changed. I confess I need someone to guide me in the matter of finance. But I have decided to return to Portugal and live in the villa my grandfather left me. There is no necessity for me to marry anyone.'

'And who, pray, *senhorinha*, is to accompany you on so long a voyage? Naturally you cannot travel without a chaperon.'

'I thought perhaps I could persuade you and one of the nuns to come with me.'

Father Dominic ran a few beads of his rosary through his thin, agitated fingers and stared at Leonora. 'But that is impossible! Even if I did decide to come——'

'Naturally, I'll pay all your expenses, Father.'

'It is not a question of expenses. It is a question of danger, not only to myself but also to you. Are you not aware that at the present time Jesuit priests and Jews are being persecuted in Portugal? If I accompany you, all your property will be confiscated. No, Leonora, I cannot go with you. Now, Senhor Mackintosh, as your husband, would be the ideal escort——'

'Perhaps you are not aware that Mr Mackintosh is betrothed to a young lady by name of Miss Fiona Mcintyre.' She was gratified to see the priest looking surprised. 'I met Fiona at Murshidabad.'

'Then it would seem you have little choice but to wed Senhor Fernandez.'

'No!'

Father Dominic shrugged. '*Sim, sim*, I know, *menina*, Pedro is old, and for that I disapprove of your marrying him. I told Dona Julia, the good God rest her soul,' he crossed himself, 'alas, he was the only man she could trust, and indeed he is your banker and oversees your money affairs. Your mother had a reason for you to marry him. Not only would you be safe from Senhor Grant, but your fortune too would be protected. Like Senhor Craig, Pedro Fernandez is indifferent to your inheritance. Dona Julia hoped he would care for you as a daughter. Except the sacrament of marriage does not allow for fatherly affections!'

Perhaps it would be best to fulfil her dead mother's wish and marry the ageing Pedro, she thought halfheartedly. Rather him than Grant. 'Where is Senhor Pedro?'

'He is at his villa by the river, but will be leaving in a sennight for Macau with his colleague Senhor Lobo.

His dwelling is not far from here. I shall fetch him after I have celebrated the dawn Mass tomorrow.'

The image of herself sharing the marital bed with Pedro Fernandez, allowing him to fondle her intimately, set her abdomen heaving. She soon had second thoughts. 'Father Dominic! I——'

'Go to sleep now, *menina*. Whatever you decide, tomorrow you have to make an early start. You and Senhor Mackintosh must be gone from these premises before Daniel, my servant, discovers you. I fear he is a notorious gossip and soon your stepfather will know of your whereabouts. For your sake I cannot allow that.'

'Then it is a mystery to me why you employ him.'

The priest's face took on a look of tender reminiscence. 'I found Daniel as a six-month-old infant lying starving in a gutter. He is like a son to me and an excellent worker. His one fault is that he has too long a tongue and is not aware of the damage he can do. Alas, I do not have the heart to dismiss him or even send him to the missions.'

She wondered if Father Dominic somehow saw his freedom in Daniel. The Sacrament of Confession bound him by the vows of silence, and he perhaps revelled in Daniel's gossip, which posed as a form of release for the priest himself from the strain of holding his own tongue.

'Meanwhile, I shall not tarry,' Father Dominic said. *'Boa noite, menina.'* With a stiff little bow that precluded further discussion, he took his leave.

Leonora believed that she would not be able to sleep, what with the dull ache of her injuries, the turbulence of her thoughts and the persistence of throbbing drums in the distance. It signalled the start of the Holi festival from Kalighat, the shrine of the feared Goddess Kali.

In fact, Calcutta derived its name from Kalighat, she mused fleetingly. Yet no sooner had she relaxed on the cushioned sofa and closed her eyes than she drifted into oblivion.

'Senhor Mackintosh, I have brought you some lime juice, preserves and buttered chapattis. This will help you to regain your strength. In a few hours you and Leonora must leave the church.' Father Dominic's urgent whisper woke Craig from a profound sleep. At first he could not prise his lids apart—they seemed to be sewn together. He rubbed his forefingers along his lashes, and opened his eyes to behold the priest bending over him like a hunched raven with outspread wings.

'Good morning, Padre,' he greeted, swinging his long legs off the settle and sitting up a little stiffly, motioning to the priest to place the tray beside him. 'I confess, I'm ravenous. But do you not have anything stronger than lime juice?' He grimaced.

'I beg you, *senhor*, to keep your voice to a whisper. Senhorinha Leonora is sleeping in the chamber beyond the curtain. We must not disturb her.'

Craig's head spun in the direction of the drape, his golden eyes wide. 'You mean she's been there all night? This calls for a dram of whisky.'

Father Dominic brought his hand up to his mouth to stifle a chuckle. 'No, *senhor*, the night is very young. It is not yet the hour of midnight. You have been asleep for only a short while. I fear the lime juice is all I can offer. The price of a jar of whisky will keep three missions in food for a day.'

'So why have you woken me, sir?'

'In four hours I will be celebrating Mass. I wish it to be a Nuptial Mass.'

Craig chewed on a bite of chapatti and washed it down with a swallow of lime juice. He shrugged. 'What has that to do with me?'

'*Senhor*, the Nuptial Mass will be for you, to join you in Holy Matrimony.'

Some of the juice spilled with the sudden jerk of Craig's hand. 'What the dev——? What the he——? What are you talking about?'

Impassively and without preamble, the priest said, 'Senhor Mackintosh, I want you to marry Senhorinha Leonora.'

Craig shot to his feet, forgetting that he was supposed to be seriously injured. 'Now look here——'

Father Dominic continued as if Craig had not spoken. 'You are in love with her.'

'Padre, I fear you do not know the implications of so serious a matter.'

'Ssh, keep your voice down, *senhor*. And of a certainty I am well aware of the seriousness of matrimony.'

'Look, I'm willing to take Leonora to my abode in the Himalayan foothills, and keep her safe there till justice has been brought to her stepfather, but as for marriage...' Craig let out a thoughtful sigh.

'Are you betrothed, *senhor*?'

Craig frowned angrily. 'No.'

'You are not enamoured of a young lady by the name of Senhorinha Mcintyre?'

'No. We are friends. What concern is it——?'

'She is your mistress?'

'What is this? An inquisition?'

'Answer the question, *senhor*,' the priest said gently but determinedly.

'Have I not said Fiona and I are friends?' Why the devil was he allowing this priest to probe into his life? Craig chided himself silently.

'The happiness of your and Leonora's future depends on your reply. That is why I ask, *senhor*. Why then do you hesitate to marry Leonora?'

Craig combed his long fingers through his fiery hair and lowered his eyes to stare at his diamond cobra ring. He regarded it as his talisman and willed it to help him out. 'A kidnapper cannot marry his victim.'

'So it *was* you, *senhor*?'

'Leonora mentioned it, I suppose.'

'No. I guessed.' Father Dominic patted Craig comfortingly on his shoulder. '*Senhor*, someone once said to me, "Father, there is always a first time for everything." Now, my son, you are fit enough to travel? I did not believe you were seriously injured. What I do believe is that you enjoyed the ministrations of Senhorinha Leonora!'

Craig chuckled softly. 'No one can hoodwink you, Padre.'

'No, *senhor*. A true priest studies people to try and gain an insight into human nature, enough to offer help to his fellow beings. Return to sleep and at dawn wake the *senhorinha* and propose to her. *Adeus* for the present.'

A light brushing of lips on her cheek brought Leonora awake. She opened her eyelids to gaze straight into Craig's eyes, their pupils black and bottomless in the flicker of lamp-light. 'You should not be out of bed, Mr Mackintosh!'

He stretched his lips in exasperation. 'You had better become accustomed to calling me Craig. We are to be married in a short while, and I'm not happy at all with this "Mr Mackintosh" coming from my bride.'

She abruptly sat up, smoothing the rumpled skirts of the dress she had perforce slept in. 'Married?' she breathed, gaping at him owlishly.

Straightening from his bent position, leaning over her, he nodded and winced. 'Father Dominic and two witnesses await us in the church. As soon as you have washed——' he raised the curtain, pointed to a basin and ewer placed on the settle, bare of its quilt '—I shall take you up. Meanwhile, I'll wait outside the door till you have completed your toilet.'

'But you are still hurt, else why did you wince, sir?'

His slow half-smile made her feel a little weak. 'I assure you, ma'am, that apart from a slight twinge when I move I'm in fine fettle. Father Dominic certainly has the healing touch.'

She had no opportunity to answer his unconventional marriage proposal, for he had left the crypt. Still dazed, she set to giving herself a thorough wash. A bath would have been ideal, she thought with a yearning sigh. From her large bag she lifted out clean petticoats and slipped on a cream silk dress with a stiff stomacher which laced in front and showed off her elegant figure. She flicked tiers of lace at her elbows and shook out the skirts to allow the lace frills to fall into place. She brushed her long hair to shining smoothness, scraped it back from the widow's peak and deftly coiled it on the crown of her head. Finding a white mantilla, she draped it over her neat hair. Her used clothes she folded and stowed in her bag. She concentrated on these minor activities to prevent herself from worrying over what would occur shortly.

Stepping out of the crypt she saw that Craig was dutifully waiting for her. As he gripped her arm and guided her up the winding steps to the church she said, 'Whose idea was this that you should marry me, sir? I am not convinced that this marriage is for the right reasons.'

He brought her to a halt and glared down at her. 'Lady, if you imagine I went down on my knees to beg Father Dominic to persuade you to marry me, you are much mistaken.'

'Then why go through with it?' she snapped, cross with herself for allowing his words to wound her so deeply.

'I'll tell you why, Leonora. I feel responsible for you since I caused you so much anxiety. It is the least I can do to safeguard your inheritance and, most of all, your life from Angus Grant. Once you are married he can claim nothing from you, even if he did decide to kill your husband. He might well leave you alone. If you prefer to marry Senhor Pedro, then who am I to stop you? But make your choice here and now and I will leave at once. Never will I trouble you again.'

'And what of your revenge on Angus Grant? You owe your father that much and I owe my mother, too. I agree to wed you, sir, even if it be in name only.'

'Then let us not tarry, Leonora.'

She felt pleased that she had accepted his proposal without loss of dignity and without revealing her emotional turmoil. His powerful attraction had linked her irrevocably to him. She suddenly realised how desolate her future would be without his strength, moral and physical, to sustain her.

Inside the church, the priest and witnesses turned towards the couple as they made their entrance. *'Bom dia,'* the three Portuguese greeted. Senhor Pedro, immaculately turned out in watered silk frock-coat and embroidered maroon waistcoat to match, shuffled towards Leonora, lifted her hand and bowed courteously over it. Unfortunately he was no credit to his elegant attire, she observed ruefully—his swarthy face resembled a turtle's under the expensive wig. His eyes, bulbous and lugubrious, imparted an impression that he was slightly offended by her rejection of him. The impeccably mannered old gentleman straightened and smiled dismally at her. 'I am delighted to see you safe and well, *senhorinha*. I wish this had been *my* wedding day—but alas!'

'Forgive me, *senhor*, if I have caused you distress,' she murmured, lowering her lashes demurely.

There was no bitterness in his quiet voice as he said, 'It was Dona Julia's wish that I should marry you, and for her, *senhorinha*, I was prepared to do anything.' Then it dawned on Leonora that this man had been in love with her mother. 'Do not worry, *senhorinha*, you can trust me implicitly with your inheritance willed to you by your grandfather, Dom Antonio Aviz. I have been assured by your future bridegroom——' here he directed a courteous nod at Craig '—that your fortune is yours; he has no need for it.'

Marriage! Fortunes! Inheritance! Events were moving too rapidly for Leonora to assimilate. Questions hovered in her brain—questions she could not formulate into precise words. In a daze she went through introductions with Senhor Lobo, a merchant friend of Senhor Pedro who had obligingly offered to be the second witness. She felt as if these men through the power of their will had charted her destiny and disregarded her misgivings. The beautiful Nuptial Mass and all its awesome implications filled her with dread; yet marriage to Craig Mackintosh was by far preferable to being hounded and molested by Angus Grant.

The vows were solemnly exchanged. Pedro gave Craig a ring which he slid on to the third finger of her left hand. She gazed at the magnificent circlet of diamonds and rubies that flashed white and red fires in the candle-light. After the Mass had ended, Senhor Pedro explained, 'Your mother entrusted me with most of her jewels when she found out that Grant had supplied his mistress with a few. This particular one, she said, was an heirloom and had been used as a wedding ring by all the brides of the house of Aviz. Once you are settled I will send up the remainder of the jewellery.'

'No, please don't, *senhor*. I would rather you use the remainder to look after my ayah and the sacked servants of our bungalow. Also, could you give something towards Father Dominic's missions?'

'Most certainly, Senhora Mackintosh.' Pedro handed Leonora a parcel. 'It contains your father's plaid and badge. I know you were much attached to him. Your mother left it in my care. Cherish it, my child.'

'Thank you, Senhor Pedro,' she said and impulsively kissed his wrinkled cheek.

Craig received handshakes of congratulation from Father Dominic, Pedro Fernandez and his friend, Senhor Lobo.

Leonora took a sad farewell of her Confessor. 'Thank you, Father Dominic, for all you have done for my mother and me,' she said through an aching throat. Kneeling on one knee, she took his fingers and kissed them.

He placed a hand on her head in blessing. His voice breaking a little, he said, 'God bless you, my child.'

In the cool of the grey and misty dawn, Craig and Leonora set out in a hired carriage. She felt relieved to see that two bags, containing her jewels and clothes, occupied the opposite seat. The jewellery gave her a sense of independence. On the street a few people walked, adroitly balancing on their heads baskets full of produce, perhaps destined for the bazaars. 'Where are we going, er...Craig? I hope you are not returning to Murshidabad.'

He slid her a sideways glance and a dry smile. 'We shall not be going there, Leonora. I'm afraid we must bide a while at the hunting lodge.'

She looked at him, her deep blue eyes round and startled. 'Pray, tell me why.'

Craig leaned back into the corner of the carriage and peered out through the slats in the window. She stole a glance at him. He must have brought his own luggage along with hers in the coach last night, she reflected vaguely; he looked magnificent in a clean change of clothes of deep green, shot silk frock-coat and brocaded waistcoat. Stroking the layers of lace on his jabot, he said, 'Because, my lady wife, we must travel in disguise, and all the apparel we'll need is there.'

Leonora groaned. 'Santa Maria, do I have to wear that tent-like *bourka* again? It will be stifling in the garment, now that the weather is warmer.' Then, feeling selfish and spoilt, she hurriedly appended, 'I'm sorry, that was thoughtless of me.'

Craig shifted his golden gaze to her, a faint, amused smile touching his mouth. 'No, there is no need for a *bourka*. You will have to dress as a youth—in fact, travel as my servant.'

'I see. Is the situation as dangerous as that?'

He sighed. 'I fear it is, Leonora. Apart from the camouflage being an ideal deflection of Angus Grant's spies, if he has set any on our trail, there is the festival of Holi. Revellers will throng the streets and squirt coloured powders and water. Where there are crowds of excited and intoxicated people there exists the danger of riots. Therefore, I'd feel easier in my mind if you were dressed as an Indian lad.'

'I understand. I should have thought of that before, but it——'

'It is all so sudden? I assure you I feel a little bewildered myself, lady.'

'I hope we can have baths at the lodge before setting out.'

'Most certainly. I see your face looks much improved. Does it hurt at all?'

Leonora felt herself colouring at his concern. She had forgotten her injuries, and now touched her mouth. It felt a little sore, but the swelling had gone down. Her jaw, too, seemed to have subsided to normal. 'Is my skin discoloured?'

'A little. But you still look very beautiful, Leonora.'

Shyly she glanced at him, aware that her face was burning. 'Thank you, Craig.'

He smiled disarmingly. 'My pleasure, lady.'

They lapsed into companionable silence and the movement of the carriage lulled her into drowsiness.

The next thing she knew was that the vehicle had ground to a halt, that her head was resting on Craig's shoulder and that his arm was supporting her against him.

'Come, sweetheart, we've arrived.' He laughed softly, chucked her under the chin and gave her a warm kiss. Her heartbeat quickened and her lips tingled. Colour washed up under her skin. Then the driver opened the door. Craig jumped down and helped Leonora out and led her to the hunting lodge. A feeling of *déjà vu* affected her.

'Wasim, could you heat up some water for the *memsahib* and me to bathe?'

'Very good, Hira Nag Sahib,' the young Muslim assented cheerfully, touching his neatly wound turban in an informal salaam.

'I would do it myself,' Craig explained to Leonora, 'but I'm afraid of starting off the bleeding again.' He gingerly felt the spot where his wound lay under his coat.

She nodded with a half-smile, and seated herself on a rattan stool. What screamed through her head was the thought that Craig might insist that they bathe together.

'You will have to help me undress.'

She jumped, her eyes wide and startled. 'What?'

He lowered himself on to a high-backed chair and sighed. 'You heard, ma'am. Look, we're married, believe it or not. You don't have to be so shocked. I thought you were a cool, controlled lady, well able to cope with most eventualities.'

'You mean a frozen madonna?' she asked drily. He smiled wickedly but said nothing and she continued, 'I would not consider marriage as "most eventualities", sir. It is an important event that's never likely to happen again in our lives unless one of us dies.'

'I agree. So, would you be so good as to help me off with this coat?'

She leaned over and eased the coat off his arms and back. A twinkle of mischief gleamed in Craig's eyes and his smile, oozing charm, revealed immaculate teeth, causing a spasm of pleasure to twist in her abdomen. Her gaze fell to the width of his shoulders.

'Now help me off with the shirt.'

She spotted the challenge in the amber of his eyes and swallowed. 'Will you be removing your bandage?' she asked, not paying attention to the logic of her question, her heart banging with apprehension.

'*You* will, of course. I also expect you to bathe me, darling.'

CHAPTER ELEVEN

INCIPIENT resentment replaced Leonora's dismay. 'I think, sir, you are singularly lacking in delicacy. You forget that I am no servant.'

'And you forget, lady, that you are my wife. It is a wife's duty to care for her husband, not a servant's.'

She detected the irritation in his voice, then he seemed to relent. Rising from the bed he came to her and, grasping her shoulders gently, lifted her to her feet. 'I suppose I'm a crass brute, but we have a lifetime to get used to each other—just as you had to accustom yourself to Angus Grant. Is that the type of treatment you appreciate?'

'Certainly not!' she exclaimed, pulling away from him. 'How much convincing do you need? Would I have screamed for help if I were enjoying his assault? Would I have married you instead of him?'

Coldly he looked her up and down. 'Perhaps your conscience wouldnae allow you to wed your mother's husband. You probably know it's against the laws of the Church, too. And after your recent rejection of me, lass, I'll need convincing of your hatred for him.' He strode to the door and stopped without turning. Squaring his back, he said, 'I'll be in the adjoining chamber. Meanwhile, have your bath alone and in peace. But remember, Leonora, I intend to consummate the marriage in the near future, even if I have to do it on the jungle floor. And you are going to be willing!'

As he opened the door to depart, she said with chilling rage, 'You forget, *senhor*, I was coerced into marriage with you. It is therefore irrational to berate me, considering you married me of your own free will—even if you didn't actually beg!'

With studied deliberation he shut the door and turned to face her, his expression hard, ruthless. 'If you must know, I was *not* willing to wed you. The old *padre* persuaded me to do so to help you.'

The mortifying blow had her swaying. Leonora had taken it for granted that he had been drawn to her more than she was to him. Therefore his reluctance to marry her increased her humiliation and undermined her self-confidence. 'I assumed you were the type of person who followed his own inclinations and not through entreaty by someone else.'

'You already know the answer to that: the marriage fulfils my vendetta, depriving Angus Grant of you and your inheritance.' She watched his magnificent eyes narrowing in speculation. 'Tell me, ma'am,' he said in a deceptively quiet voice. 'Tell me, why did you not betray me to the priest? You could have told him I was your kidnapper and had me gaoled.'

Before replying she struggled to collect her composure. Clearing her throat, she said, 'Perhaps it has slipped your mind, sir, but I—I did promise not to betray you if you returned me to my home, despite the fact that your venture failed.' She lifted her chin proudly. 'I do have principles and I have been brought up to keep my pledges.'

He appraised her, his gaze so boldly sensual that it summoned in Leonora a peculiar sensation of pleasure mixed with discomfort. That she had spoken without careful consideration, she felt certain. Yet years of practice had schooled her to hide, on most occasions, her emotions beneath an impassive veneer. She returned his scrutiny with equanimity.

He raised an eyebrow slightly. 'Really?'

Leonora dropped her gaze to her restless hands, and knew she had blundered somewhere, listening to the underlying triumph in his voice. She could find nothing to say.

'In which case you should have no trouble honouring your recent vow to fulfil your conjugal rights.' And then, collecting his coat, he executed a deep bow and was gone, leaving Leonora stunned.

The dawn mist had dispersed when they set out that morning through the forest. Rays of the sun streaming down between the foliage of towering sal trees spread a dappled carpet of light and shade on the leaf-strewn ground. It looked idyllic, but felt like hell in the torrid atmosphere.

In spite of the heat, Leonora had felt refreshed after enjoying a tepid bath before getting out and garbing herself in clean male attire, which Wasim had carried in when he had delivered the water. There had been no mirror in the lodge for her to examine herself, but the grey pyjamas, loose shirt, large cotton shawl to hide her curves and ready-wound turban under which she had tucked her thick hair had been comfortable. The outfit had stirred in her a sense of freedom, daring.

Only the natural sounds of the forest disturbed the quiet as Wasim, Craig and Leonora walked their horses over crackling leaves. She enjoyed the antics of the langurs as they leapt from tree to tree, chattering and coughing, the exquisite trilling of numerous and colourful birds interspersed with the twitter of ubiquitous yellow-beaked mynahs.

'You did not tell me where you are taking me, sir,' she remarked, feeling a surge of excitement not unlike that of a child about to set out on a thrilling venture.

He turned slightly in his saddle to view her. 'We have a long journey ahead of us, lady. It might take all of two months, but, I can promise you, once we reach our destination it will be pleasantly cool. Our route will be in the vicinity of the forest, away from roads and *serais*.' He smiled disarmingly at her. 'Willing to rise to the challenge?'

She nodded and smiled back, a radiant smile showing an array of perfect teeth. Slowly his face grew serious and for just a moment their eyes held. A magical sensation, wild, alien, possessed her body. For a fanciful moment she imagined him to be a flame-haired god evolved from ancient mythology, or an archangel sent to guard her. Leonora took a grip on herself and could not for the life of her understand what had taken her imagination to such dizzy heights. She dragged her gaze from his and stared ahead, absently watching grey, striped squirrels racing up and down tree trunks. 'What other choice have I but to rise to the challenge, sir?'

His jaw hardened, a muscle pulsing. 'None,' he said, his voice brusque. 'We might have to spend tonight sleeping on the forest floor if we don't find a hospitable forest dweller who is willing to spare us a hut for the night. The forest people, few though they are, sometimes have a spare abode for lost or passing wayfarers— at a price, of course. Except the tribe I happen to know might well have decamped and moved elsewhere.'

Her spine tingled with foreboding. 'If we are forced to sleep in the open forest, what about wild animals?'

'A good question, Leonora. In that event we'll have to find a glade and build fires in a circle round us for protection. Tigers, panthers and lions do some of their hunting in darkness. I know what you're thinking, ma'am,' he said softly, sending her a swift backward glance. 'You're wondering how we'll be able to fulfil our marriage vows in the midst of danger and with Wasim around.'

'I wasn't thinking that at all, sir. I am puzzling over whether we shall live to see another dawn.'

He laughed deeply, attractively. 'You have no worry on that score, my fair bride. I have been through this area often enough and know all the tricks and skills required for survival.'

'I suppose you come to the forest to hunt?' She could not control a shiver of distaste—the slaughter of the magnificent wild cats he had mentioned she considered cruel and wasteful.

'No, to sketch and later paint.'

Leonora had forgotten that he was a talented artist. Somehow she had judged him from his powerful build to be a man more suited to physical action. He seemed too virile to engage in the gentle art of painting.

'You find that too mild a pastime for me?'

'I do. You seem more suited to hunting than painting.'

'Oh, I am—I am, lass. That is, in one respect; in others I'm an admirer of natural beauty, and the forest is beautiful.'

She said nothing, her thoughts trying to work out in what respect he considered himself a hunter. Then it suddenly dawned on her and she felt her skin growing hot.

'Aren't you going to ask me what manner of hunter I am, Leonora?'

'No. I already know. Your quarries are women.'

'Just one, darling.' Craig threw his head back and laughed till the sound echoed through the forest, setting up a cacophony of disapproval from birds and beasts. He saluted a langur running halfway up a tree trunk. 'Sorry. I forget I'm trespassing.' The monkey turned and showed all its teeth in fierce chastisement. 'That's a caution for us not to laugh too loudly or we'll have the whole troop down on us,' Craig warned in Urdu for Wasim's benefit.

The gurgling of water led them to a clear stream.

'Let us fill up the goatskins, *sahib*,' Wasim suggested. The moment Leonora dismounted she raced for the welcome coolness in the heat of the afternoon, drank her fill, and splashed her face, hands and feet. They ate some cooked lentils, thick chapattis and fruit. While Leonora washed the utensils, Craig and Wasim unsaddled the horses, rubbed them down and tethered them to feed on a patch of lush grass nearby. After a short siesta the trio remounted and resumed their journey.

Craig knew relief when they all lapsed into silence. He needed to think. They were in a precarious situation and he had withheld information from Leonora who, he gathered, had enough trouble trying to cope with the trauma of being married to him. He dared not mention that the forest provided a haven for miscreants—the more hardy types who were well versed in jungle survival. She had already undergone a nasty experience with *thuggees*, and now, with the advent of the Holi festival, these gangs would be active in their nefarious cult of strangling and robbing wayfarers. The British East India Council in Calcutta was deeply involved in abolishing these killers from their territory. But since thuggery was part of a religious cult they were having difficulty suppressing it. The Goddess Kali had to be pacified.

It was in this forest that the *thuggees* of Bengal gathered, and from here they branched out in groups to attack travellers. Aware of this, Craig had worked out a route with Wasim which would take them into the density of the jungle where there was least likelihood of human habitation. It was also the shortest distance to his property in the Khasi mountains. Even so, the journey would be extremely hazardous. This forest stretched from the mangrove swamps in the south at the delta right up to the foothills of the Himalayas. And, as if that were not enough, he had a premonition that Angus Grant had set spies on his trail. The man would not easily surrender Leonora.

Leonora! He breathed in deeply. She was an enigma. Why had she not protested vigorously against marrying him? Dared he hope that she cared a little? He shook his head in bafflement. She wasn't his type of woman. Hitherto he had been drawn to lively, laughing women, not cold, highly intelligent and deep ones of Leonora's ilk. Craig confessed that it had taken little persuasion from the priest to press him to marry Leonora. And the old *padre* was right, he had fallen in love with the lass. It was a question of his pride that prevented him from wooing her; he believed that she was indifferent to him. A deep shudder racked his body.

*   *   *

The trio had met with no mishap during the day-long trek through the jungle, Leonora thought thankfully. They passed under towering trees and through natural glades where chital, spotted deer, sambar, large golden deer and black buck grazed serenely as the sun passed its zenith in the azure sky. She would not have believed that ferocious animals inhabited the wild area of rampant undergrowth, had she not noticed large pug marks embedded in the wet mud edging the tributaries the party came upon, where they filled their goatskins and watered their animals. But Leonora was no novice; she possessed a good knowledge of the vast subcontinent teeming with dangerous beasts. At night they emerged to eat, creeping up on unsuspecting prey.

Yet she experienced no fear. As much as she begrudged it, she had to own that the man riding ahead conveyed to her his protectiveness, a feeling of safety she had not known with any other man, and now she basked in it. But she cautioned herself not to take him for granted. He might be her husband—however, that did not mean that he harboured any keen sense of duty towards her; he did not love her, scarcely liked her, probably resented being lumbered with her. And the thought filled her with wretchedness.

To avoid troubling herself further, she detached her mind from brooding over him and perforce concentrated on the natural beauty of her surroundings. Her gaze fell on orchids growing on tree trunks, the flowers breathtaking in glowing colours of orange, purple, yellow, red and speckled shades. Flowers she had never seen before grew among the undergrowth and gave off a heady perfume intensified by the steamy heat. She warded off the temptation to unbend a little and ask

Craig if he appreciated this wealth of beauty no gardener on earth could produce. Of course, he was an artist and no doubt enjoyed this visual feast. Yet any attempt at friendliness, she presumed, he might interpret as encouragement that she was willing to consummate the marriage. And as yet she had no intention of doing so—certainly not in the jungle—least of all on its floor!

The scents of the forest seemed to have a drugging effect on her, curtailing her thoughts. Soon she found herself drowsing, head sinking on to her chest.

Craig's sharp voice startled her into wakefulness. 'Wasim, we had better dismount here. Look, I can see a path made by humans.' He had twisted slightly in the saddle, his eyes cast down, inspecting the ground.

'Ji han, sahib,' Wasim agreed. 'It is as you say.' From the squeak of the saddle she knew that he had already dismounted.

Leonora watched Craig swing down with an agility that affected her with flutters of pleasure in her abdomen. He then moved back to her and lifted her down. 'Now please lead your horse and follow me, lass. No talking,' he said just above a whisper. She nodded, aware that they had entered an unknown zone which presaged hidden dangers. In single file they trekked along the footpath snaking ahead endlessly. The sun had now sunk low in the western sky, its remaining rays slanting through the branches of the trees and barring the forest floor with elongated shadows. The deeper they delved, the darker it became, no doubt from the closely growing trunks and density of foliage. In the twilight she could just make out the tall form of Craig pushing ahead. He moved with easy grace and fearlessness. She could not say that for herself, though she was grateful for his presence.

A deadly silence descended, prevailed, ominous in its unnaturalness. She could feel the hairs rising on her nape, sense unseen eyes boring into her, and knew it was no trick of her imagination. She forcefully quelled the irresistible urge to glance up into the branches. God knew what she would behold. Keeping her gaze riveted on the rough path and a prayer on her lips, she trudged on behind Craig.

Darkness was upon them when the forest erupted with piercing, birdlike whistles. The vague forms of man and horse pushing on in front of her came to a halt and her own animal began sidling and snorting, making it difficult for her to hold on to the bridle. Possibly she had conveyed her nervousness to him, she surmised, and could not control the tremors of fright attacking her body. Craig came to her rescue by grabbing the restless animal's reins and soothing him.

'Whatever you do, Leonora, do not show fear,' he whispered calmly.

'Do not worry, Craig, I will not panic,' she whispered back. 'Can you tell me what danger we are up against?'

'We are about to meet a tribe, and I cannot promise it will be on a sociable footing.' He called out softly to Wasim, 'Can you hear me?'

'*Ji, sahib.*'

'No acting hastily. Keep your dagger hidden. You and the *memsahib* remain exactly where you are. It might be for quite some time. We are being closely watched. Any moment we may find ourselves surrounded—or we may wait half the night, till they've made up their minds about us one way or another: friends or foes.'

She felt her mouth go dry with rising terror, but managed to whisper, 'How do you know humans and not animals are on our trail?'

'Experience, lady. Those whistles we heard were human ones.'

Despite the oppressive heat, a cold sweat broke out on Leonora's brow and trickled down her face to dampen the loose end of her turban, used to cover her mouth. Years of controlling her emotions now stood her in good stead, else she felt sure she would have panicked, raced off into the jungle and screamed till her voice collapsed.

A faint scraping reached her ears. She knew then that the unseen people were climbing down the trees. Santa Maria! What if these men were *thuggees*? Now even if she wanted to move she could not—the thought of being strangled to death held her petrified.

Shadows closed round them. Leonora could hear Wasim's rapid breathing—her own breath she held. She could sense the presence of bodies which emitted heat and the strong odour of coconut oil, a favourite lubricant in this country, she knew.

Suddenly a light flared and a lantern was held aloft. If she had not been so terrified, Leonora felt certain that she would have been fascinated by the sight that met her eyes.

The tribe of a dozen or so men who formed a circle round the trio were of a type of people she had never encountered before. They were short, sturdy men with sallow skins and Mongoloid features. On their straight, oiled hair they wore a band of animal pelt that rested on their foreheads. Round their necks dangled rows of beads that matched those tied on their muscular upper arms, and the only clothes they wore were loincloths.

Their expressions were impassive and fearful in the light of the lamp that threw eerie light and shadows across their features. What made Leonora quail were the fierce-looking spears that the group held levelled at them.

One of the men stepped forward and shouted something in a tongue she could not understand. But the tone of voice sounded disapproving, and suggested that he was asking a question—perhaps demanding to know who they were. She fully expected Craig to use signs to explain the circumstances. Obviously the trio were trespassing on these people's property, and they objected. She jerked in astonishment when he replied fluently in the same language.

A rapid question and answer session ensued and was kept up for some time. Of a sudden the discourse ceased, and to her utter relief Leonora saw the stranger smile, lift his hand in a salaam and motion to his men to lower their spears.

Craig returned the salutation. Then he turned to Leonora and Wasim. 'This is a Khasi tribe. They usually live farther north, nearer the Himalayas. I'm surprised to see this isolated group so far south. The man I was talking to is their chief and he has agreed to let us use a hut for the night. They live on wild honey, fruit and venison. That's what we'll be having shortly. The payment is that we give them cloth, beads and salt. I keep bolts of cotton at the lodge. I brought two along and I always carry beads and salt to meet eventualities such as this.' He raised an eyebrow and looked critically at her. 'Did I advise you to keep your eyes lowered? They're too feminine. No, don't speak, lass.' She could not even if she had wanted to, not after the ordeal of tension she had experienced, and she gazed sheepishly at him. 'No matter. But please, come the morning, try and make yourself as inconspicuous as you can and keep your eyes lowered.' He caught his horse's bridle and said, 'Let's proceed.'

Accompanied by the group, the trio followed the headman to a hut on the outer perimeter of the dozen or so similar abodes comprising a small village in the confines of a natural glade. Craig ordered Wasim to bring a bolt of cotton, beads and salt from the luggage on the servant's horse. Then he spoke to his quaint host, pulled out a drawstring purse and tipped a gold coin into the headman's hand. The man grinned his delight, waited till Wasim had handed over the promised commodities to his men and strode away with them.

Craig explained to Leonora and Wasim that they could tether the horses to one of the nearby trees, and some Khasis would bring the animals newly cut grass.

The hut they entered, Leonora noticed, had been swept clean and only a large rush mat covered the mud-tamped floor.

'Since the tribe thinks we're all males, we have to share this mat,' Craig said with a trace of amusement in his voice. He had spoken in English, but now repeated what he had said in Urdu to Wasim.

The servant's nostrils flared and his thin mouth fell open in shock. *'Arre nahin,'* he objected. 'I will sleep outside, *sahib*. You and the *memsahib* use the hut.'

'No! You will sleep in here, Wasim, near the door. These people must not become suspicious. They might not be as friendly as we imagine.'

'Very good, *sahib*,' he agreed. 'I will fetch our mats from holdall.' He began sorting out the luggage he had brought in.

So, after supper of delicious honey and fruit, Wasim unrolled a long prayer mat, said his prayers and settled down to sleep across the threshold. Soon he was snoring.

Craig and Leonora lay in the centre of the hut on the large woven mat—at a respectable distance from each other.

Except that Leonora could not sleep, even though she was weary enough to do so. Apart from the floor being uncomfortably hard, she felt grimy and sweaty from their journey.

'Would you like to bathe?' Craig murmured, and she marvelled at his uncanny ability to read her thoughts.

'Is it possible?' she asked eagerly.

'Indeed it is.'

She raised herself on one elbow and whispered into the darkness, 'Where?'

'There's a clean tributary not far from here. The headman said we are welcome to use it. No one else bathes at this time of night for fear of the nocturnal hunts of snakes or predators. Come, sweetheart, let's find it.'

'I'm not so sure. What if *we* are attacked by snakes and predators?'

'We won't be. Come.' He caught her hand and raised her to her feet.

'What about Wasim? Should we leave him here?'

To her surprise, the servant spoke out of the dark in Urdu, 'I will look after the baggage, *memsahib*. When you and the *sahib* return I, too, will take bath.'

A short walk along a path brought them to a narrow river. She knew why she had not heard it rushing—it lay as placid as glass, reflecting the moon. They found a spot that provided privacy. Craig hunted around for a dried branch and poked at nearby bushes to ensure that no dangerous reptiles lurked in them. Kicking off his sandals, he tested the water with his feet. 'Let's go in,' he invited, casually pulling off his shirt.

Leonora looked at him, appalled. 'What?'

He flung off his shirt and glared at her. 'You wanted to bathe—so, now, come on.'

'I dare say you misunderstood me, sir. I desired to bathe *alone*.'

He let out his breath in an angry hiss. 'Woman, this is no time for false modesty. We have to be quick. What do you expect me to do? Turn my back while you undress?'

'Most certainly I do! I will not bare myself to you like some——'

He clicked his tongue in mock sympathy. 'Like some wife? Darling, I'm no callow youth. I've seen all there is to see in a woman.'

CHAPTER TWELVE

CRAIG began moving slowly towards Leonora. He looked magnificent enough to take her breath away, his bare body shining in the moon's radiance. A silver god from classical mythology, she thought fancifully. She stood transfixed before him as if in a bewitched dream, yet alive to his nearness, his actions. She made no attempt to stop him while he removed the stole from her shoulders, and even lifted her arms while he took off her shirt. He untied her pyjamas and let them fall to her ankles and she gingerly stepped out of them. She watched with an enthralling heat growing in her loins as he stripped off the last of his clothing. Leonora swayed towards him, her body consumed by a fierce hunger to be in his strong arms, to feel his mouth on hers. Rationality played no part in what promised to be a rapturous communion of body and soul. Her brain succumbed to the oft rejected call of her heart.

Except that he disappointed her by taking her upper arms and holding her away from him. 'Let's bathe,' he said gruffly. Catching her hand, he pulled her towards the river.

The water was gloriously cool, but neither of them splashed about lest they should waken the forest folk. Craig and Leonora waded out till the river was deep enough to wash in. They did not stay long. She was the first to head back to the bank, with Craig following soon after. When they reached the silver patch of warm sand, he turned her to face him. His eyes shimmered in the light of the moon. His hair, free of its turban, lay slick against his well-formed skull. A balmy breeze kept mosquitoes at bay and softly caressed her skin. Slowly he passed his fingers through her long, black tresses, squeezing out the excess moisture, then along her face and neck. Her nipples sprang out and tingled in arousal as the hairs on his chest brushed them. She sighed her pleasure as his arms came round her, pressing her yet closer to him, making her aware of his strength and desire. A moist heat pulsed in her body. Leonora tilted back her head to stare up at him, eagerly awaiting his lowering mouth. It was like a touch of fire when it met hers. Gently, insistently, he parted her lips, opening them to receive his deep and probing kiss.

All the while his hands moved restlessly down her spine, over her hips, caressing, rocking her against the hub of his passion, reaching the very depths of her sensuality. His male scent, his healthy breath, the erotic hardness of his body, the rapidity of his deep kisses, the strength of his lovemaking carried her into a vortex of ecstasy she had never experienced before.

And then, as she felt ready to explode, he lifted his mouth and Leonora drew in a deep breath. Her eyes sought his face, wondering if she had disappointed him. 'Craig, I . . . I——'

'You want me? Say you want me, Leonora darling.'

'Craig, I . . . You make me want you,' she whispered.

He laughed softly in triumph. 'I'll do better, sweetheart.'

He laid her on the warm sand and traced his mouth along her throat, gently sucked the pulse hammering at its base. Then slowly he moved his lips over the swell of her breast, kissing, arousing, and finally closed his mouth over the jutting nipple. Tenderly he nibbled and sucked it. He repeated the treatment on her other nipple till she moaned in pleasure, holding his head against her to prolong the rapture.

As their mouths fused again, she opened her legs to him and wound them round his hips. And then he thrust.

The stabbing pain filled her with momentary anger. She pushed at him. 'You hurt me!'

'It always hurts the first time, my love. Relax, darling, it will be all right.' He waited a while till their breathing slowed, then began arousing her again. His hand closed over her breast, fingers moving, igniting the fire in her blood, causing her to arch back in response. She gasped when his hand dropped to the erotic nub of her femininity. Leonora clung to him, feeling their hearts drumming in unison. He tightened his arms around her and thrust slowly till her pain subsided and only the ache for fulfilment remained. As her passion mounted the blood pounded in her head, her pulse hammered erratically. Their bodies slick, they moved in an erotic love-dance of pure bliss. He seemed to be rocking her to the moon and the starlit sky, there to climax in a glorious explosion.

In the aftermath they stayed locked together till their breathing and heartbeats returned to normal. Craig lifted himself to settle beside Leonora and held her in a loving embrace, pressing her cheek against his.

Exhaling a long sigh, she whispered in his ear, 'I should hate you for what you are doing to me, Craig Mackintosh.'

He moved his mouth to just above hers and whispered back, 'But you don't, Leonora darling. You enjoyed my lovemaking, and that's how it should be between husband and wife. If your hate is like this, my bonny lass, I'm content to do without your love.'

Craig, Leonora and Wasim set out in the cool dawn of the following day with the whole village seeing them off. Mackintosh had bought from the headman some wild honeycomb, forest fruit and a sack of dried tea-leaves that grew wild in bushes. It was not as tasty as the costly China brew, but equally refreshing. A tributary of the Brahmaputra River ran along the route Craig had worked out, so there would be no dearth of water.

Leonora took little interest in these practical matters. She was filled with compunction over what had occurred with her full consent last night, with the man whom she had once regarded as her enemy and partly held responsible for her mother's death. She had to keep reminding herself that he had bluntly informed her that he cared not a whit for her love if she wantonly surrendered her body to him. All he had married her for was to spite Angus Grant. But then, she had done the same in marrying Craig, she was forced to own. It was a confusing state of affairs. Her attitude towards him in the following days was one of remoteness, a cloak to cover the shame, the guilt she experienced. Hitherto she had secretly enjoyed herself in the role of a frozen madonna, but now it seemed an affectation, had become pathetically ridiculous and passé. A futile display, she reflected sourly, like locking the door after the rest of the house had fallen down. Moreover, to her chagrin Craig too assumed an air of polite coolness.

In the ensuing fortnight no opportunity arose to afford them privacy; they were compelled to sleep in the open with Wasim not far away. Furthermore, they perforce remained alert, all their senses attuned to ever-present dangers lurking in their wild surroundings. But Leonora could not suppress the frustration of her body despite her niggling shame. She yearned for Craig's exquisite lovemaking culminating in blissful union. While she went about her duties of cooking, she could not help herself from stealing glances at him whenever he was looking elsewhere or attending to the horses. Instead of resenting his aloofness she found that it attracted her ever more to him. I must be in love, she concluded. The reluctant acknowledgement stunned her.

Hell and damnation! Craig swore to himself. He could not believe that this beautiful woman, who had opened to him like a rose to the sun, allowing him to drink of her nectar, had resumed her frigid role. God! She made him feel as if he were a cad who had taken her by force. Even so, despite her complicated nature he could not resist her, could not live without her and, if they did not arrive at a dwelling tonight, he would have to find somewhere private to make love to her. Except there was Wasim's presence to consider.

What the hell could he do about the servant? He should have asked him to bring his wife along to keep him out of the way—too late. He sighed. He had never felt this way about a woman before he met Leonora. They had always taken a secondary place in his life. Perhaps being deprived of a mother from an early age and living in a predominantly masculine world might have had something to do with his lack of opportunity of learning more about the opposite sex. His jute and cotton businesses and painting had occupied his mind.

Oh, there had been women—he was no monk. But he had existed without deep commitments and without hurting anyone. Then Angus Grant had reappeared in his life and subsequently there had been his enforced meeting with Leonora. Fate had mocked him by effecting the fiasco of the kidnapping, which had ended in the irony of his marrying this woman with whom he had reluctantly fallen in love. He was filled with remorse for misjudging her, for assuming that she had been Grant's mistress. The night of the consummation had proved otherwise, to his great joy. Now the pleasure was short-lived because of her cold attitude.

A roar shattered the night, reverberating through the forest. He heard Leonora gasp and Wasim yell, 'Oh, Allah!'

'Ssh!' he hissed, reining in his horse and raising his hand in a command for the other two to halt. Very quietly he dismounted, came to Leonora and whispered, 'We are being stalked by a tigress. Now do exactly as I say.'

She leaned down and gripped his hand in fright. 'How do you know it's a tigress?'

'Look,' he said softly. 'Look behind Wasim's horse. There are two half-grown cubs following us. The mother cannot be far behind. It was she who roared.'

Leonora nearly ricked her neck twisting her head to stare beyond Wasim. No moon lit the way, but in the bright, star-spangled night she glimpsed in the distance two figures like dogs silently crawling on their bellies towards them, stopping every now and then. 'Santa Maria! What are we to do?' she asked almost inaudibly.

Craig crept to where the servant was. 'Wasim—give me that lamp and the torches. Are the wicks oiled?'

'*Ji, sahib,*' the servant said tremulously, unwrapping two wooden torches from their oilskins.

'Good. Now I'm going to light these from the lamp. Meanwhile, Wasim, tie the horses to that low-hanging branch and unload the baggage. The steeds might break free and bolt and we'll lose all our belongings.'

Her heart slamming in her throat, Leonora dismounted and helped Wasim tether the horses and remove the baggage. The cubs were nowhere in sight, but she could feel their presence not far off.

Craig had lit both torches and now faced the direction in which the cubs had been seen, with Leonora, Wasim and the horses behind him. She slipped up to Craig and said as calmly as she could, 'I know you are going to try and frighten them away with the flaming torches. Wouldn't it also be helpful if Wasim and I built up fires?'

'Aye, lass, good idea. Wasim should have a bundle of faggots and kindling.'

But when she looked back the servant had conquered his terror and was already laying small bundles of twigs and lighting them. 'What if they disregard the flaming torches and fires, Craig?' How brave he is, she thought, her heart lifting with pride.

'Then as a last resort, and only then, there's the pistol, but it means reloading for the next shot. By that time the tigress will have killed at least one of us if we've blasted her cubs.'

'There must be some other way,' Leonora remarked, trying to stifle the fear causing her skin to break out in goose-bumps.

Craig nodded, holding the flaming torches aloft, trying to locate the animals. 'There is. I could fire into the air, which hopefully will frighten them away. Animals are terrified of loud sounds. You could help by using the cooking utensils to create a racket. But don't do anything till you actually sight the cubs.'

A tension-racked silence descended. All was ready for the attack. Craig stood braced with the two flaming torches, Leonora held cooking pans in her hands, ready to bang them together, and Wasim watched over the two small fires he had built. The shivering horses were the first to sound the alarm by sidling and whinnying in fright.

Beyond them, Leonora's alert eyes spotted the cubs crouching in the long grass. She tensed, gripping the pans tighter, her heart banging rapidly. A low snarl coming from Craig's direction made her look towards him. The tigress had emerged, a superb, striped creature, her ears back, eyes ablaze. She paced some distance in front of Craig. The torches were keeping her at bay and the two fires built by Wasim were doing the same to the cubs. But how long would this state of affairs go on? Leonora wondered in alarm. They were now wedged between the mother and the cubs. Obviously the horses were the main attractions—they would provide the tigers with food for several days. And if three dead humans were thrown in, so much the better.

Suddenly Craig bawled, 'Make as much noise as you can!'

Leonora banged the pans, Wasim clapped and shouted and Craig yelled with all his might, waving the torches which formed arcs of fire. The cubs were the first to leap back into the jungle; the tigress was not so eager. She roared and snarled, mouth wide, showing enormous fangs, but eventually she loped away, though not far— they could hear her threatening snarls and the yowls of the hungry cubs, who had now teamed up with their mother.

'This is just a respite,' Craig said, backing to where Leonora stood. Perspiration streamed down his face and she reached up and dabbed it away with her shawl. 'Thanks, lass.' He leaned down and kissed her on the cheek. He called out to Wasim, 'Make some more fires, nearer the horses. We are in for a long, arduous night.' He handed Leonora the torches. 'Hold these, my love, while I scoop out a couple of holes to stand them in.' She took them from him and watched while he used his long dagger to dig. He worked fast and soon the torches were planted in their earth sconces. Returning the knife to its leather sheath dangling from a thong under his sash, he wiped his brow and, smiling tiredly, said to Leonora, 'Let's sit for a while till the opposition have decided on their next plan of attack. Aye, listen to them—they're having quite a discussion!'

His good humour dissolved some of her fear and made her laugh a little sadly under her breath. This might be their last night on earth and he was treating their predicament with amazing flippancy. Only the courageous, she believed, could jest in the face of death. He cleared a space for her beside him and she sat down with her knees drawn up. 'You are truly brave, Craig.'

He lifted a corner of his mouth in a one-sided smile and took her hand, staring for a while at the ruby and diamond wedding ring scintillating in the firelight. 'And you, my lady wife, are a marvel. You would shame many a man with that inner strength I have noticed since I abducted you. As for the women, most would be panic-stricken, fainting with terror—at least, the ones I have known.'

'Including Fiona?' The words had slipped out before she could stop herself.

His eyes, as golden and glowing as that tigress's, narrowed. 'Why bring her in?'

Leonora shrugged. She had no opportunity to answer as the tigress bounded out of the undergrowth and crouched some yards away from them. Her nose wrinkled back in a ferocious snarl. Craig leapt up and snatched the torches from their holes. The trio repeated their racket. This time the tigress crept closer on her belly, as if determined to ignore the fires. But Craig moved forward half-bent, thrusting the torches at her. It proved too much for the animal and, her tail lashing, she retreated.

Then from the depths of the forest came another roar. 'Arrrroum!'

'Save us!' Craig shouted. 'There's another grown tiger. They don't roam in prides like lions. What the devil is going on?'

'Come back, Craig!' Leonora entreated. 'Come back in the circle of fire! They might attack you. Craig, please, for my sake!' She let out a sob.

He returned to the ring and stared at her. 'Now, now, my love. Where's my brave wife gone?'

'We must think of what to do, Craig. Their hunger might force them to overcome their fear of fire.'

'*Sahib*, you give Wasim torches. You use gun.'

'Aye, Wasim. I was just about to tell the *memsahib* that. Here, take these.' He handed the torches to the servant.

Craig whipped out his pistol just as another roar vibrated the air. Then, to Leonora's astonishment, two grown tigers came into view. A snarling contest ensued.

The big male didn't attack the female but appeared to be threatening her. She lashed out at him, her claws extended, but he dodged and gave a deafening roar. There was no sign of the cubs. After more snarling, the tigress backed away and fled into the jungle. To Leonora's utter amazement, the male sprawled out not far from them, his big head upright, and began panting.

'The devil!' Craig exclaimed. 'That's my good friend, Rajkumar.'

'You mean the yogi's tiger?'

'That's right, lady. What the devil is he doing so far away?' Craig stuck the pistol back in its holster and stepped out of the ring of fire. 'Let's make sure.'

Leonora grabbed his arm. 'No! Please, Craig. You can never be sure with wild animals. He might have forgotten you.'

'Never! After that magnificent display of defending us?'

'Then let me come with you—please, Craig.'

He placed his arm round her. 'Come.'

'*Sahib*, where are you going?' Wasim wailed in alarm.

'Stay where you are, Wasim. You'll find a pistol in my bag. I happen to know this animal, but if he shows signs of aggression fire into the air.'

The servant consented reluctantly.

As the couple advanced towards the tiger, Craig called softly to him and spoke in Hindustani as the old yogi did. 'Rajkumar. You were excellent, boy. Where's Sri Ajuna?'

The animal screwed his face up and snarled softly. Craig released Leonora and crouched down to stroke the large head.

Simultaneously a man stepped out from the under-growth. It was Sri Ajuna. He hurried towards the tiger. 'Where have you been, Rajkumar?'

The animal rose with lazy grace and gave a soft 'aroum', and gently rubbed his head against the old man. Sri Ajuna smiled and patted the animal. All the while he peered closely at Craig. 'You are the good Hira Nag Sahib, are you not?'

'Aye, and this is my lady wife. Do you remember her?'

The old yogi chuckled, showing his very white teeth. 'I do not recognise the lady, for she is in different clothes, but I remember she was troublesome. She is now obedient, is she not?'

Craig laughed. 'Aye, for the moment. Pray, what brings you and Rajkumar so far from your part of the forest?'

'I have been looking for you, *sahib*. The Khasi headman told me you had stopped at his village and he thought that perhaps you were following the river.'

'He's right. But we cannot talk here. Let's return within the ring of fires and sit in comfort.'

The yogi gave Rajkumar the command to stay where he was and followed Craig and Leonora to their temporary encampment. Wasim pulled out a large mat from the luggage and they all sat on it after Leonora had brewed some tea, which the trio drank from brass cups, but the yogi politely refused all refreshment. 'Now, Sri Ajuna, what takes you out of your way to seek me out? It must be of the gravest importance.'

The old yogi wagged his white head. 'It is, it is, *sahib*. You and the *memsahib* are in great danger. It is as well that Rajkumar and I found you first.'

'What sort of danger, sir?' Leonora asked when the old man paused.

'The Khasi said a *sahib* and a woman of Hindustan are looking for you. They are travelling by cart pulled by mules and tended by five armed servants.'

'So, if the headman told you in what direction we were heading, he must have told the others the same,' Craig said, looking anxiously at the yogi.

'He did not, *sahib*. The white man and the woman were rude and threatened the Khasis if they did not say where you had gone. The intruders and their servants had guns trained on the villagers. The woman said her brother was head of a gang of *thuggees*, and if the Khasis did not reveal your whereabouts they would be strangled by the gang.'

'The man and woman must be Angus Grant and his mistress, Kamila! My ayah said she had connections with the *thuggees*,' Leonora told the yogi agitatedly.

'Did the tribe betray us?' Craig asked. 'I wouldn't be surprised, if they were threatened with *thuggees*.'

'No, *sahib*. The headman was angry but did not show it to the strangers. He told me you had been good guests and had given him ample payment for your night's stay at the village. Because he liked you, he informed the white man that you were crossing to the Arakan. That is due east and will take your enemies off your trail.'

Touched by the yogi's kindness, Leonora said, 'We are truly grateful to you for going out of your way to shield us, Sri Ajuna. How can we repay you?'

'It is I who must do the repaying, *memsahib*.' He spread a veined hand, indicating Craig. 'Hira Nag Sahib helped my kin. They would have starved to death, as none wanted to share my lonely life in the forest.'

'I think you had better stay with us tonight, Sri Ajuna. We have food enough for several days.'

But the old yogi shook his head and rose from his crossed-legged position in a single movement. 'I thank thee, *sahib*, but I came here to help you. If you would reload the horses and follow Rajkumar and me, I will lead you to safety if only for tonight.'

So while the old yogi went over to his tiger and talked with him, the others packed away their belongings, doused the fires—with the exception of the lamp—and mounted their steeds.

'But will the horses move with Rajkumar not far ahead, following his master?' Leonora asked Craig in a concerned voice.

His golden eyes viewed her with admiration. 'I had not thought of that. It would be best if we lead the horses instead of mounting them.' He swung off his stallion.

The old yogi strode to the head of the file and, holding his staff high, signalled to the trio to follow as he strode briskly through the forest. However, his tiger seemed to have disappeared.

'Where is Rajkumar, Sri Ajuna?' Craig called.

'He is keeping out of scent of horses, *sahib*. They will not trouble you now.'

Leonora and Craig exchanged relieved glances. The wise old man thought of everything. 'Are you all right, Wasim?'

'*Ji, sahib*. Allah takes care of all who fear him.'

Leonora felt exhausted from the recent ordeal and she prayed her thanks for their safe deliverance. She sat upright in the saddle, giving no hint of her aching back and lack of energy, exacerbated by the heat of the night. It should not be long, she reflected, before they came to a village or wherever the old man led them. But it was a long time before the yogi led them into a paved courtyard, with plants pushing up between flagstones, and surrounded by broken walls and tumbledown rooms with doors torn off or hanging on their hinges. Ajuna lifted his staff and called a halt. Leonora saw Craig dismount and go up to the old man. They exchanged words and he came back to her. 'Sri Ajuna says this is a disused *serai*. In years gone by it was on a main road that ran along the river. Apparently there was a diamond mine around these parts, but it is now defunct and so is the *serai*. He thinks it's a good place to shelter for the night.'

'Oh, I'm glad. I'm sure we could all do with a good night's sleep.' She was about to dismount, but he stayed her by touching her thigh.

'Wait here for a while. The old man and I decided it would be better if he and I went over the place first. Make sure it's vacant and safe.' He turned to Wasim. 'Stay with the *memsahib*, till I return.'

The servant assented, and Leonora watched in some trepidation as the yogi and her husband strode into the darkness.

A fair length of time elapsed before they returned, evoking in Leonora a feeling of uneasiness. Both men were silent, both looked stricken in the dim light of the lamp.

'Craig, what is the matter? What has happened?' Sheer instinct kept her voice low.

'Quick, we must get out of here. You ride with me and let Ajuna take your horse. *Thuggees* are grouped in one of the rooms. They have just ritually killed two men.'

CHAPTER THIRTEEN

'*NAHIN, sahib*, I do not know how to ride on horse,' Sri Ajuna stipulated, just as Craig was about to help Leonora down.

'Then how will you manage to get away fast?' Craig enquired.

'I will ride my tiger. He is watching us in the bushes. You go, *sahib*. Do not delay! The *thuggees* are coming after you!'

'Hold tight!' Craig told Leonora, and gave her steed's rump a thump. Her mount plunged and surged forward. She sent up a silent prayer of thanks that she had been obsessed with riding as a child. It stood her in good stead now.

Leaning forward in the saddle, she glanced back to see the other two thundering close on her heels. She could not see Sri Ajuna, but in the distance behind she spotted flaming torches and heard the yells of the *thuggees*. She was relieved to notice that they did not possess horses.

Eventually, after what seemed a good length of time, Craig called a halt. He patted his stallion's sweat-lathered neck. 'We cannot overwork these animals, else they'll go lame. We too need a night's rest, so we'll camp in that glade yonder.'

If they had gone any further, Leonora thought, she would have collapsed; every bone in her body ached and she all but tumbled out of the saddle. She did not wait for Craig to help her down—he had enough to contend with.

Even so, there was still much to be done, she reflected: a ring of fires to build to safeguard themselves against wild beasts, a meal for her to cook, while the two men fed and watered the horses. Forcing her exhaustion aside, she began unloading the cooking utensils and a bag of wholemeal flour.

'Wait!' Craig said, taking hold of her wrist.

'I have to prepare something to eat. You and Wasim must be hungry.' Another blessing was that she had been fascinated with cooking and had pestered the cook at the bungalow to teach her. She could not have envisaged how handy it would prove, and felt pleased that she could make some use of her talents instead of being an additional burden on this journey abounding with hazards.

'We'll manage with fruit and honey, lass. You look far too tired. Go lie on the mat I've spread for you. I'll bring you the fruit.'

Leonora made no demur, but, once she had lain down, she knew nothing till dawn. She woke to find herself pleasurably ensconced in Craig's arms. Wasim's reassuring snores told her that he was not far off. The fires were still flickering, which caused pangs of guilt to trouble her. The two men must have taken it in turns all night to keep them lit while she enjoyed an undisturbed sleep.

Ever so quietly, so as not to disturb Craig, she pushed her head back to gaze at him. He looked young and vulnerable in sleep, and distractingly handsome. His hair, damp in the dawn mist, was attractively tousled and a couple of locks fell on his smooth, high forehead. The nostrils of his narrow nose flared slightly as he breathed.

His mouth, which had excited her so pleasurably, lay with sensual lips a little parted. Her eyes travelled down to the hard chin, jutting jaw bristling with dark red stubble and the strong neck with a pulse beating at the hollow of his throat. She inhaled his smell of horses and sweat, mingled with the freshness of early morning outdoors. Her gaze returned to his eyes. She started when she saw him observing her through his long, meshed lashes.

A slow smile curved his mouth. 'Had a good sleep?'

She nodded. 'But I fear you have not. I can see you and Wasim were probably up half the night tending the fires.'

'My lovely, sympathetic wife,' he said with a laugh, giving her a hug. 'Wasim and I have gone without more than a night's sleep before now.'

'I think I had better cook some breakfast,' she offered, attempting to hide her confusion in being caught studying him.

'Aye, I confess I am ravenous—for this.'

His husky voice caused her heart to dance, his lowering mouth made her breath seize up in anticipation of his kiss. Wasim's sudden cough warned her of his presence. She put her finger on Craig's mouth and followed her eyes in the servant's direction.

Craig moved her finger from his lips. 'He's asleep. And even if he is awake, he'll keep his back discreetly turned to us.'

'I—I couldn't. Not with Wasim so close. I mean——'

'He's a good few yards away. Stop struggling, sweetheart. I'll not disgrace you.' His mouth touched hers softly. 'Just a taste to keep your appetite alive.'

'Mm,' she murmured dreamily as he half rolled on her, his leg pinning both hers. No longer did his mouth linger softly, but hardened till she opened hers in willing response.

Leonora yielded to the deep exploration of his kiss, suffered sweet torture knowing there would be no fulfilment. His hand slid beneath her shirt and glided over her bare skin to cup her firm breast and caress the swollen peak. Her body throbbed with the heat of arousal, brought to fever pitch as his hand left her breast to massage the silken skin over her ribs, her stomach, and dipped under the corded waistband of her pyjamas to fondle the enticing triangle below.

They broke apart when they heard Wasim stirring. Abruptly they sat up and stared at each other, their faces flushed. 'I—I think I had better cook some breakfast,' she said, coiling up her hair and shoving it beneath her turban.

Smiling wryly, Craig nodded. 'Aye. Next time perhaps luck will favour us.'

During the meal, Leonora received the impression that all was not well with Craig and Wasim, for they looked uncommonly morose. She tried to shrug it off, assuming that they were still tired from insufficient sleep, but the sensation of uneasiness persisted. Leonora decided to take the forthright way of finding out. 'Craig, is something wrong?'

For a moment he stopped chewing the fresh chapatti spread with clarified butter and looked at her, startled. He washed down his food with the last of his tea, put the pewter mug down with concentrated deliberation and then looked steadily at her. 'We're lost.'

A coldness crept into her veins, despite the warmth of the sun's rays which had dispersed the mist and penetrated the leafy roof of the towering foliage. The glorious birdsong which had lifted her spirits a second ago turned into a dirge. 'Lost,' she breathed, gaping at him in disbelief. Surely this strong man could never be lost. It brought home to her the immensity of the faith and trust she had unconsciously placed in him.

'Not irretrievably, I might add. There's no need for panic.'

'What are we going to do, Craig?'

Wasim glanced from one to the other of the two people he had lived in close proximity with and whom he liked. He could not speak English, but did understand a word here and there. His presence, he decided, was superfluous. He rose from the circle of three and mumbled that he would put out the fires.

Leonora hardly noticed him. She stared about her, at the vastness of the forest and the giant sal trees. 'What are we going to do, Craig?' she repeated.

He squinted up through the branches. 'Nothing, for the moment,' he replied with astonishing mildness. 'We have enough food and there's plenty of grass for the horses. The main trouble is water. Wasim gave you the last drop to brew the tea. None of us will survive for long without water, especially the animals—they need a lot to drink.'

She shook her head. 'No.'

'No, what? We don't need water to survive? Is that what you're trying to say?' he asked, a touch of cynicism underlying his tone.

Leonora licked her dry lips and flung her hands out. 'I didn't mean that. What I'm trying to convey is that there must be water. Look at these towering trees, their green foliage, the lush grass and undergrowth. They cannot grow without water.'

'Aye. It's all underground, drawn up by the roots of the trees. Perhaps if we dig deep enough we'll come across some. Alas, we donnae possess tools.' He spotted the hurt in her eyes and suppressed his sarcasm. 'But don't be too distressed. We'll look for animal spoors. They usually lead to a river, stream or lake.'

She felt slightly heartened, but then gloom set in again. 'How are we going to get out of this forest?'

Craig rose in one agile movement, caught her hands and hauled her up. 'We won't, I fear. But once we've found water we'll get back on course using the sun. If we move in a north-east direction, we cannot go far wrong.'

They all agreed to walk beside their mounts to relieve the animals of the extra burden, but it was nearing sundown when they came across a spoor and far ahead a herd of spotted deer, the chital, heading west. The trio followed the animals at a cautious distance, till suddenly the trees fell away from view and the vista of a broad belt of sand and wide river, golden in the sunset, confronted them.

Leonora cried out with joy and the horses whinnied and plunged, shaking free of their reins to dash headlong to the water.

Craig laughed exultantly, swept Leonora up in his arms and ran into the inviting coolness, closely followed by a grinning Wasim.

*   *   *

They returned to the jungle on Craig's advice. 'We're too exposed on this stretch of sand. It won't take long for our pursuers to find us.'

'You think we are still being followed?' Leonora asked, squeezing the water from her hair, her eyes wide and dark in surprise and fear.

'The *thuggees* might have abandoned their chase, but Grant won't give up so easily. I believe he's out to kill both of us, whether he gets your fortune or not. Perhaps I should stay and accept his challenge of a duel.'

Leonora shivered in apprehension. 'No! Didn't Sri Ajuna say Grant had several armed men? You will be tempting fate, sir. What if...?'

'What if he kills me?'

'It's not impossible.'

'No, that's true, lass. Then you'll be on your own. And, of course, I couldnae allow that.'

'I wasn't thinking of myself, Craig, but you also.'

He grimaced. 'I'm too young to die?'

She laughed. 'That's one of the reasons.'

'And the others?'

She shook her head, signalling the end of the discussion, and busied herself cooking a light supper. The cooking fire soon dried out their clothing and they sat replete and pleasantly drowsy round it. Wasim offered them betel-nut from a small silver box, but Craig and Leonora politely refused and watched him place the cut-up nuts and lime paste in a round *pan* leaf, fold it into a triangle and pop it in his mouth. Leonora shifted her gaze to the horses tethered nearby, contentedly cropping the grass beneath a tree. Mosquitoes buzzed around, but the ring of fires kept them from harassing them.

'Have you decided on what we should do, Craig?' she enquired, returning her eyes to stare into the hypnotic flames.

'Aye, I know where we are now. We have come back to the Hooghly River and can proceed north, come dawn.'

Her eyes softened as she gazed at him. 'Oh, Craig, I knew you would rescue us from this mess.'

He let his scrutiny appraise her. Her newly washed hair hung thick and straight to her waist from the enchanting widow's peak. The fire cast a rosy glow on her cheeks and parted lips, and the deep blue eyes enhanced by their thick fringe of lashes held him entranced. Her masculine garb was wrinkled from the recent dip and she smelled faintly of fresh water and wood smoke. He had to admit that she had completely captivated him. Lifting a large, rough hand, he gently stroked her cheek and lightly ran a finger down the cleft in her chin. 'Did you, lass?'

'Aye, m'lad. I couldnae do aught else,' she replied, mischievously imitating his Scottish accent. He chuckled softly and Leonora joined him—so did Wasim. They both glanced at him in surprise.

'You understood what we said, Wasim?' Craig asked.

'A little, I am knowing, *sahib*. But you are happy and that makes Wasim happy, no?'

Craig smiled at him affectionately. 'You'll be rewarded well if we do arrive safely at Hira Nag Palace.'

'We will, *sahib*. It is the will of Allah. *Insh'Allah*.' He straightened, bowed slightly and reverently touched his forehead, lips and heart. 'If you will excuse, I must go now and say prayers.'

*   *   *

Within the next few weeks they were back on course and making good progress. Craig consulted the map for streams and tributaries to ensure the constant availability of water. But the weather grew steadily hotter though they were travelling north. 'It'll not get cooler till we reach the foothills. Not long now. So bear up, my love.' He smiled at Leonora to cheer her up.

His 'not long now' turned out to be several weeks, in which Leonora learnt the true fight for survival. They had avoided villages where they could have stocked up with flour, because there was the danger that Angus Grant would stop there to make enquiries about his quarries. In consequence, Leonora was forced to ration the number of chapattis per person. The honey had long been depleted but, mercifully, wild berries and papayas grew in plenty.

Craig had decided against carrying tents at the start of the journey, stating that the support poles were too cumbersome and the canvas bulky and heavy even when tightly folded. He calculated that they would arrive at their destination before the advent of the monsoons. Alas, he had not allowed for the odd shower. One day it came down in torrents and lasted till sundown.

They hurriedly dismounted, for the trees provided little shelter in the hard downpour. The two men hastily erected a makeshift tent with mats and broken branches they searched for on the ground. By the time their shelter was ready, all three were soaked. Leonora did not mind her wet clothes since they helped to keep her cool—the forest had become a cauldron. Wasim alerted them to the danger of snakes. 'If their holes fill with water, *sahib*, they will come out. Sometimes they look like branches across the forest floor. Therefore, I say beware!'

He failed to take his own advice. One of the branches that held up their temporary tent snapped. 'I will fetch another,' Wasim offered, and ran out into the dusk.

A scream rent the air.

For a fearful moment, Leonora assumed that the *thuggees* had discovered Wasim and were strangling him.

'Stay here,' Craig ordered and darted out. She ignored his words and followed close behind him.

'I'm not sitting there alone,' she said when he glared at her.

They had gone a short way when they met Wasim limping towards them.

Craig eyed the servant with concern. 'What's wrong, Wasim?'

'I bent to pick up a dead branch, *sahib*,' he said, gasping.

'And you touched a snake.'

'*Ji, sahib.*'

Leonora could only stare in horror.

Craig carried Wasim back and laid him on the mat inside the dilapidated shelter. Then he drew out a knife. The sight of it made Leonora's blood freeze. 'What are you going to do to him?' she asked faintly.

'I'm not going to kill him, but try and *save* him. Now watch, lest you should have to do this to me!'

She stared in frozen horror as Craig snatched off his turban, tore a strip from it and tied it tightly above Wasim's knee, then cut across the punctures of the bite on his calf, which had begun to swell. He incised several gashes above and below the wound. Wasim groaned but made no effort to protest. Craig applied his mouth to the bite, sucked in as much venom and blood as he could, then spat it out. He made no attempt to stem the flow from the other wounds he had deliberately gashed.

Leonora impelled herself into action and rummaged in one of her bags till she found a petticoat. She tore the fine lawn into strips and made a wad to soak up the blood streaming from the cuts. She could not imagine why he had made the incisions. As she bent to stem the flow, Craig shouted, 'Leave it! Let them bleed!'

'Why?' she asked in a defiant voice, affronted by his shouting.

He paused for a second from his gory task, looking macabre with his mouth covered in blood. 'To let the venom flow out.'

Wasim had stopped groaning and Leonora glanced anxiously at him. 'Craig, I think he's unconscious.'

'Slap him! Don't let him die on us, for God's sake!'

Leonora did not hesitate. She struck Wasim several times across his thin face. For a while she thought he had gone, and panic seized her. 'Wasim, wake up!'

'I—I am awake, *memsahib*,' he said wanly, giving her a strained smile. 'Could I have little water to drink?'

The amount of blood Wasim was losing probably made him thirsty. 'Would you prefer tea, Wasim?'

'Ji, memsahib. Shukriyar.' He thanked her.

Craig lifted his mouth from the wound. 'Make enough for all of us. It will help to get rid of the taste of blood.'

'First I'll give Wasim a drop of water, then you can rinse your mouth. Have you finished...?'

'Yes, I have sucked the bite dry.'

He sounded as if he had sucked the juice from a mango. It made her feel sick.

Leonora brought a goatskin of water and Craig took it from her. 'I'll give it to him.'

She left them, then lit a fire and boiled water in a pan to brew the tea. She made it strong and sweetened it with honey for all of them.

By suppertime, Wasim was delirious, raging with a fever. Neither Craig nor Leonora felt hungry and both took it in turns to minister to the servant, placing wet cloths across his forehead to reduce his heat. But it was two days before the crisis was over. At dawn on the third day, the servant asked for something to eat. Leonora stretched out her hand and caught Craig's. 'Oh, thank God. He heard my prayers,' she said with tears in her eyes.

His face softened despite its lines of fatigue. 'How could He fail to, coming from someone as lovely as you are, darling.'

She let out a long sigh and allowed her shoulders to droop. 'How much longer are we to remain in this forest?'

'Hira Nag Sahib, Allah has thought to spare me. I am feeling well. We can travel as soon as we are packed.' Wasim startled them both by speaking.

'You might be feeling well, you old rogue, but I assure you, you are in no condition to travel for at least another couple of days, if that. You must recoup some of your strength.'

However, Craig decided to move on the next day. Water was running out and the food supply was low. Fortunately the short, life-giving spurt of rain had brought out an abundant crop of spinach and grass, and had replenished streams and rivers. This kept humans, horses and no doubt the rest of the forest well fed and watered.

They moved slowly at first, stopping periodically to let Wasim rest. After a few days the trio pushed relentlessly forward.

Leonora's first sight of the Himalayan foothills astounded her. She had been thinking in terms of hills, but these were mountains soaring into the vivid blue sky. She held her breath, marvelling at the grandeur and majesty of the giant massifs. As the three climbed the narrow, hairpin-bend trails, with sheer drops on one side and a wall of trees growing tightly up the other side of the mountains, towering to unseen heights, Leonora noticed a distinct change in the atmosphere. Gone were the humid heat, dust and insects. An idyllic coolness surrounded everything, brought colour to her cheeks and energy to her body. She breathed in deeply of the pure air.

A few days later, when the sun was at its zenith, they entered a high valley, and there spread before them was a palace that resembled one which she supposed could exist only in the realm of dreams. Here was a fairy-tale edifice of gilded domes and turrets. She realised that her mouth was hanging agape when Craig spoke to her with quiet amusement. 'Surprised, are you?'

She blinked and stared again. 'And—and that belongs to you?'

'You have my word on it. But if you are doubtful ask Wasim.'

She did not have to as the servant was wildly jubilant, revealing a toothy, *pan*-streaked grin.

They passed through a towering gateway with scalloped archways, and through courtyards and gardens with sunken pools abounding with giant lotuses and golden carp.

Wasim galloped ahead to announce their arrival and, by the time Craig and Leonora had walked their steeds up to the scalloped, dome-shaped arcade, a few servants had rushed out to meet them.

Craig helped her to dismount. 'I'll see you later. You'll need some rest.' He gave rapid orders to the group as more people emerged in the marble portico.

Soon Leonora found herself separated from Craig as three women guided her to a suite of rooms of a resplendence that made her gasp in awe.

'You like, *memsahib*?' one of the servants asked. They were all young and dressed in glittering saris to match the opulence of the chamber.

'Yes—yes, indeed.' She smiled at them and their happy expressions dispelled some of her weariness.

'You will be wanting to have bath, *memsahib*. We will have water put in bathroom and then help you to bathe. That is all right, no?'

She did not argue, but allowed herself to be led into a circular, marble bathroom with two huge marble water jars fixed to the floor, which gradually sloped towards drains.

Leonora luxuriated in the warm, scented water being poured over her, the perfume rising with the steam to envelop the whole room. Finally, she enjoyed a brisk rub-down, let the servants enfold her in a soft, red wool robe, generously embroidered with gold thread, and take her back to the gold and green satin-draped bedchamber.

It was time for a couple of hours' rest. She dismissed the servants, but one insisted on bringing in a meal. She ate it seated on embroidered silk cushions at a low, fretted ebony table with silver claw-feet.

At last the tray was carried out and she was left alone to study her surroundings. She crossed the deep-pile indigo carpet covering the marble floor, and stepped out through a jutting, dome-shaped window with a fretted balcony that overlooked a garden courtyard. She breathed in the sweet, pure air, and watched the sun sink between two mountains.

A sigh of contentment escaped her lips. She turned and made her way to the vast four-poster of European design, draped with the same gold and green material that graced the walls. Sinking back on the green satin quilt, she wondered if Craig had undergone the same pampering she had. Perhaps he would come to her in a little while. She smiled complacently and closed her eyes.

Soft swishing of skirts woke Leonora. For a moment she could not recollect where she was, then it flooded in with a rush. She watched a woman light a low lamp suspended from the ceiling, and a couple placed in gilded niches. Raising herself on her elbow, she glanced out of the projecting window and saw an indigo sky awash with enormous stars.

'Have I slept very late?' Leonora asked the woman, who had her back turned.

'*Salaam, memsahib.* You have slept well!' the servant replied in a familiar voice.

With a soft cry of delight, Leonora swung off the bed and hugged the woman. 'Rumi! Oh, I am glad to see you!'

'And I you, *memsahib.* It is very good to know that you and Hira Nag Sahib are married. I said he was good man. No?'

Leonora's eyes sparkled and she laughed out loud with happiness. The rest had done her good. All her aches and stiffness of muscles had vanished. She felt alive, like a dying fire fanned to a blaze.

Rumi eyed Leonora critically, shook her head and tutted ruefully. 'Ah, but you are too thin *memsahib*. We must feed you up. Dinner is still an hour away. Would you like some sweetmeats?'

'Dinner an hour away!' Leonora exclaimed. 'Have I slept all that time?'

'*Ji*. I will fetch sweets.'

'No, Rumi. I would rather wait till dinner.'

'Then come, *memsahib*. I will help you dress.' The servant pointed to a brocaded sofa that was placed up against a wall.

Leonora had expected to see one of her own dresses on it, but was surprised at the sight of the gown spread out. She knew that the crimson colour would suit her, though she had never worn so bright a garment.

'Where did you get this?' she asked, without lifting her gaze from the gown.

'While you slept I unpacked your bags, *memsahib*. If you remember, I told you my brother is tailor. He came here with my family from Murshidabad, *memsahib*. He sewed this gown while you slept.'

'He must be a genius!' Leonora marvelled. 'And where did he get the material?'

'There are many cloth merchants in the palace bazaar.'

'And you chose this?'

'*Nahin*, the *sahib* sent a small piece of cloth to me with money to buy same kind and pay my brother for the sewing. The *sahib* told me to use one of your dresses for fit.'

Leonora laughed. 'Santa Maria! So many frills and flounces. It's more suitable for a royal ball.'

The colour enhanced the pearly sheen of her magnolia skin, emphasised the glow on her cheeks and suited the blue-black of her hair, which she coiled up on the crown of her head with wisps lying in spirals in front of her ears. She rummaged in her bag, looking for the purse of jewels, when she spotted the package Senhor Fernandez had handed her, stating that it had been her father's plaid.

Removing the covering, she gazed at the length of material. The tartan was of green, red and thin yellow lines, and lying on top was a gold brooch engraved with the Maclean clan badge and inscribed with its motto. She touched it lovingly. I'll substitute this for jewellery tonight, she told herself.

She remembered her mother wearing the plaid at an official dinner once in Portugal. Now she pleated it diagonally over her breasts and back and secured it with the brooch on her left shoulder. She admired the effect in a full-length mirror, twisting and turning in her voluminous skirts. Rumi's effusive praise made her chuckle with delight.

A knock sounded on the door. 'Come in,' she called gaily, assuming that Craig had come to fetch her for dinner.

As she turned to face the caller, her heart slipped.

Looking radiant in yellow stood a smiling Fiona Mcintyre.

CHAPTER FOURTEEN

HITHERTO, before meeting Fiona, Leonora had never known jealousy of another woman. The acid sensation corroding her abdomen which she failed to suppress brought a flush of shame to her cheeks. She felt helpless to deal with the situation, and silently reproached herself for taking the coward's way out by pretending that nothing was amiss.

'Good evening, *senhorinha*. I had not expected to see you here,' she said, forcing her frozen lips into a semblance of a smile.

'Of course you did not, Leonora. Father and I recently escaped a massacre at Patna, thanks to Robert Murray, and were forced to find shelter here with Craig, who has been our friend for a number of years,' Fiona said defensively. A hint of defiance crept into her voice as she continued, 'After all, Father helped Craig when he was struggling to cope as a merchant.'

So the girl was not deceived by my false attitude, Leonora thought. 'I'm sorry if I gave you the impression that you are not welcome——'

'I could scarce blame you if you did, ma'am. No new bride wishes to have visitors intruding on her privacy.'

A bizarre situation had materialised, Leonora mused: she liked Fiona, whom she considered her rival, yet felt jealous of her; but, most preposterous of all, Leonora had grown to love her erstwhile abductor. How could she deal with her dilemma?

Suddenly Fiona's face lit up with happiness. 'But I didnae come to argue, I came to tell you I——' Her words were cut off by Craig's appearance.

Leonora's heart jolted with pleasure—he looked superb in his clan outfit of predominantly red tartan. He, too, wore his plaid as she did hers, across his chest, anchored at the shoulder by a brooch depicting the Mackintosh coat of arms and motto. His head was bare, the flame-gold hair waving back and caught at the nape with black velvet ribbon which matched his waistcoat. Throughout the journey in the forest he had managed to keep his beard to a stubble, but now that was shaved off and his clean-cut chin and jaw made him look devastatingly handsome.

He appraised both girls with admiration, his golden eyes agleam with good humour. 'Good evening. I see I have the honour of escorting two of the most beautiful ladies to dinner.'

Craig and Fiona stood side by side. To Leonora's jealous eyes they looked magnificently well-suited to each other. In normal circumstances she would have observed courtesy and taken his offered arm, but the green serpent coiled in her breast incited her to break with convention. 'Please escort Miss Mcintyre,' she said, trying hard to hide the mockery in her voice and failing. 'I have a few words to say to Rumi. She will show me the way to the dining-hall.'

Smoothly, blandly, he said, 'There is plenty of time to discuss whatever you have in mind with Rumi. But I fear dinner cannot wait indefinitely, ma'am.' He then spoke gently in Hindustani to the servant. Rumi brought her palms together and departed.

It was his scarcely definable stress on the 'ma'am' that told her he was furious at her breach of etiquette. Fiona glanced from Craig to Leonora, her light green eyes clearly revealing her embarrassment.

He strode up to his wife, caught her hand and placed it in the crook of his arm. He did not have to repeat the action with Fiona—she automatically took his arm when he came abreast of her, and the three of them passed along cusped arcades to a large chamber.

It could have been a European state banquet hall, not part of an Indian royal palace. 'This used to be the Durbar hall when this was a raja's palace,' Craig informed his companions, 'but I have made a few renovations.' Leonora heard Fiona voice her approval of it but she herself remained silent. Vaguely she noticed, at the far end of the hall, Fiona's father and a young man standing near an ornate sideboard, holding cut-glass tumblers and sipping amber liquid which she assumed was whisky. Her attention had been caught by the large portrait within a gold frame above the marble fireplace. She knew at once that the man in the Highland garb of the Mackintosh clan sitting straight and proud was Craig's father, despite the difference in colouring. The man in the picture had black hair and black, probing eyes, whose shrewdness the painter had cleverly captured, but the features were identical to Craig's. She knew she had no need to ask him if he was the artist. He certainly possessed great talent, and this must be his masterpiece.

'Like it?' he asked softly.

She became aware that Fiona had left them to join her father and his companion. 'It's a great work of art. If your father were alive he would be exceedingly proud of you.'

'Ah! Observant of you to spot the likeness. Aye, he would have approved of it. I'll take you to the gallery one of these days and ask your opinion of the other paintings. For now, can I offer you a drink?'

'Thank you, sir. I would appreciate a claret.'

He caught her elbow and guided her to the other guests.

Fiona's father put down his tumbler and caught both her hands. 'Good to see you again, lass. If ever there's a bonny one, you are.'

'Thank you, Mr Mcintyre. I'm pleased to see you looking well, in spite of the ordeal both you and Fiona endured.'

'Aye, thanks to this laddie, here——' he slapped his companion lightly on the back '—we were able to salvage most of my jewels and escape from Patna. But I fear other English people fared ill. Most of them died.'

'Oh, I'm so sorry.'

Fiona broke the ensuing silence by introducing the young man. 'Leonora, this is our friend, Mr Robert Murray, who saved father and me from the massacre. Rob, this is Leonora Mackintosh, Craig's wife.'

Leonora smiled and offered her hand. 'I'm delighted to meet someone as brave as you are, sir.' He was a handsome young man with pale hair and brown eyes, a few years Craig's junior. He also wore the uniform of his clan, like the other two men. 'Have you been long in India?'

He bowed formally over her hand, just as Craig held out a wine glass of claret to her which she accepted with her free hand. 'Aye, a good few years. The company sent me as a clerk to Patna, but I resigned and went into a business partnership with Mr Mcintyre.'

A gong sounded indicating that dinner was ready to be served, and a liveried servant led them to their seats, placed at one end of the long banqueting table.

A large leg of venison was dished up and set before Craig, who as host did the honour of carving. Once everyone had been served, Mr Mcintyre asked for all the glasses to be replenished. He raised his and said, 'I have great pleasure in announcing the betrothal of my daughter, Fiona, to Robert Murray. Cheers!'

On hearing the good news, Leonora's heart sang with joy—she believed she must be the happiest person alive. She stole a glance at Craig to see how he had taken it, and was relieved to see him smiling.

'On behalf of Leonora and myself, I wish you both the best of luck and happiness. Congratulations!' They all stood up. 'But before we drink——' He asked a servant to fetch a bowl of water.

Baffled by the strange request, Leonora tried to catch Craig's eyes, but he was staring up at the portrait of his father.

When the bowl arrived, he held his tumbler over it and said in a voice filled with nostalgia, 'To the king over the water.' And she knew he wasn't toasting the English monarch. They all drained their glasses, and after the refill complimented the engaged pair.

'When will the wedding be?' Leonora asked, leaving her seat to kiss Fiona. She felt it was the least she could do to compensate for her needless jealousy.

'Not long, I hope. We intend to buy premises to build our house and business in Calcutta. Meanwhile, we must rely on your and Craig's hospitality,' Fiona said, smiling radiantly.

'Where in the palace are you staying?'

'Where we always stay when we visit Craig here, in the summer.'

'It's a separate building which used to be the *zenana* where the women and children were housed,' Craig explained to Leonora.

'You never mentioned how you came to possess this palace. Was it in lieu of a portrait you painted of the owner?' She felt that in this congenial atmosphere it was the right time to ask him.

He smiled at her indulgently. 'Partly, but most of it was bought with gold and silver from the profits of my jute and cotton trade.'

Leonora brought her arched brows together in a frown of perplexity. 'Why would the raja leave so pleasant a climate and site, I wonder.'

'He wanted to move out of the British sector, afraid lest the new conqueror should confiscate his property,' Craig said. 'I met the raja in Murshidabad at a nobleman's palace where I was painting his portrait. The ruler was suitably impressed and commissioned me to do one of him. In fact, I travelled back with him here. Then I learned that he was anxious to sell the estate and was prepared to let it go cheaply. I saw that this was an ideal climate to produce fruit and vegetables when it became too hot and dry in the plains to grow anything. So I bought the estate with help from my good friend, Ian Mcintyre.' He waved an elegant hand to indicate Fiona's father.

'Tosh! 'Twas but a trifling. You've paid it all back, lad. But enough. No one has thought to congratulate bride and groom. This calls for further toasts.' Ian Mcintyre held out his tumbler for the servant to refill. 'Drink up, drink up, m'lads and lasses!'

By the end of the evening Mcintyre had sent for his bagpipes, and marched round the table while Rob and Fiona sang a Scottish ballad that went well with the skirl of the pipes. As the night wore on only Leonora and Craig remained sober. They were about to slip away when a liveried servant informed Craig that Wasim wished to speak to him.

Wasim was waiting near the door just outside the hall. He greeted them by touching his forehead. *'Salaam, sahib, memsahib.'*

They both returned his greeting and Craig asked, 'What is it you wish to say?'

'I have told all the people who would listen to me in the bazaar,' Wasim began, 'about how you cured me of snake-bite and they are filled with wonder. We, all of us, believe you are rightly called the Hira Nag Sahib, for have you not shown your power over serpents?'

Craig laughed and clapped the skinny but wiry Wasim on his shoulder and Leonora smiled with amusement. 'Naturally, I'm honoured that they brand me a miracle-worker. However, this is not the case. The snake that bit you was not as venomous as a cobra or krait, else you would be nurturing the trees in the forest. Even so, I appreciate your faith in me—but don't make me out to be a god.'

'Never, *sahib*!' Wasim looked appalled. 'There is only one god—Allah.'

'Aye, aye, of course. Now, the *memsahib* and I are about to retire. I suggest you do the same. You must be as fatigued as we are.'

'One moment, *sahib*. The people are wanting to have celebration in honour of your wedding and to welcome you home. They ask your permission to hold rejoicing in main courtyard of palace and for you and the *mem-sahib* to be guests of honour. There will be much feasting, tumblers, jugglers, music and dancing, men and women!' He at last stopped for breath.

'You have my permission. But I forbid any celebrations till the *memsahib* has had a few days' rest. Meanwhile, I'll have a word with the *wazir*, the chief minister, to release funds to pay for the feast.'

'*Nahin, sahib,*' Wasim vociferously refused, waving his hands about. 'We, the people, will pay for it!' he said, sounding affronted. 'Already we have collected many rupees and the rich merchants in the bazaar have given gold. This will be our wedding gift to you and the *memsahib*.' Here he bowed respectfully to Leonora.

'We are greatly touched, Wasim,' Craig said gruffly. 'We appreciate what you and the rest of the people are planning for us. Now go home to your family and don't come near the palace for at least three days. And don't overdo the organising for the celebrations.'

Wasim grinned and wagged his head. 'Very good, *sahib. Khuda hafiz.*' He wished them goodbye and departed.

Craig had not released Leonora's hand while he spoke to Wasim, and she experienced the tingling of pleasure passing along her skin as she felt Craig's thumb moving in circles on the back of her hand. She knew what to expect once they reached the confines of her chamber. Did he have a separate suite of chambers for his own use? she wondered vaguely. The overpowering sensation of anticipation of being in his arms shortly sent the blood racing with excitement in her veins.

Once they reached her room, Craig shut and bolted the ornate double doors. 'I'm not opening these for anyone.'

A single dim lamp in a niche shed feeble illumination in the room, but enough to see his face and its expression of yearning. He reached out his arms to circle her waist and shoulders, drawing her close to his strong chest. As she heard the heavy beat of his heart, a tremor of delight rippled through her body and a sigh of happiness escaped her parted pink lips. His amber eyes with their brown flecks grew dark, seeming to draw her into their bottomless depths, holding her spellbound. A sorcerer could not have matched the magic Craig successfully cast over her. Closer and closer his mouth came. She closed her eyes, lifted her face, opened her lips in joyous expectation of his kiss.

It never came.

The magic silence was disturbed with shuffling from all the unseen areas of the room. Shadows emerged.

'What the devil is going——?' Craig did not get the chance to complete his question. A loud crack on his head seemed to slice his brain in two and rendered him senseless.

As Leonora opened her mouth to scream for help a wad of cloth was shoved into it. Although she fought to free herself from what felt like dozens of hands clutching at her wrists, arms and even ankles, she was soon overpowered. Her bonds seemed to be leather thongs which bit into her flesh at her slightest movements. Worst of all, she had been blindfolded before she could catch a glimpse of her attackers. There appeared to be a good number of them. And—oh, Santa Maria!

Her stomach curled in horror—had they killed Craig?
No, no, good Jesus, she prayed, don't let it be.

She felt herself hoisted over a shoulder and heard
whispers in a language she did not understand. Or
perhaps her horror-struck brain could not assimilate the
words. From the cold air touching the exposed skin of
her face, she knew that she had been taken outside. And
then she could feel herself being carried downwards. Was
it down a ladder or into the pit of hell?

And Craig! What had happened to Craig? Oh, God,
let him be alive. I cannot live without him. I love him.
He was snatched away from me just as we were about
to enjoy that love.

The jolting of her body suddenly ceased, and she knew
that the man who bore her had stopped. Then she heard
the call of the night-watchman, 'Beware! Beware,
evildoers!'

Leonora wriggled off the man's bony shoulder and
began rolling away from him. A swathe of grass protected her body. Despite her gag she tried to emit some
sound. She must have succeeded because she heard the
watchman's challenge, 'Who is it?'

But by now she had been caught and held down pain-
fully. And then something crashed down on her head
and she knew no more.

Leonora came to her senses, her head throbbing, her
body shivering in the cold. Still bound and gagged, she
lay on her back upon grassy ground; she could feel the
blades prickling through her gown, but could see nothing
because of the blindfold. A sixth sense warned her not
to move, despite the fleeting moment of disorientation
she experienced on first regaining consciousness. Once

her memory returned, she assumed that she had been knocked unconscious for attracting the watchman's attention. A low rumble of voices brought her senses alert. She strained to hear what was being said or to at least try to identify a particular voice—Craig's. He must have been taken prisoner like herself. From the crack she had heard in the apartment, she presumed that he had been knocked on the head.

Suddenly she stiffened. She recognised one of the voices. She could not distinguish the words, but the tone was familiar—she had lived with the sound of that voice for thirteen years from the age of ten. Angus Grant! Of course, how could she have forgotten that he had been tailing her and Craig for the past three months?

Dampness from the grass seeped through her silk dress and the thick plaid, and brought on a bout of shivering which she found impossible to curb.

'Grantji, I think your stepdaughter has revived.' A woman's voice startled Leonora. It came from close by. 'Shall I remove her blindfold? And perhaps her gag? Do you not wish to speak with her and hear what she has to say?'

Muffled footfalls sounded and then Grant's hateful voice said, 'Aye, but do not remove the bonds. Get your men to watch her, for she is a wily bitch.'

A low, attractive laugh followed. 'Like me, Grantji?'

He snorted. 'Look, woman, there's no time for games. I've yet to confront her lover when your brother has dealt with him. The bastard interrupted me at the bungalow all those months past just as I was about to...to...'

'Violate her? You do not fool me, Grantji. But it matters not to me. It is the money I require. Once you pay the fifty thousand rupees you owe me I will not trouble you again.'

'Liar! You said that when I paid you the last lot.'

The woman laughed, not in the least offended. 'Ah, but a courtesan must make as much money as she can while she is still young. I do not wish to spend my old age begging, *sahib*. But I shall not ask more from you once you pay the fifty thousand rupees. This I swear. Even I know my limits.'

At last Leonora's blindfold was removed. She blinked and squinted till her eyes grew accustomed to the sudden brightness. She stared up at the woman bending over her.

Leonora was forced to admit that the Indian possessed exceptional beauty, the sort that took a man's breath away. She could imagine the power such exotic good looks could exert over an ageing hedonist of Grant's calibre.

This must be the renowned Kamila. She smiled at Leonora, displaying immaculate teeth, but the smile did not reach the thickly fringed, liquid black eyes with their latent gleam of cruelty. In between her fine eyebrows was a red dot. As she leaned over Leonora to loosen and toss away the gag, the strong scent of musk clouded about her bright pink sari with its wide border of gold embroidery. Her hands were tiny, the beringed fingers slender and tapered, and her skin glowed a deep golden colour.

As soon as her mouth was free, Leonora swallowed several times to eliminate the dryness caused by the wadding. She said to the courtesan, 'You must be Kamila.'

'Ah, you know about the famous Kamila?' She sounded genuinely pleased at her notoriety.

Leonora decided that it would be to her benefit to flatter the woman. 'Who has not? Look, Kamila, I shall give you the fifty thousand rupees. I do not have it on me, as you can see. If you free me and take me back to the palace——'

'Poppycock! She lies!' Grant roared, glaring down at her. 'She has no money—she is entitled to none till she marries, or attains the age of twenty-five in two years' time. Do you not recall how she connived with her lover to stage her own kidnapping and had the temerity to demand ransom from me?'

Leonora sighed and struggled to sit up. 'I cannot carry on a discussion lying flat on my back. Kamila, if you please.' She smiled beguilingly at the woman.

Kamila looked baffled but assisted the girl to raise herself. 'Where is this money you promised me?'

'I have said it is in the palace——'

Impatiently Kamila interrupted, 'Tell me where in the palace and I will send one of my men to fetch.'

Leonora became aware of a group of men seated in a clearing, taking it in turns to smoke a hookah. 'Who are they?' she asked.

'They are *thuggees*. My brother leads them.'

Waves of fear swept through Leonora. 'And what have they done to Senhor Mackintosh? I refuse to give any money till you release him and me!'

The black eyes, outlined with kohl, narrowed menacingly. 'Are you not afraid that I will have you killed, *missahib*?'

'And what will it gain you, Kamila? Only my death, and no money, because I swear that I shall not reveal where my wealth is hidden no matter how much you torture me!'

'You don't need to be tortured, you stupid bitch. I intend to forcibly marry you, and then everything you own will be mine. Kamila knows my plans and she is agreeable.' Grant grinned at her hideously, triumphantly, and Kamila laughed cruelly.

'And who, pray, is to marry us?'

'Oh, I'm prepared for that. We'll take you to Patna where there are a couple of parsons.'

'I'm afraid you're too late. The Europeans in Patna have fled.' It was her turn now to look victorious. 'Moreover, I am already married.'

Grant's eyes seemed to leave their sockets, and his mistress looked thunderstruck. 'You're at your lies again, lass,' he said, his bloodshot eyes scanning her face uneasily.

Craig came to from the shock of cold water hurled in his face, his head near to bursting with the hammering pain. Unlike Leonora, he was not blindfolded and gagged, but was nevertheless securely tethered at elbows, wrists, knees and ankles. He too lay on coarse grass, wet from the dawn dew.

He stared up into a dark face with merciless black eyes, and knew at once he was looking at a *thuggee* from the knotted scarf the man wore slung over the shoulder of his brown robe, tied at his waist with a twisted cloth girdle similar to the material of his turban.

'So you are the rich Hira Nag Sahib?' the *thuggee* said, his thick, upward-curving moustaches rising higher as he smiled darkly.

Automatically Craig glanced down at his hand, and was surprised to see that his cobra ring had not been removed. He sat up awkwardly and saw the wide circle of thugs sitting cross-legged facing him. Unlike their leader, none smiled. Why, he wondered, had they not killed him? Craig looked squarely at the leader who had questioned him. It would be dangerous if he showed fear. 'That's right. Whom do I have the courtesy to address?' he said in fluent Urdu. He reckoned that these were not the same gang of *thuggees* who had attacked Leonora and Rumi. They would have recognised the ring and killed him for deceiving them. This lot must be hired by Grant.

'It matters not what my name is, *sahib*. But you may call me Ram Lal. I have been asked by my sister to kill you and bury you here in this forest. See, we have already dug a grave beneath that large oak tree. No one will find your body here. You are knowing who we are?'

'Aye. You are *thuggees*.'

'You are not afraid that we will kill you, *sahib*?'

If they could hear my heart thumping with fear they would enjoy a feast of torture, Craig thought, eyeing the man fearlessly. 'Every man values his life. But you do not intend to kill me, else you would have done so the moment you captured me. What have you done with my wife?'

'Your wife?' Ram Lal looked surprised. 'We were told the woman was your mistress.'

'Who told you?'

'My sister and her white man.' Here the *thuggee* spat in disgust. 'But if you do as we want, you and your wife will be safe, *sahib*.'

'Where is she?'

'She is with my sister. Not far from here.'

If he were not bound, Craig thought, rage bubbling in his chest, he would have strangled this fool with his own scarf. Calmly he said, 'What do you and your men want from me, Ram Lal?'

The leader gave a shrill laugh and wagged his head. 'We want gold, *sahib*. If you give it to us, we will spare your and your wife's lives and find other victims,' he said with a nonchalance that chilled Craig.

'And how am I to fetch the gold, trussed up like a turkey cock?'

'We have a servant of yours and his family here. I will send him with a note from you to your chief minister to give him the gold. If he does not return with it, then all his family——' He unsheathed his curved dagger and drew it lightly across his throat. 'You are understanding, *sahib*?'

Craig had difficulty stifling his fury. 'You will have to supply pen and paper and untie my wrists. Once you receive the gold, what assurance do I have that you will set my wife and me free?'

'We will, never fear, *sahib*. You have power over serpents and you are a friend of the yogi Sri Ajuna who has power over tigers! Such men the gods favour. We do not choose them as our victims. But we need gold to live.'

The necessities for writing the note were supplied to Craig. When he had scribbled a couple of lines to his minister, stressing the urgency of the matter, Ram Lal gave the order for the servant to be brought in.

It was Wasim they dragged out from the forest, his face swollen and bruised, his shirt covered in blood. 'Take this note to the *sahib's* minister, dog! If you don't return with the gold, and you bring the palace guards, your wife and children will be slaughtered.'

'Forgive me, *sahib*!' Wasim pleaded, tears streaming down his cheeks.

'There's nothing to forgive. Do as they tell you, Wasim. Bring the gold. Our lives and those of our loved ones are more important than valuable metal.'

Once Wasim was despatched with the note, Craig looked about him. He was in a small glade of long grass in the forest. 'Where is my wife, Ram Lal?'

'Not far from here, *sahib*. I will direct you to her after the gold arrives.'

Time lagged. Though the morning was cold, Craig could feel the sweat beading his brow as he watched the *thuggees* fidgeting about impatiently, tugging off their strangling cloths and examining the knots.

But to Craig's relief Wasim staggered into the clearing with a sack. The *thuggees* fell upon it, biting on the gold coins, testing for authenticity. Then, without much ado, Ram Lal slashed Craig's bonds, pointed to where Leonora had been held captive and vanished with his men. Wasim touched Craig, who was flexing his muscles trying to get his circulation back.

'*Sahib,*' the servant whispered, 'my family are behind those trees. Before I go to them, take this. The minister gave it to me.' He drew out a pistol from his girdle. 'Those fools of *thuggees* were so greedy for the gold, they did not think to search me.'

Craig felt touched. 'Thank you, Wasim. You took a foolish risk. I'm going to look for the *memsahib*. You take your family back to the palace.'

'Do you not want me to come with you, *sahib*?'

Craig shook his head and moved in the direction the *thuggee* had pointed.

'Then I will send you help,' Wasim promised.

Within a short time Craig heard voices and crept towards them. He took up his position behind a tree and saw Leonora being harassed by Grant and his mistress.

'I am not lying, Angus Grant. I am married to Craig. Where is he—what have you done with him?'

'He's as good as dead——'

An amused chuckle cut him short. 'Sorry to disappoint you, sir. But as you can see I am very much alive.'

Craig stepped out from behind a tree, his pistol primed and pointing at Grant.

CHAPTER FIFTEEN

LEONORA uttered a cry of joy, but because of her bonds she was helpless to reach Craig.

'Stand away from my wife, both of you,' Craig commanded the gaping Grant and his astonished mistress. They instantly obeyed as Craig held his pistol steady and drew nearer to Leonora. With his free hand he pulled out the dirk hidden in his sporran and with rapid strokes slashed at her fetters.

'Call your men, woman!' Grant bawled at Kamila. 'We can't let these two escape.'

Leonora had forgotten about the group of *thuggees* seated a short distance away smoking a hookah. Her heart thumped with anxiety as she twisted her head looking for the men but could see no one.

'You're wasting your time,' Craig said drily. 'They've gone.'

'Gone? Gone where? Kamila, why would they leave? Did we not promise them gold?' Grant demanded.

'They've received it——' Craig began but was interrupted by a furious Grant.

'From whom? Who gave them gold?'

'I did,' Craig owned, his voice cool, unperturbed.

The vein in Grant's throat looked as if it were about to burst.

'While you were busy interrogating Leonora,' Craig went on, 'I did a deal with the leader of the *thuggees* who I believe is Kamila's brother. Am I right?'

The courtesan looked too dumbfounded to speak. She stared at Craig and nodded.

'You gave him gold?' Grant roared, saliva spraying from his mouth. 'You had no gold on you! I know, I searched!'

'Which you did so thoroughly that you left me with the dirk?'

'You're lying, Mackintosh. You had no gold on you!' Grant looked frantic.

'True. But, as I've said, I did a deal with the *thuggee*—ask him if and when you see him again.'

'But why did he desert us?' Grant whined, turning a malevolent look on Kamila.

'I'll tell you why, Grantji,' the courtesan said, her lip curling in contempt. 'He was once a worker of yours at the warehouse in Calcutta. You accused him of stealing a bolt of cotton and dismissed him. Wrongly, it would seem. He swore he would take his revenge on you. Now he has accomplished that. Think yourself lucky he has spared your life. And now,' she said, backing away, 'I must leave you and join my brother. Do not try to shoot me, Hira Nag Sahib, because this forest is full of my brother's men and they will kill you if you harm me.'

Grant lunged forward and grasped Kamila's slender wrist, making the gold and silver bangles on her forearm jangle. 'What do you mean, join your brother? You're with me!'

Kamila shook her head and snatched back her wrist. 'No. This has been planned! Once you received your stepdaughter's fortune and paid me my dues... But since this is not to be——'

'You would have left me?'

'I was never with you, Grant *sahib*. I belong to no one.'

'Stay where you are, Kamila; my palace guards will be here soon and I intend to take you and Grant prisoner. You will then be escorted to Calcutta, where you will both stand trial for Dona Julia's murder.'

Kamila gave a scornful laugh. 'You are not a man to shoot women, *sahib*. But I have warned you what will happen if you harm me.'

Craig helped Leonora to her feet and she clung to him as he hugged her to his side.

'Let her go, Craig,' Leonora entreated. 'Why risk your life?'

'I think she's bluffing.'

But Kamila was already hurrying through the forest.

'*I'm* certainly not! Drop that gun, Mackintosh.'

The couple stared at the pistol Grant levelled at them.

Craig cursed himself for allowing his guard to drop, but refused to relinquish his gun. 'Don't be a fool, Grant. My men will be here soon. Now drop that pistol, and come quietly to the palace.'

'Oh, no, you're not taking me prisoner. But never be it said that I am a coward. I'm not leaving till you accept my challenge to kill you in a duel, Mackintosh. I'll not give up Leonora without a fight.'

'You never owned me, Angus Grant.' She could hear horses moving through the forest and voices calling out. 'Put that gun down, sir.'

'When I kill him, then your fortune becomes mine,' he proclaimed loftily. And to Craig, 'Do you accept my challenge?'

The blood went out of Leonora's face. She was aware of Grant's expertise with firearms and swords, and had no idea how accomplished Craig was in the use of these weapons.

'Fortune or no fortune, it has never been my practice to refuse a duel. Even though I dislike fighting aged men like you.'

Grant's face became florid, so incensed was he. He choked, spluttered and finally burst out, 'I'll fight you to the death. You'll not get away with what you've done, bastard!'

Craig raised his eyebrows. 'It is I who should say that to you. Have you forgotten your treachery that caused my father's death?'

'And did you not admit to murdering my mother?' Leonora interposed. 'I'll not forget that, sir!'

'Then let's settle the score and fight that duel!'

'Name the venue and weapons, Grant,' Craig suggested in a steady and sober voice.

Grant bellowed with maniacal laughter. 'Swords, sir! Swords! I want to see you dance in your own blood before you fall, you bastard!'

Leonora stared at Craig to gauge his reaction to Grant's confident forecast. How good was he with the sword? And what would she do if he died? The thought made her feel sick with despair and caused a weakness in her legs.

Craig's expression appeared placid, but his arm tightening round her waist conveyed that he was not wholly unaffected. 'And the venue, Grant?'

'The venue, Mackintosh, will be here in this glade. Tomorrow at dawn!'

'What about seconds?'

'We'll fight without them.'

'What? Is it to be nothing short of a brawl without witnesses?' Craig asked, striving to keep the irritation out of his voice.

'Then bring whom you wish to witness your death. And I'll bring my sword!'

'So be it. You had better be gone before my men appear on the scene. I can hear them now.'

'Don't forget our appointment at dawn, Hira Nag Sahib! And mark you this—the winner goes free!' Grant sneered, and ended with a laugh of gleeful malevolence that sent chilling fear up Leonora's spine.

Craig and Leonora watched him back away, still keeping them both covered till the forest swallowed him up.

Back in the palace, Leonora winced as she allowed Rumi to bathe the lump on her head and apply a soothing unguent. The throbbing ache had subsided, but her anxiety about Craig's head wound grew.

Halfway to the palace after Grant had left them the couple had come upon the palace guards, who had been alerted to their predicament by Wasim.

Craig had carried Leonora back to her apartment and had left her in Rumi's care. He had brushed aside her insistence that he have his injury dressed. It had appeared much worse than hers—she could see the blood clotted in his flame-gold hair. He had smiled, kissed her lightly on the forehead and remarked that he had much to see to.

'Has the *sahib's* wound been attended to?' she asked the servant.

'I am not knowing, *memsahib*. I have been here with you.'

'Yes, yes, of course. I'll make enquiries myself. Fetch me a clean dress, Rumi, while I tidy my hair.'

'*Memsahib*, I do not think it wise for you to move too much.' Rumi crossed the thick carpet to the cupboard and picked out a yellow day-dress of fine cotton. 'Will you wear this?'

'Yes,' Leonora agreed absently.

'I will find out about the *sahib*, *memsahib*, while you rest on the divan.'

Leonora sighed as Rumi helped her wash and change into clean clothes. 'But I cannot bear to be idle while the *sahib* is in agony.'

Rumi said nothing, concentrating on helping Leonora to complete her toilet. She took no notice of her mistress's protests as she gently but firmly guided her to the brocaded divan set against a wall near the projecting window.

Just at that moment a guard placed outside the chamber announced Fiona.

'Oh, Leonora!' she cried, gliding towards the divan, her pretty face pale and marred by a frown. 'What is this I hear, that you and Craig were kidnapped by *thuggees*? Ach! It's a miracle both of you are alive!'

Leonora nodded. 'But how is Craig? He received a nasty wound on his head. Rumi has promised to find out for me.'

'There's no need. Papa and Rob are with him now. They forced him to have himself treated. But he refuses to lie abed, so they insisted on accompanying him round the estate.'

Leonora released her breath in a long sigh of relief, and politely asked Rumi to bring some fruit juice for her visitor. She patted the divan, inviting Fiona to be seated, admiring the girl's lavender dress.

'Oh, I'm happy to know Craig isn't alone, Fiona. I fear he cares nothing for his injuries.'

Fiona's eyes softened. 'You love him very much, don't you?'

'Yes. Else I would not have married him.' In retrospect, she decided, this must have been true since she had not put up much of a resistance to marrying Craig—considering what she had undergone to avoid marriage with Pedro Fernandez. 'I wonder what he's up to now?'

At that moment, Craig had completed his toilet and felt almost back to normal. He had impatiently succumbed to Ian Mcintyre's demand to have his wound washed and tended. The older man's insistence that Craig rest in bed had met with derisive laughter and rigid refusal. 'Look, I've got to inspect the gates in the palace walls and recruit some more guards. It seems that any number of devils can get in and make off with what and whom they choose.'

'Then Rob and I will come with you. With a wound on your head, you might come over dizzy.'

Craig grudgingly consented. He would have to be quick with this inspection, because there was the urgent matter of practising fencing to prepare himself for the contest with Angus Grant. Ian Mcintyre was adept with the sword and, although Craig felt reluctant to confide in his friend, he had no other choice since he knew no one else who could fence in accordance with European fencing rules.

He had to win. He had much to live for now that he knew Leonora was not indifferent to him. She had not said so outright but her behaviour, her anxiety for his safety, had proclaimed it as thunder foretells rain.

It was noon by the time he and his compatriots had finished their inspection and Craig had recruited more guards to safeguard the palace.

During luncheon, at which the ladies were absent, Craig said to his friend, 'Ian, can you spare me a few moments alone?' Hastily he added to the younger man, 'No offence intended, Rob. You'll learn about it soon enough.'

'Ach! That's all right, Craig. Willing to help if you need me.'

After they had eaten and Rob had taken his leave, Craig led Ian into a small antechamber. There were a few straight-backed chairs with brocaded seats. Craig lifted forward a couple from their places against the draped walls, and invited his friend to sit down.

'I need your help, Ian.'

'Aye, I had a feeling something was amiss, my friend. What is it?'

'I need to practise fencing.'

The older man's grey eyes narrowed speculatively. 'Be more specific, Craig.'

'I am to fight a duel at dawn tomorrow.'

Ian Mcintyre's eyes protruded, his grey brows rose high with alarm. 'What? With whom? Surely it cannot be with a *thuggee*!'

Craig smiled faintly and squeezed the bridge of his nose. 'No. It's with Leonora's stepfather.'

'I think you need to do some explaining, Craig.'

'Aye. It all started at the New Year's ball...'

Ian listened attentively to the narrative, occasionally interjecting a question. At the end, he scrutinised his handsome compatriot and emitted an incredulous laugh. 'You surely played with fire, m'lad.'

'Aye, and I'd do it again if it meant winning Leonora.'

'Gallant of you, but look at the morass you've plunged into. Have you thought of the dire consequences for yourself tomorrow?'

Craig gave a short, sardonic laugh. 'Aye. I may be killed. In the event I ask you, my friend, to see that all my possessions are passed safely to Leonora.'

'What has she to say to all this?'

'I haven't had the opportunity to discuss it with her. She, too, received a knock on her head. At the moment she is resting and I don't want to disturb her. I believe Fiona visited her this morning after breakfast.'

'Talk to Leonora tonight. She'll no doubt persuade you to abandon the duel.'

Craig's jaw hardened in obduracy. 'As much as I love her, I fear she'll not succeed.'

'Aye, I feared as much,' Ian said, and then with a resigned sigh added, 'All right, lad, where are those swords?'

In spite of her efforts to stay awake during the day, Leonora could not prevent her eyelids from drooping. After Fiona had taken her leave this morning, she had promised herself a short nap. She woke when Rumi brought in her lunch, but had scarcely eaten a few mouthfuls than she dropped right back to sleep again. Now she opened her eyes and saw the rays of the setting sun streaming into the room. She felt her head gingerly and found it a little tender to the touch, but the swelling had gone down and the headache had vanished. Carefully she rose from the divan lest an abrupt movement should cause it to start up again. She made her way to the door and asked the guard on duty to fetch Rumi and also have a brazier brought in, for the room had become chilly.

While waiting, she crossed the chamber to the projecting window and marvelled at the beauty of the snow-capped mountains to the north tinged with the gold of sunset. She breathed in deeply of the crisp air, its purity generating a pleasurable feeling of light-headedness. But the sensation soon disappeared when her thoughts focused on the ordeal Craig would face tomorrow.

Rumi entered then, and Leonora requested that hot water be placed in the bathroom. She needed to be fresh and groomed when Craig called to take her to dinner.

It was dark when she had finished dressing. In the light of the lamps and the glowing charcoal brazier, she gazed at her reflection in the full-length mirror with its gold, dome-shaped frame. She approved of the dark green velvet gown she had donned, with its tiers of lace falling from elbow-length sleeves. For jewellery she had chosen emeralds surrounded by diamonds fashioned into earrings and necklace. She had to look her best for him tonight—she might never... No! He *had* to win. Despite her determined optimism she could not disguise the disquietude mirrored in her dark blue eyes.

She spun round as the double doors were flung wide and Craig strode into the chamber. He nodded to Rumi, and taking his cue she departed.

He came up to Leonora, lifting her hands to his lips, kissing each one in turn. 'How does my lady wife feel?'

For a moment her breath caught in her throat. He looked devastating. She had expected him to appear in his kilt, but tonight he had opted for a fawn velvet coat that flared from waist to knee. His well-shaped legs were encased in matching velvet breeches and stockings. She had only ever seen his feet shod in boots, but tonight he wore highly polished shoes with diamond buckles to match the only other piece of jewellery on his person: the diamond cobra throwing out iridescent sparks from its coils on his finger. Unlike her, he appeared unmoved by the ordeal he would face on the morrow.

Her lips quivered in a half-smile. 'Bodily, I feel well. The headache no longer troubles me, as I fear I have been excessively lazy and slept all day. And you, sir, how is your wound? You do look a little pale.'

'I assure you, Leonora, I am in fine fettle. Unfortunately, I could not find time to rest. However, I'll acquire that in our bed tonight.'

His amber eyes smiled into hers and he placed one of her hands in the crook of his arm. 'Time enough for that later. Come, the others are waiting for us.'

Her cheeks grew hot, the flush emphasising the sparkle in her eyes of the promised love the impending night would bring.

As she had fully expected, dinner turned out a fiasco. The game pie which Fiona declared she had herself prepared for the cook to bake seemed to have indeed been created for a game, rather than for eating. All five of them, seated at one end of the long table, pushed their portions round their plates and placed little of the food in their mouths. Though the whisky and wine were generously imbibed, a pathetic pretence at optimism prevailed. Leonora recognised that these kind people were overplaying their parts in trying to cheer Craig and herself. The only reality in this absurd drama was the proud, unsmiling man in the portrait who gazed steadily down at her. Help him, she asked the picture, he has been a wonderful son and has done all in his power to avenge your death. Let him win against your enemy and mine, I beg you.

At last everyone rose, and exchanged goodnights as if nothing unusual were about to take place in a few hours' time. The others, Leonora observed, looked pale, their smiles stiff, unnatural. Her own heart wept tears of blood. Oh, Santa Maria! How can I bear this?

When Craig, with Leonora on his arm, entered the bedchamber it felt pleasantly warm from the heat the brazier emanated. Wicks of the lamps in niches had been lowered, and a subtle scent of jasmine and roses permeated the air. This should have been the ideal setting for a night of romantic love, except the poignancy of what could be their last night together brought Leonora near to breaking point. She turned to Craig, her eyes huge, distraught. 'Is this *our* bedchamber?' she asked, the few inconsequential words helping to keep her tears at bay. But for how much longer?

'Aye. For tonight, at least.' She detected the slight crack in his deep voice.

'Oh...oh, C-Craig!' She felt helpless to restrain her tears.

With an agonising groan he caught her in his arms, crushing her to him, kissing away her tears. 'Leonora! Darling, please don't cry.'

'Craig, don't go, I beg you. Don't meet Angus Grant tomorrow.'

He rubbed his cheek, slightly rasping, against hers. 'You know full well, Leonora, that I must. It is a matter of pride to honour Grant's challenge. Would you have it put about that your husband is a craven?'

'I don't care! I want you here with me.'

He lifted her chin and stared into her eyes. 'Why, Leonora? Tell me. Tell me why?'

'Oh, Craig,' she burst out, 'I love you.'

CHAPTER SIXTEEN

CRAIG held Leonora away to scan her face. 'You do?'

'I do, Craig.'

'Show me.'

Leonora flicked her gaze up at him and her heart stilled for a beat or two before pounding on. His golden eyes with their brown flecks blazed in rapture down at her. She hesitated, uncertain of how to start.

'Show me,' he prompted again.

Shyly she raised her hands and placed them on his nape, lightly caressing the thick hair lying loose below the velvet bow.

Her soft touch held him in thrall. He experienced difficulty in controlling his erratic breathing, enjoying to distraction the exquisite play of her hands along his neck. The banked fires of passion revealed in her half-closed eyes of deepest blue sent the blood smouldering in his veins. Craig's hands rested weightlessly at the sides of her slim waist. He resisted the temptation to take the initiative and satiate his rising desire, allowing her to entice and seduce him in her own way.

Leonora brought his head down to her uplifted mouth and pressed her pliant body against him. He could no longer keep from enfolding her in his arms, feeling vibrations of elation rippling along his spine. But when her soft lips met his and opened to receive his kiss, a mild explosion of bliss took place in his virile body.

He had both their clothes off in as short a time as it took to discard his coat, breeches, stockings, shirt, jabot and her heavy gown, layers of petticoats. Everything lay on the carpet.

Sweeping her off her feet, he lay her on the soft, rose-scented quilt of the fourposter. 'I've dreamed of making love to you in these splendid surroundings, my beautiful madonna,' he told her in a tender, caressing voice while he lounged on his side next to her with his head propped on his hand. His golden gaze drank its fill of the perfect curves of her body, his hand moving down her throat, smoothing her shoulder, gently fondling her breast, stroking the nipple with his thumb till it stood out. He watched her close her eyes in enjoyment and his whole body throbbed in arousal; yet he controlled the ache for fulfilment till he had brought her to the peak of desire. His hand left her breast and moved over her abdomen, the curve of her hip, along her thighs, and then his fingers gently aroused the hub of her femininity.

Craig's gaze never left her delicately flushed face, delighting in every response she made, the gasps, the sighs of pleasure, the slow closing and opening of her eyes. This picture he would carry with him to the grave—perhaps tomorrow. Emotion welling up inside him, Craig repeated the movements of his hand over her body with his lips. He kissed her throat, then caressed her breasts, gently sucking the nipples, and on downwards. She was shivering when he brought his face up to stare into her sparkling eyes. 'Now do that to me, Leonora,' he whispered, letting his back sink into the quilt.

Leonora did what he asked without restraint, till he felt himself aflame with desire, just able to hold back the burning ache she had aroused in him.

He caught her in his arms and rolled her on to her back. Of her own volition she opened her silken thighs to him. He laughed in pure delight as he thrust into her.

His mouth came down on hers, seeking her honeyed depths with his probing kiss while they both moved in an erotic dance. He felt her soft arms tighten round his body and he crushed her to him as they both climaxed in what seemed like a glorious sunburst of bliss.

In the aftermath she nestled against him and he held her close. Leonora felt poignant fear, haunted by the shadow of death, by the sword hovering about Craig, which had effected a bitter-sweet poignancy in their lovemaking.

'Leonora darling, whatever the outcome is tomorrow, remember that I love you. I think I loved you when I first saw you at the ball.'

She pushed her head back to let him see the happiness in her face. She knew that he was a man who meant every word he spoke and was not given to shallow declarations of love. 'That makes me very happy, Craig.' She paused. 'But you don't have to confront Angus Grant tomorrow. Can I not persuade you not to go, my love? We could leave India and live in Portugal, or perhaps sail to Brazil. Why leave yourself open to danger in a duel with a worthless man?'

'I thought we had been over all that before,' he said coolly, which sent pain cutting through her heart.

'Yes, you are about to do what my father did to my mother and me—leave to fulfil a foolhardy mission,' she accused bitterly. 'What makes honour and patriotism so important that they come before duty to wife and family?'

'Maybe I can show you. Where are the robes?'

Leonora found the woollen garments, which they donned.

Craig caught her round the waist and together they left the chamber. He took her along a corridor and up a flight of narrow steps which led to a large chamber. 'This is my picture gallery,' he said with a dash of pride. In a niche near the door, a gold filigree lamp, its wick low, burned. Craig removed it, turned up the flame and held it high, enabling Leonora to see the large, ornately framed paintings. He ignored most of them and led her to the largest, which was a battle scene and took up half the space on the wall.

'You painted that?' she asked in awe.

'Aye. Now look carefully at it. Study the men's faces. What do you see?'

She scanned the huge scene. On the right-hand side was an army in red uniform; on the left were men in kilts and tartans of the various clans. She could almost hear their war cries, mouths wide, faces contorted with grimaces of hate as they, the Scots, held their claymores aloft and raced to meet their foe.

'I suppose you have guessed that I've portrayed the battle on Drummossie Moor. Do you see the dedication on the Highlanders' faces? The chiefs knew they were doomed, but that made no difference to the fulfilment of their honour.'

'Yes,' she whispered, but her gaze had stopped absorbing the picture as a whole, the horrendous slaughter, the blood, the dying. Not even the attention-drawing inset Craig had detailed of the young Prince Charles had the power to captivate her. Only one figure stood out, right there in the front line of battle, his face and frame thin, ravaged with hunger and hardship, his kilt and tartan torn and dirty, yet he held his shield and claymore with pride and defiance. His black hair was partly hidden beneath a cap bearing a bedraggled cockade. The dark blue eyes were what held her riveted. They blazed with a ferocious zeal that depicted the full meaning of pride, honour, patriotism and bravery. Those eyes blazed straight at her.

Tears welled up in Leonora's eyes. 'Oh, Papa,' she called softly. 'Oh, *Pai*!'

'Leonora, what are you trying to say?' Craig asked with deep consternation. He placed the lamp on the marble floor and took her in his arms, gently rocking her.

'Look, Craig, you've painted Papa. See, he wears the Maclean tartan. And he has given me his answer.' Her voice rang clear as she added, 'You must fight Angus Grant tomorrow.'

Craig looked at her in wonder. Slowly he lifted the lamp to the picture. 'Where is he?'

With a trembling hand she pointed to her father. 'Did you ever meet him?'

He drew in a sharp breath. 'No, but he impressed me the most. I couldnae forget him any more than I could forget Prince Charles.'

They returned thoughtfully to their bedchamber and made poignant love again. Leonora lay awake watching Craig as he slept. She vowed that, unbeknown to him, she would be at the scene of the duel.

Leonora feigned sleep when Craig rose to dress for his assignment. It was still dark and, in the dim light of the lamp which burned perpetually, she saw Ian Mcintyre creep in. She heard the two men whisper and then soundlessly leave the chamber. Immediately, Leonora swung out of bed. Rapidly she selected and dressed in a velvet riding habit, also flinging a hooded cape round her shoulders for she knew it would be cold outside at this hour.

She quietly pulled open one half of the double door and stepped out to—confront two palace guards. They had not been there during the night when she and Craig had visited the picture gallery. They must have been on their rounds, she supposed, and consequently she had forgotten all about them. Lamps in the corridor illuminated their faces and they looked questioningly at her. Feeling disconcerted, Leonora could think of nothing to say for the moment. It must appear most unseemly to these men for the wife of the ruler to behave in so furtive a manner, like a common felon.

With as much aplomb as she could muster, she said, 'Would one of you be so good as to lead me to the stables? I wish to take a ride.'

The guards exchanged worried glances with each other. Then one of them spoke respectfully. 'Hira Nag Sahib has given us strict orders to guard the chamber, and you, *memsahib*.'

'Did he order you to keep me a prisoner here?'

'*Nahin, memsahib.*'

'Then perhaps one or both of you can accompany me on my ride.'

'Alas, *memsahib*, we cannot ride.'

She frowned. Here indeed was a difficulty. She thought for a while till an idea took shape. 'Would you fetch Wasim? He is the servant who accompanied the *sahib* and me on our journey up here. And ask him to have a mount saddled for me.'

'*Ji.* I know him. He used to be a sepoy in the *sahib's* army. I will fetch.'

Leonora returned to the chamber and began pacing it restlessly. She felt tempted to race past the remaining guard and make a wild rush for the stables. Except she had no idea where they were. Meantime, what was happening to Craig? she worried. Perhaps he had arrived at the venue. No, it could not be so soon. Santa Maria, this waiting was agonising. By the time Wasim arrived the duel would be over and the victor—she swallowed to relieve the pain in her throat—who would be the victor?

A knock on the door proclaimed Wasim's arrival. He came in with one of the guards. 'You sent for me, *memsahib*?' He was neatly attired and looked as if he had been up for some time.

'Yes. Wasim, will you ride with me to...to...where the *sahib* is going this morning? I wish to surprise him. Take me to the stables now.'

Wasim looked pleased. '*Memsahib*, I too wish to follow the *sahib*. He would not let me go with him and the old *sahib*. He is saying I will cause trouble. So I thought to follow him. My horse is prepared and I have asked the syce to saddle up a mare for you.'

'I am ready, Wasim—I have been ready for some time. Come, let us be gone. Pray, lead the way.'

The two guards looked perplexed. '*Memsahib*, what will we tell Hira Nag Sahib when he returns? He will be much enraged with us for not guarding you.'

She wanted to cry, Not *when* he returns, but *if* he returns. 'I'll see to it that you do not get into trouble. However, I would like you to send word to Fiona *missahib* that I have gone to see the *sahib*. Else she'll worry.'

Both guards salaamed and one said, '*Ji, memsahib*.'

Leonora nodded politely and followed Wasim to the stables.

She was thankful for her hooded cape, which protected her against the winds sweeping down from the Himalayas, during the long walk to the stables situated quite a distance away near the main gateway. It was a clear, cold and windy dawn. Stars and the moon were still bright in the indigo sky. Amid all this beauty would soon be a gory death, she thought with chilling horror.

The syce brought a mounting block for Leonora, who used it to ascend the mare side-saddle. She could see Wasim, already astride his horse, talking softly but animatedly to some guards. And then he was leading her past them. They came to attention and saluted her smartly as she passed.

Once the riders had crossed the drawbridge, Wasim broke into a canter and she followed suit. She could not at first recognise the direction they were travelling, but as the sky began to lighten in the east she recalled the familiar route. Only now she realised that she would in a short while witness a duel to the death. Moreover, it hit her that this journey was a wasted effort—there was nothing she could do to avert her husband's death—if he should prove the loser. Of course, there was something she could do. She could pray, and she did. She prayed that Angus Grant would not keep the assignment.

They were now in the thick of the forest and nearing the glade. She could faintly hear voices and reined in, calling softly to the servant. 'Wasim, I think it would be safer if we left the horses here and moved forward on foot.'

Wasim reined in, nodded and dismounted. She slid off the saddle before he could help her. They each tethered their mounts and crept forward. And now for the first time she saw a long curved sword in Wasim's right hand. She wanted to question him about the weapon but was afraid to even whisper lest the sound should carry. Instinct told her that the assignment about to take place would not be an ordinary duel.

The glade for the rendezvous had now come into sight and Leonora concealed herself behind a massive oak. Wasim decided on taking cover behind one a little ahead.

Cautiously Leonora peered from behind the trunk. The morning had brightened enough for her to catch sight of the scene in the clearing. Her fervent prayers had not been answered, she reflected with a feeling of despair. Dressed in conventional black, Angus Grant manoeuvred his gleaming épée, testing it with mock feints. Leonora's heart slipped; he looked alarmingly confident.

Her gaze swept to her husband. He and Ian Mcintyre also wore black, but Craig, as always, looked superb. Her heart jolted as she watched and yearned for him. She felt a little hope when she observed that apart from the pallor of his face he stood easily, holding his épée with a casualness that proclaimed him as adept. But was he?

The snapping of twigs made her spin round. She could see nothing, yet the prickling of her skin told her that danger lurked near by.

Then an order rang out, shattering the silence. 'Get ready, gentlemen!' It was Ian Mcintyre's voice. She watched the two enemies discard their coats and move to the centre of the glade where Ian stood. The duel was about to begin.

If this were a mock fight, with the contestants using blunt weapons, she would have found it exciting. But this was a duel to the death and the sensation churning in her stomach was the sickness of fear. Even so, she could not release her gaze from the two antagonists.

They stood facing each other. After lowering their swords in a salute they assumed a sideways position, knees bent, sword arms bent at the elbows, épées held erect.

'On guard!' Ian Mcintyre yelled, and moved out of the glade into the shelter of the trees.

Straight away Grant lunged. It was so unexpected that it made Leonora jump. But Craig had obviously guessed at Grant's tactics—with graceful agility he side-stepped and parried the thrust. It soon became apparent to Leonora that Grant's claim to be an expert was not an idle boast. At this stage he was leading, with Craig on the defensive. Cut, parry, feint, thrust, the two men moved in a wide circle round the glade with Angus Grant relentlessly in pursuit. The sun had risen and flashed on the épées as they clashed and sang. Both men's faces were streaming with perspiration. Grant's expression exhibited dark triumph and, every so often when he saw Craig twist to avoid his thrust, he barked with laughter. Craig on the other hand displayed no emotion; his face seemed carved from rock.

Leonora bit her lip and clenched her fists. Angus Grant appeared to be too good for Craig. The older man left no opening for his opponent, yet by some extraordinary quirk of fate he had not succeeded in wounding or disarming him.

And then, unexpectedly, Craig slipped on the dew-sodden grass and fell. Grant gave a bellow and lunged forwards to finish off his target, even as Leonora gasped. She felt glorious relief when Craig rapidly rolled out of the way, leaving Grant's épée deeply embedded in the earth. A quick twist of his wrist enabled Craig to knock the hilt from Grant's hand. Now Craig was on his feet, the tip of his épée held firmly under the older man's chin.

A tenseness prevailed. The wind stopped, the forest was silenced. Everything seemed to be waiting. Waiting like Leonora's held breath.

Then Craig's voice rang out, remarkably clear, unperturbed. 'Get your sword, Grant.'

Leonora could not believe what she had heard. Could Craig not see the expertise of his opponent? She found it difficult holding her anger in check. What on earth was Craig up to, sparing Grant? She was about to yell at him not to throw away his life, when the fighting restarted. And now she perceived a marked difference, a sudden turning point in the contest.

Grant's movements became laboured. He could not regain his lead and was now on the defensive. The triumph once visible on his face had changed to surprised alarm. His breath rasped, the spring in his footwork vanished. He appeared to move on leaden feet, while his opponent acquired the agility and strength of a tiger.

Her spirits spiralled in elation. Craig had astutely tired out his foe. For a while longer the contest dragged on, till Grant stumbled and fell heavily, his épée flying out of his grasp. Once more the older man was subjected to the point of Craig's weapon, but this time it was pointed at his heart. Swiftly Craig bent, retrieved the fallen épée and tossed it to Ian Mcintyre, who had emerged to witness the kill.

His face grew red with annoyance. 'What the devil are ye waiting for, Craig? Finish off the bastard! If you don't, I surely will!'

'No, no, please, kind sirs!' Grant whined.

Leonora could scarcely credit that this man, who had strutted with such bravado for most of his life, lay at Craig's feet, a squirming, cringing mass, his flabby face as white as the lawn shirt he wore and his eyes bulging in pure terror.

'I'll not trouble you and Leonora, Mackintosh,' he howled. 'I'll leave this heathen country. Just give me a few pieces of gold and——'

Craig removed his épée from its position over his opponent's heart, stood astride Grant, flung back his head and roared with laughter. 'Not content with my sparing your worthless life, you dare to ask for gold! Get up before I change my mind.'

Leonora felt pleased that Craig had decided to spare Grant's life—it proved that the bitter vengeance he had carried in his heart was fully sated. She knew that her stepfather had accepted defeat and would leave Craig and herself completely alone—if he was allowed to. Craig would probably contact the governor in Calcutta and return Grant for trial. She watched her stepfather rise slowly and awkwardly to his feet. Then she stepped out from behind the tree. As she moved forward, she was suddenly brought to a halt by the sharp point of a dagger pricking the side of her neck under her ear. She froze.

'Do what I tell you, *memsahib*,' an unfamiliar voice ordered quietly.

Her terrified gaze darted to the tree behind which Wasim had hidden and saw with alarm that he too had a dagger held to his head by an individual who wore the garments of a *thuggee*.

As she was led into the glade, Leonora saw that Grant had been shoved back and held by two *thuggees* and that the remainder of the gang surrounded the three men.

'Craig!' Leonora called and tried to run to him, but the *thuggee* closed iron fingers round her arm, preventing her from moving.

She saw Craig's face turn a sickly grey. 'Leonora! What the hell are you doing here?' He and Ian Mcintyre raised their swords, obviously in an attempt to fight their way out of the circle of men, but the man who held Leonora soon stopped them.

'The *memsahib* dies, Hira Nag Sahib, if you and your friend try to break free. Now, hand your weapons to my men.'

Craig sighed and tossed his épée to one of the *thuggees*, and nodded to a dismayed Ian to do the same. 'Look, Ram Lal, I assume you want more gold. Just release my wife and——'

'*Nahin, sahib*. It is not gold we want——'

He was interrupted as the palace guards dashed into the glade, their curved swords drawn, apparently intent on arresting Angus Grant and rounding up the *thuggees*.

'Call your men off!' Ram Lal shouted. 'Or the *memsahib* dies!'

Leonora closed her eyes as she felt blood oozing from the sharp poke made by the dagger.

Craig shook his head and ordered his men not to act. The guards stood by helplessly, their sabres useless.

'Order them back to the palace, *sahib*. It will go badly for you and the *memsahib* if you let any of your men harm mine.'

Craig patiently issued another command, and warned the guards not to return or all their lives would be in jeopardy. Once his men had withdrawn he turned back to Ram Lal. 'You were saying?'

'We want Grant Sahib.'

Craig's eyes widened in surprise. 'But he's yours, Ram Lal!'

By now Leonora was finding difficulty remaining upright, her knees beginning to buckle.

Vaguely she heard Ram Lal say, 'We watched the fight. Why did you not kill him?'

'Because I don't think he's worth killing.'

'Then I will kill! He deprived me of my livelihood. For that he must sacrifice his life!'

The *thuggee* let go of Leonora and in a few strides Craig reached her, lifting her into his arms as she sagged to the ground. She struggled up to him, at the same time watching the chief of the *thuggees*.

'Bring the dog here!' Ram Lal ordered the two men who held Grant captive. They dragged him forward and forced him to his knees.

He began whining and pleading for his life. 'Your sister loved me. She would not see me done to death. For her sake spare me, Ram Lal!'

The *thuggee* laughed. 'My sister? That whore? You want to be reunited with her?'

'Aye, aye,' Grant replied, his eyes darting about. 'Where is Kamila?'

'You will soon be with her, Grant Sahib,' Ram Lal said with ominous kindness. He came up to Craig and said softly so that Grant could not hear, 'Go home, *sahib*. Take your wife and your friend. I thank you for providing the two victims for our mother goddess.'

'Who are they, Ram Lal?'

A fanatical gleam came into the dark, handsome eyes. 'Grant Sahib is one and my sister, Kamila, the other.'

'Where is Kamila?' Leonora asked tentatively, almost afraid of the answer.

He dragged off the strangling cloth on his shoulder and tautened it between his hands in a meaningful gesture. 'She's in hell!'

Craig, Ian and a shocked Leonora left the glade with Grant's howls for mercy ringing in their ears. By the time they came upon their horses, the horrifying screams had stopped, the forest resumed its tranquillity and the clear air trilled with birdsong.

CHAPTER SEVENTEEN

IT was dinnertime when Leonora, Craig and their guests climbed the marble steps leading to the Hall of Public Audience, a large, flat-roofed marble pavilion of scalloped archways supported by ribbed marble pillars decorated with arabesques of precious stones. A flamboyantly dressed usher banged his jewelled mace and announced to the crowd thronging the courtyard, 'His Honour, Hira Nag Sahib and his *memsahib* are here to salute you with their presence and to partake in the festivities.' A roar went up as Craig and Leonora took their places on embroidered and gold-tasselled cushions spread over a spacious marble throne in the shape of a lotus which stood on a pedestal in the centre of the hall. Below the throne were a number of couches to which the other three Scots were shown, along with state officials.

Leonora observed with intense fascination that the pavilion faced the main courtyard, lit with lamps suspended from the surrounding walls showing the people colourfully arrayed in sparkling garments. To please the people Craig had requested his compatriots and herself to wear traditional Indian dress. So, with Rumi's help, Leonora had draped herself in a scarlet sari sprinkled with brilliants and edged with gold lace, complemented by gold and ruby jewellery. Fiona's mauve sari and the amethyst and diamond set, given to her as a betrothal gift by Leonora, went well with her auburn colouring. The three Scotsmen looked exceedingly elegant in their brocaded knee-length coats, tight pyjamas and bright turbans with jewelled aigrettes, worn with aplomb. Leonora was happy to see that Ian had graced his neck with the Vasco da Gama cross she had insisted he accept.

Craig rose and gestured for silence. He spoke in fluent Urdu. 'I am indebted to all of you for this great festivity you have taken so much pains to prepare in honour of our wedding. On behalf of my wife and myself I thank you from the bottom of my heart. Enjoy yourselves!' A roar of approval went up.

Leonora appraised Craig with pride. He looked magnificent in a leaf-green brocaded surcoat and green turban embellished with an aigrette of a large diamond cobra supporting a plume of peacock feathers.

Huge trays heaped with all manner of exotic food were brought in and distributed to the honoured guests and the people in the courtyard.

Craig sent for Wasim and handed him his promised reward: a purse of coins. He salaamed profusely. 'May Allah shower His blessings on you, Hira Nag Sahib.' He was followed by a line of people climbing the steps of the pavilion to place garlands of sweet-smelling flowers round Craig and Leonora's necks.

Dancing girls, tumblers and acrobats performed their stunts and were heartily applauded by all present. It was late when Craig and Leonora rose to bring the festivity to a close.

Suddenly a commotion at the far end of the courtyard near the entrance gateway made Craig pause before wishing everyone goodnight. 'What goes on?'

It was Wasim who pushed his way through the crowd and mounted the pavilion. '*Sahib*, the yogi Sri Ajuna, asks to speak with you, but his tiger Rajkumar will not leave him!'

'It's a relief to know the old yogi is alive,' Craig told Leonora. 'I was worried the *thuggees* might have killed him.'

'Yes, indeed, I too felt anxious,' she stated.

'Let Sri Ajuna through!' Craig ordered the crowd. 'Do not touch him and the tiger will not harm any of you.'

They fell back like grass before the wind.

'He would not listen to me, Hira Nag Sahib,' Sri Ajuna complained, as he finally reached Craig and steepled his hands in greeting. Few looked at the yogi; all eyes fastened on the magnificent gold beast with his striking black stripes and long tail, its black tuft flicking as he followed his master.

Leonora heard Fiona gasp and her father and fiancé draw in their breaths. 'It's all right,' she reassured them. 'Rajkumar won't harm any of us. Not while he is with the yogi.'

'I have come with a message from the chief of the *thuggees*,' Sri Ajuna was saying.

'And?'

'And, Hira Nag Sahib, he has sworn by the Goddess Kali that he will not harm you or your people. With the gold you gave he has vowed to open a carpet shop in Oudh and employ his followers as weavers.'

Craig chuckled in disbelief. 'Thank you, Sri Ajuna. But owning a carpet shop is no guarantee that he will stop being a *thuggee*.'

The yogi lifted his thin shoulders in a half-hearted shrug. '*Ji*, it could well be, *sahib*. But of a certainty he will not trouble you again.'

'What makes you so sure?'

Sri Ajuna nodded his white head enigmatically. 'I have ways, *sahib*.' Rajkumar let out a snarl as if in agreement with his master, and everyone cringed.

Craig then ordered retainers to give the old man some flour and raw vegetables. 'Thank you for all you've done for my wife and me, Sri Ajuna. In return, I invite you and Rajkumar to live on the estate.'

To everyone's relief the old man refused the offer. 'I thank you, *sahib*, but my destiny is in the forest.' He then bade farewell, 'The gods go with you.' And, calling to Rajkumar, he took his leave.

The night had grown quiet when Craig and Leonora finally exchanged their finery for night robes. He placed an arm around her and said, 'I have a wedding gift for you.'

'Can it not wait till tomorrow, Craig?'

'It is good to know I have an enthusiastic wife,' he teased, 'but I fear we'll not be leaving our room tomorrow. I've given orders for us not to be disturbed.'

He ignored the yawn she stifled and guided her again to the gallery, this time to the far end, and brought her to a stop in front of an easel covered with a cloth.

'Close your eyes, sweetheart.'

Leonora thought she had guessed what the painting would be. 'Craig——'

'Ssh!'

She heard the careful rustle of cloth and then he said, 'Open your eyes, darling.'

Leonora viewed the portrait in awe. It was of herself in the pink muslin dress she had worn on the barge, against a backdrop of the river, a temple silhouetted on the bank and the gold and scarlet of sunset. 'Oh, Craig! It's magnificent!' She put an arm about him and nestled her head in his shoulder. 'This was what you hid from me on the barge?'

'Aye. I was besotted with you then, though I was reluctant to own up to it.'

'We were both smitten with each other, I think.'

'And pride, darling.'

'What are you going to call it—"The Frozen Madonna"?'

'You're that no more! You have become a warm, glowing woman in keeping with the portrait and its background. I've decided to call it—"My Lady of the Sunset".'